By ELIANA WEST

A Paris Walk
Compass of the Heart
Dreidel Date

EMERALD HEARTS
Four Holly Dates
Summer of Noelle
Falling for Joy
Be the Match

MOCKINGBIRD BRIDGE
The Way Forward
The Way Home
The Way Beyond
A Hidden Heart

THE
WAY
Forward

MOCKINGBIRD BRIDGE

BOOK ONE

ELIANA WEST

Published by
SECOND PRESS
info@secondpress.com

The Way Forward
© 2024 Eliana West

Second Edition
First Edition published by Tule Publishing, August 2020

Cover Art
© 2024 Elizabeth Mackey
Cover content is for illustrative purposes only and any person depicted on the cover is a model.

Trade Paperback ISBN: 9781963011036
Digital ISBN: 9781963011029
Trade Paperback published June 2024
v. 2.0

For Neva—the librarian, my sister, my heart.

ACKNOWLEDGMENTS

I AM honored and humbled to be a part of a wonderful community of authors and I am thankful for your generosity every day. Anne Turner, Marie Tremayne, Tess Thompson, Aliyah Burke, and Rebecca Zanetti, your encouragement and support mean the world to me. Thank you for answering all my questions and offering words of wisdom. I am beyond lucky to have your friendship.

Fire/EMS Officer Dan, thank you for being an awesome friend and technical adviser and being so patient with all my questions.

Thank you to my beta readers for your time and wonderful notes.

To my book mom (you know who you are), thank you for the lunch dates and unwavering support. No one could ask for a better mentor and friend.

To my husband David, thank you for always believing in my dreams. I love that I have you by my side on this journey. Jackie and Satchel, your strength and compassion inspire me in everything I do. I am proud that I am lucky enough to be your mom. Thank you.

Carmen Cook, the greatest gift I have received along this journey is your friendship. Thank you for listening to all my crazy plot scenarios, talking me out of the depths of self-doubt, and believing in the magic that is the plotting journal. Thank you for pushing me past my fear and for your unwavering support through my successes and failures. I'm looking forward to sharing many more plotting sessions over good bottles of wine as we craft more stories of love and friendship.

CHAPTER ONE

TIME STOOD still in Colton, Mississippi, or at least it seemed that way every time Dax Ellis came back to visit. Nothing in his hometown had changed since he left. Like many small towns in the South, Colton was a place where folks were afraid of letting go of the past and fearful of moving forward into an uncertain future. The only thing that changed over time was the worn welcome sign showing the population, which only went down.

When Dax Ellis drove across Mockingbird Bridge, it went up by one.

He rolled down his window, taking in the cool morning air. His gaze swept over the small patch of green with a gazebo at its center. Absolem Madden Colton Park was the centerpiece of Colton's downtown. His mouth began to water as he drove by the Catfish Café. Sometimes the fact that nothing changed was a good thing. He'd have to stop in for some of Tillie's pecan pie if she'd let him in the door. Hopefully, it tasted as good as he remembered. The barbershop pole continued its lazy twirl on one side of the town square while the neon lights for Walker's Pharmacy flickered a dull orange glow. The K blinked twice and went dark just as he drove past. Seven years since he came home for his father's funeral, and the town had faded even further into obscurity since then. He'd come back to do his best to make sure it didn't disappear altogether.

Dax nudged his charcoal-gray Ford F-150 into a parking spot next to its much older twin. A man wearing a pair of worn overalls and a huge grin stood next to the vintage truck. Dax jumped down from the cab and pulled his uncle into a bear hug.

"I didn't expect to see you this early. Welcome home," Uncle Robert said, his voice gruff.

Dax looked into a pair of dark brown eyes that matched his own, framed with a few more wrinkles from squinting into the sun. He rubbed his chest where a sudden ache formed. He'd forgotten how much his uncle and father resembled each other. They shared the same straight brown hair, only now more silver poked out from beneath Uncle Robert's baseball cap than brown. If his father had lived past sixty-five, would he have looked the same? He shuddered when he thought of where he would have ended up without his uncle's guidance.

"Once I hit the road, I couldn't wait to get here. I didn't even mind the speeding ticket I got along the way," Dax confessed.

His uncle cuffed him on the shoulder. Dax grinned. "I've missed you, Uncle Robert."

"Seven years is way too long for you to be gone."

"It is," Dax agreed. "You know it wasn't about you." He looked around the town square, his gaze zeroing in on one building he'd always admired. "It's good to be back."

"I've got the keys to the Barton Building if you want to take a look now." Robert jangled a set of keys in front of him.

Dax rubbed his hands together. "I sure do."

They walked across the park toward the building he'd loved since he was a boy.

"Are you positive you want to take this on? It's a big project," Uncle Robert asked.

"I'm ready for the challenge now."

"What's changed?"

"The Army has given me the skills to start my own business, and the last few consulting gigs have given me the money I'll need to fix this place up and make it my home."

Inside, the sun barely penetrated through the dust and grime on the windows; the scent of age mixed with mustiness filled his nose. Dax coughed, waving the dust particles out of his eyes. They wandered around the main floor, their voices echoing in the empty space as they discussed the repairs Dax would need to make. The building was in surprisingly solid condition, and it wouldn't take much to restore the main floor to get his cybersecurity business up and running. They climbed the creaking staircase to the second floor. Standing in the middle of a large open space with rotting floorboards and crumbling plaster, Dax rested his hands on his hips, admiring the large arched window that faced the street and flooded the space with light. Converting the cavernous space into apartments would be an enormous task, a challenge Dax was ready for.

Uncle Robert kicked at one of the rotting floorboards. "You're right. It's gonna be an expensive project, but it will be worth it."

When his uncle mentioned several months ago that the building was going up for sale, Dax jumped at the chance to buy it. Next to the courthouse, she was the tallest building in Colton, standing proudly over the rest of the single-story buildings in the town square. Built in the Beaux-Arts style, the Barton Building once served as an office for cotton traders in the early 1900s.

The main floor would serve as headquarters for Ellis Technologies, his cybersecurity consulting firm. He'd convert the top floor into an apartment for himself and the second floor into four apartments, hoping to convince a few of his friends that Colton was a town worth saving and that moving in would be a good investment. His mother would throw a fit when she found out that Dax bought the building and didn't have any intention of moving into the family home, but sometimes a man just had to follow his heart.

Robert Ellis stroked his salt-and-pepper beard. "This place has sat empty for too long, and once you're done with her, she'll be a queen."

"Does anyone know I'm the one who bought the Barton Building?"

Uncle Robert shook his head. "Nope, you asked me to keep it quiet and that's what I've done."

"Good."

The Army had kept him on the move for the last thirteen years and he'd loved every minute of it, but it was time to settle down, and with an agreement to continue as a private contractor, he had the income secured not just to invest in the Barton Building but the town as well. *It's time to rebuild this town after everything I tried to do to destroy it.*

Dax crossed over to one of the windows and looked down at the deserted street below, thankful there weren't many people around. He wasn't ready, not yet. He'd left with a reputation he was ashamed of now.

"You're going to need help," Uncle Robert said.

"My buddy Jacob Winters is coming down just as soon as he gets his discharge papers."

"Does your friend have the right skills to help you out here?"

"Jacob is good with a hammer and has always been able to make something from nothing."

Uncle Robert joined him at the window. "How do you feel about ending your career with the Army?"

"It was time," Dax said. "I'll be happy to have Jacob's help and I'm hoping there will be opportunity for a few other guys I served with to move here. Jacob wants to set up a contracting business. He can look for other jobs while he helps me rehab this place."

Uncle Robert studied him thoughtfully. "There's plenty of work around here for a good carpenter. I can think of one off the top of my head; the librarian could use some help with a bookstore she's trying to open."

"Since when did you start hanging out at the library?" Dax asked, picturing his uncle flirting with a gray-haired lady.

"Don't look at me like that, boy, I know how to read."

Dax laughed and nudged his shoulder, surprised to find solid muscle beneath his hand despite his uncle's age. His uncle would never admit it, but he was slowing down just a little bit. Dax wanted to be around to help him and repay him for all the kindness and guidance he'd given him when he needed it. But if there was a sweet, older librarian in the picture, he'd happily share the duty with her.

"I've got to get back home," Uncle Robert said, "but if you have time, you might want to go over and meet the librarian and tell her about your friend."

They walked back downstairs and across the park.

"I hope the folks will give me a chance to show that I've changed."

Robert swung his truck door open and climbed inside. "Remember who you are, not who you were," he said through the cab's open window.

Dax watched his uncle drive away as the soulful notes of Coltrane drifted from the truck before turning to take a closer look at the little library. The colorful display in the window stood out from the papered-over abandoned storefronts on the rest of the block, piquing his curiosity. Opened in the sixties by Richard Colton, the Colton Public Library was Richard's pride and joy. Colton, Mississippi, started out as the Colton Plantation, the town growing out of the rubble of the Civil War. Two families dominated the town, both Coltons.

One Black and one White.

The descendants of the slave owners and the slaves still lived and worked on the same land as their ancestors. Dax frowned. Unfortunately, there were those who still remained segregated. Some by history, and some by choice. A descendant of one of Colonel Madden Colton's slaves, Richard Colton had been a well-known figure in town. Returning after leaving for Chicago during the great migration, he'd brought a drive and determination to bring the sleepy town back to life. He insisted that the town needed a post office, a clinic, and a library—the last of which he funded with his own money. "For the young people," he always said. He made sure all children, no matter the color of their skin, had a book in their hand when they came into town.

Downtown may have withered away over the years, but the library was the one business that never closed. Taking a closer look, Dax admired the restored brick façade on the building. Cream paint on the window had been redone, the vintage lettering proudly declaring "The Colton Public Library" outlined in gold. The windows had fresh robin's-egg-blue trim that matched a new awning and a bench out front. On one side, another storefront had papered windows and a sign announcing, "Bookstore and Coffee Shop Opening Soon." Dax's lips curved slightly. He wouldn't be alone in trying to revitalize his sleepy hometown.

He entered the air-conditioned coolness of the library. The old wood floors had been refinished and polished into a dark rich sheen. The original bookshelves were given the same treatment. A long table took up the middle of the room, hugged by two long benches on either side. Two overstuffed chairs covered in a blue floral print sat in one corner with a small bookshelf and floor lamps beside each one, inviting readers to stay for a while.

The pale cream walls and schoolhouse light fixtures made the space feel warm and inviting. Dax stopped at the small counter by the door. Everything was neat and tidy. A new computer and bar-code scanner sat at one end. The old library had finally caught up with the times.

His hand hovered over the bell on the corner of the desk when he caught sight of a head of deep golden-brown curls popping through a doorway at the back of the room. Dax froze as blue-gray eyes that had haunted him since childhood stared back from a light brown face frozen in shock, her expression quickly changing to fear. The stack of books she had been carrying fell to the floor and she put a hand to her mouth.

Numbness washed over him. He wanted to leave, but his feet refused to cooperate.

She was the one to take a step back, her eyes locked onto him, wide with anxiety.

Breaking eye contact, Dax forced his fingers to wrap themselves around the warm metal of the door handle before wrenching the door open. He turned and fled.

The actions of getting in his car, of driving through town, were a blur as his heart raced from the shock of seeing her in the flesh.

Callie Colton—of all the people he'd hurt, he hurt her the most.

Rocks flew as Dax slammed on the brakes, pulling up to his uncle's house.

On the outskirts of town, Uncle Robert lived in a two-bedroom cabin surrounded by seven acres of cornstalks that already came up to Dax's waist. Clearly expecting him, his uncle sat in the same rocker on the wide shaded front porch that Dax remembered from his childhood.

"Damn it, Uncle Robert, you knew Callie Colton worked at the library!" Dax charged toward his uncle like a guided missile.

Robert continued to rock, a book open on his lap. Dax stood in front of him, his heart pounding in his ears, drowning out the dull chirp of cicadas in the heat. "How could you just let me walk in there like that?" he asked, voice low.

Robert closed the book and set it aside. "Wasn't my place to tell you."

"Bullshit, you could have given me a heads-up."

Robert jumped up, standing toe to toe with Dax. "You're a grown man, and I'm not here to hold your hand."

Each poke of Uncle Robert's finger in his chest took Dax back to the first time his uncle confronted him about his behavior on this very same porch. That confrontation led to a lot of long talks that ultimately saved him. Dax took a deep breath and let the anger drain from him. He had no right to be mad when he was the one who'd caused all the hurt. "You're right."

They remained silent for a minute, giving Dax a moment to gather his thoughts.

Dax stepped back and leaned against the porch railing. "How long has she been here?"

"'Bout a year. Her grandparents were killed in a car crash, and they left her the whole block of buildings including the library. They knew how much she loved it."

Dax shifted his weight on the railing. Of all the things he was prepared to face moving home, he wasn't ready to face Callie Colton again.

His uncle went into the cabin and returned with a couple of beers. He grabbed the bucket of peanuts by the front door, setting it at their feet before he leaned against the railing next to him.

"I expect you're going to want to stay here tonight," Robert said, handing him a bottle.

Dax took a long swig. He dreaded going home knowing his dad wouldn't be there. Many things about Colton felt like home; his mom wasn't one of them. Their relationship had always been complicated. She loved him, but it wasn't until he left home that he realized her love was conditional.

Dax nodded and took another drink. "If you don't mind."

"Always happy to have you here, you know that," Uncle Robert said, handing Dax a handful of peanuts.

Dax cracked open the nuts and threw the papery shells out into the yard. A cardinal swooped down to peck at the remains.

"Sorry, buddy, didn't mean to fool you," Dax muttered, throwing a peanut next to the shell. He glanced toward Robert. "I didn't think she would be here." He studied the pattern of squares on the peanut shell in his hand for a moment before he threw another treat to his new friend. "I wasn't ready. If I had known—"

"Would it have made a difference?" Uncle Robert cut him off. "She's here, and the two of you would've run into each other sooner or later."

"You're right, I know that, but I would have preferred later."

"You've had plenty of time to prepare for this day. If you weren't ready, why did you come back?"

"Because I realized even after all the trouble I caused, Colton is home. I want to be part of a community and do my part to… to help the town survive. Too many small towns are dying, disappearing, only remembered as a forgotten spot on an old map."

The cardinal flew back, hopping a little closer to the porch. Dax threw another peanut, and with a flash of red, the bird caught it before it hit the ground. It never occurred to him that Callie would feel an attachment to a place she'd only visited during the summer. He squeezed his eyes shut, trying to block out another wave of memories. They weren't easy memories, either.

"Let it go, son." Robert's voice washed over him.

"What do I do? How do I...?" Dax rubbed his hands over his face, trying to get the image of stormy-gray eyes out of his head, but they were burned into him. "She has no reason to forgive me—no one in the town does—but Callie...." How could he explain the way he'd treated her haunted him through the years?

Dax jumped up and paced the porch. The cardinal hopped a little closer, tilting its head to look up at him, waiting, while Robert sat forward with his hands clenched. Like a baseball player standing in the outfield waiting for the pitch. Years ago, his uncle sat in the same position, waiting for Dax to decide which path he was going to take in life.

"How am I going to avoid her?" he asked, turning to face his uncle.

"Colton is too small. You can't avoid her, so you're going to have to figure out a way to talk to her."

"Easier said than done. You didn't see the way she looked at me."

Robert's eyebrows shot up. "No, but I can guess." He glanced at Dax, adding, "She's grown into a beautiful young woman, hasn't she?"

Dax swallowed hard "You're not helping." *Beautiful* was an understatement. The luminous gray eyes were still there and still looked at him with wariness, but the gangly arms and legs were gone, replaced by soft curves. Daily life in the Southern sun had turned her skin a tawny brown and the curls that cascaded over her shoulders a deeper shade of golden brown. Callie Colton was a stunning woman. "I need to figure out how I'm going to approach her again and start with an apology."

"She's not going to want to talk to you at first, so start by being a part of the community and show you care."

"Any suggestions?" Dax asked.

"There's a meeting next week you might want to go to, for a start."

Dax frowned. "Meeting? What kind of meeting?"

"Book club."

"Book club? What the hell are you talking about?" Years working for the CIA had made his uncle a master manipulator, a skill that had always driven Dax crazy.

Robert went inside and returned a few moments later carrying another book in his hands, which he handed to Dax. "The next meeting is Tuesday night. You better catch up."

Dax arched a brow. *"The Barista Mysteries: M is for Macchiato?"* He held the book up. "This doesn't seem like something you'd read."

"You need to be more open-minded." Robert sat down in his rocking chair. "The book is good, but that's not important. Book club meets at Callie's house."

Dax turned the book over in his hand, reading the back cover blurb. "I've heard of this author before. She's popular."

Robert nodded. "Katherine Wentworth books are always popular with the book club."

Dax thumbed through a few pages and then flipped it over, reading the back copy. The cardinal flew back, landing at his feet. Dax held his empty hands up. "I don't have anything more for you." The bird cocked its head as though believing that if he waited long enough, Dax might change his mind. Instead, he held up the book. "Besides, it looks like I have some reading to do."

Uncle Robert left him alone on the porch, and Dax sat down, opened the book to the first chapter, and began to read. The chaos of his first day in Colton gave way to the quiet calm of the end of day. The leaves of the giant oak tree began to rustle in the evening breeze. Reading a romantic mystery on his uncle's front porch wasn't how Dax expected to spend his first night back in Colton. But this was home—the good and the bad— and he knew he was in the right place.

It was also the only place where he could make amends.

CHAPTER TWO

TEARS BLURRED Callie's vision after Dax left. She took deep, measured breaths, trying to block the memory of the names he'd called her in the past. *Freak, stupid mutt, mongrel.* The words came back in a flood that threatened to drown her. She looked around the room. What was she doing before Dax came in? She picked up a stack of books and shoved them onto the shelves haphazardly. It took all her focus to keep moving and not give in to the shock of seeing Dax Ellis again. She didn't notice her cousin until she gently grasped her arm, turning Callie to face her.

"Callie, honey, what's the matter?"

Callie looked up at her cousin's face. "I… I just saw a ghost," she whispered.

Mae guided Callie to one of the chairs in the corner and grabbed a bottle of water out of her tote bag. She opened it and pushed it into Callie's shaking hands. Mae knelt beside her. "What happened?"

She shook her head. "I knew I would see him eventually. I just thought…."

"Who?" Mae asked.

"D-Dax Ellis." Even saying his name was hard. "I shouldn't be this upset after all these years."

Mae stood up. "You have every right to be upset even after all these years. Dax was horrible to everyone in Colton, but you got the worst of it. He hasn't shown his face around here since his dad died. I wonder what he's back for now?"

"I don't know." Callie took a deep, shuddering breath. "I'm okay now. I was just so shocked to see him. Honestly, I hoped it would never happen."

"I can't believe he had the nerve to come in here," Mae said, following Callie back to her desk.

"It's still his hometown." Callie sorted the stack of books that had been returned to the library that morning, wishing she could sort her feelings about seeing Dax again into categories the same way.

Mae perched on the edge of her desk. "Let's hope he's here for a short visit and we don't see him again for a long time. And," Mae straightened her shoulders, "if he tries anything while he's here, I'm ready to give him the setdown he should have gotten when we were kids."

Callie smiled at her cousin. Mae Colton was a head shorter than Callie but ten times braver. She understood better than anyone else how much Dax hurt her. Mae had become her best friend on her first summer trip to Colton. Callie's grandparents never approved of their daughter moving so far away from home, and when she married a White man, their already strained relationship almost broke. Sending Callie to stay with her grandparents every summer kept a fragile peace in the family.

Even with all the love and attention her grandparents lavished on her, her time in Mississippi was not always pleasant. The light brown hair and striking gray eyes she inherited from her father set against golden-brown skin reflected the mix between her mother and father and set her apart. The White kids in town considered her a freak. And the Black kids wanted to know why she "talked funny" with her lack of Southern accent. Both sides were always asking the same question: "What are you?"

It would have been a lonely childhood if it weren't for Mae.

Callie's grandfather was one of seven children, so Colton cousins were as numerous as cotton flowers on the stem. Richard Colton was the root that held them all together. Callie and Mae were the youngest of the bunch, and the first time they met, Mae stood in front of her with her tiny hands fisted on her hips, smiling at her.

"Your dress spins." Mae reached out and grabbed Callie's hand. "Come on, you're going to be my best friend," she announced, pulling her outside to make princess fairy mud pies.

The two were inseparable every summer after that. Eventually Callie spent all her school breaks and her summers in Colton with the people she loved.

"Are you sure you're okay?" Mae asked Callie, not ready to drop the subject.

Callie gathered the rest of the books that needed to be shelved and began placing them back with more care this time, ignoring her cousin's skeptical look. "I'm fine." She tried to sound confident even though her words sounded hollow to her own ears.

Mae crossed her arms over her chest. "We're not kids anymore. It's gonna be different this time."

"You're right," Callie said more firmly. "I've changed. I'm not the same person, and I'm not afraid of him anymore." She smiled at Mae. "Now stop worrying and let me get back to work."

As soon as Mae left, Callie leaned against the bookshelf and blew out a long breath. She'd put on a brave face for Mae, but Callie wasn't okay. Seeing Dax Ellis after all these years had rattled her. He was the reason for every bad dream she'd had as a child. He'd made her life hell.

Callie debated closing early, but that would only bring another harsh censure from Dorothy Ellis. One visit from an Ellis was enough for today or any day.

Callie locked the library door at the end of the day and headed home. The front wheel of her bike wobbled as it dipped in and out of a pothole in the gravel road on the ride to her house. She glanced over her shoulder again and again, expecting to see Dax jump out from behind every tree and bush she passed. She gripped the handlebars until her fingers began to ache, pedaling faster until she pulled into the driveway of her grandparents' house, breathless.

Instead of going right in, Callie went to her favorite spot. She sank down onto the porch swing with enough force to start a gentle sway back and forth. Callie wished she had her grandparents on either side of her the way they used to be, with her grandfather telling her stories about his childhood while she sat cocooned in her grandmother's arms. Their love had made Colton home.

Her grandparents left her a nice inheritance when they died. Her parents wanted her to sell the library and the rest of the buildings on the block, but Callie knew she could never do that to her grandparents. Besides, you can't put a price on unconditional love. Her parents couldn't even spare a full day to attend the funeral. Instead, it was Mae who stood with her graveside while she said her final goodbye.

Callie never questioned her decision to make Colton her home. Not until today. She could handle Dorothy Ellis and her "queen of the South" attitude, but her son? Callie shivered, wrapping her arms around herself. She didn't know how she would handle Dax. She tipped her head back, looking up at the night sky. Looking for the North Star, she gave the swing another push with her toe. Why had he looked so shocked to see her? Didn't he know she would be there?

"Evening, Miss Callie," a deep, gravelly voice called out.

Callie jumped, putting her hand over her heart. "Oh, Uncle Robert. I didn't see you there."

Anyone under thirty in Colton called Robert Ellis Uncle Robert. If someone needed help planting a garden or mending a fence, Uncle Robert was always happy to lend a hand. He had become a guiding force in the community, and in many ways reminded Callie of her grandfather.

He came up on the porch and took a seat next to her on the swing.

They rocked in silence for a few moments before he finally said, "I just wanted to make sure you were okay."

Callie raised her eyebrows, looking at him. "News sure does travel fast."

He nodded. "I've been talkin' to Dax. He's pretty shaken up."

Callie snorted a laugh. "That's ironic."

"He'll be fine." Robert waved his hand. "You're the one I'm worried about."

Callie leaned back, looking up at the beadboard ceiling. "I thought he wouldn't come home. I should have known better, with his mother living here. How long is he staying for?"

Robert stood up, making the swing jerk and creak. "He's here for good, honey."

"What?" Callie jumped off the swing to face the older man. Her heart pounded in her chest. She could handle Dax being in town for a few days, but living here?

Uncle Robert patted her shoulder. "He's not the same boy and you're not the same girl," he said with a quiet calm.

She leaned in for a hug, resting her cheek against the rough denim of Robert's shirt, taking in the faint scent of earth and tobacco. Her lips twitched. "I thought you were going to give up smoking."

Robert's low laughter vibrated through her. "It's the right of every old Southern gentleman to sit on the porch and smoke a cigar every once in a while."

"Maybe." She pulled away and sat back down. "I wish you would have told me Dax was coming."

Robert joined her on the swing. "You're right. But I didn't want to upset you."

"I don't know that I can be anything but upset and… angry. I've worked hard to make a life for myself here, and he doesn't get to just come back and act like nothing's changed."

"I promise you it's not going to be the same as it was before."

Callie nodded, but in her mind, time stood still, and nothing had changed.

"Dax isn't here to start any trouble," Uncle Robert added firmly. "Do you honestly think I would stand by and let Dax do anything to hurt you?"

She sighed. "No, I don't. It's just hard for me to trust people."

"Can I ask why?"

"Sometimes people would pretend to want to be my friend, and then a few weeks or months would pass and they would slip me their demo tape or their friend's tape asking me to take it to my father."

"Oh, honey. That couldn't have been easy, but I suppose it comes with the territory when your dad's a well-known producer."

"I learned the hard way that some people don't want to be friends with me for the right reasons."

"And that's why you use your mom's maiden name," he answered.

She nodded. "It's easier to blend in when you're Callie Colton instead of Callie Fischer."

"Some people would love that kind of attention."

"Not me." Callie's jaw firmed. She spent most of her childhood being raised by nannies while her parents flew around the world, immersed in the music scene. Living in Colton gave her the normalcy and stability she craved.

"You have good friends here who can see past all of that. Dax doesn't care about that stuff, either. He just wants to have a fresh start."

"So, we're just supposed to start over?"

"It's not gonna be easy. I expect my sister-in-law is going to crow even louder now that her favorite son is home, but I'm here for you whenever you need me."

Callie smiled. "I know, and it helps."

With a last pat on her shoulder, Robert rose and headed home.

Callie dug her toe into the floorboards, sending the porch swing into a gentle rocking motion, and watched the lightning bugs dance for a while, creating a ballet of light in the darkness.

Uncle Robert was right, she couldn't avoid Dax—you couldn't avoid anyone in a small town.

Robert was also right about Dorothy Ellis. Mrs. Ellis acted like the sun rose and set on her youngest son. For years, Callie didn't even know Dax had an older brother. Reid Ellis had been sent away to boarding school the first summer Callie spent in Colton. One time she walked in on her grandparents furiously whispering something about "that poor Ellis boy." The conversation ended abruptly when they noticed she was in the room. Callie must have been about seven and too young to understand what was going on. Her grandparents never mentioned Reid Ellis's name again.

Sometimes she wished she could ask her mother about the Ellis family and her time in Colton. But her mother acted like Colton didn't exist. It was just one more way she and her mother were so different. Callie loved the place her mother couldn't wait to get away from.

Callie wandered into the house. Sometimes she still expected to see her grandmother standing at the vintage stove making hot water corn bread because it was her favorite. She'd updated the kitchen with new cabinets and sage-green paint on the walls, but she kept the stove for sentimental value. She looked over at her grandfather's rocking chair, another memento she couldn't bear to part with. She could still picture him sitting in his favorite chair, nodding in agreement with whatever he read as he rocked. She turned on the light in the spare bedroom she'd converted into an office. Sitting down at the antique desk in front of the window, she opened her computer. She had a book review to write and a blog post to finish.

Forty-five minutes later, Callie closed her laptop. She was hungry but too distracted to prepare dinner. Everyone always assumed she would work in the music industry like her father, but it was books that she loved. Her eyes scanned the first editions that filled her bookshelves. They were her one real indulgence, building on the collection that started when her grandparents gave her a first edition of *Anne of Green Gables* when she was a girl.

Callie grabbed the next book on her to-be-read pile and climbed under the covers. It didn't matter how compelling the story was, tonight she struggled to focus. After reading the same page twice, she gave up and closed her eyes.

Her feet pounded on the dirt road as she ran toward her grandparents' house, desperately trying to escape the boy throwing rocks at her. The farther she ran, the larger the rocks grew. Her grandparents stood on the front porch, her grandmother holding her arms out, calling to her, but Callie couldn't run fast enough. The rocks became boulders, battering and bruising her until she couldn't run anymore.

She woke up sweating, heart racing, skin damp. For a moment she didn't know where she was; she dug her fingers into the quilt her grandmother made for her, grounding herself.

The nightmares were back.

CHAPTER THREE

DAX SLIPPED in through the back door of his childhood home, ignoring his mother's preference for the formality of the main entrance. It was a small act of defiance—one that he was too old for—but he did it anyway. His mother had been over the moon when he told her he was moving home; the words were barely out of his mouth when she began to outline what was expected of him. Duty. Responsibility. Obedience. If he'd just listen to her, she knew what was best. Every conversation since then, he'd tried to make her understand that he was coming home, but on his terms, living the way he chose. His mother had a way of hearing and seeing things only the way she wanted. She was as rigid and set in her ways as the toughest drill sergeant he'd faced at boot camp.

The pristine white exterior accented with dark green shutters and framed by a deep covered porch may have appeared inviting, but Dax knew better. Most people cherished their childhood home, but he only felt remorse. There was no love in this house and there never had been. His mother had made it clear during their many conversations about him moving back to Colton that she expected Dax to move in with her, but that was impossible.

He would suffocate here.

Ripe, red cherries still hung in clusters on the wallpaper, and his mother's precious copper pots, polished to spotless perfection, hung above the large island in the center of the room. He was the only thing that had changed over the years. He found his mother in the dining room, setting the table. The large oak table in the kitchen sat unused—that table was only for show, so people would think they were a normal family. As usual, they would be eating in the more formal room. Dax clenched his teeth, watching her place each knife and fork with precision, making minute adjustments only she would notice. She glanced up at him and then examined the place setting with a critical eye, turning the plate a quarter turn so that the pattern set straight. That's the way Dorothy Ellis liked things. Keeping up appearances meant more to his mother than greeting the son she hadn't seen in years.

"Welcome home, Dax," his mother finally acknowledged, placing a kiss on his cheek, forgoing a hug that might wrinkle her suit.

"Hello, Mother." Dax looked down at the table. How many forks did a person really need to get through a meal? "Looks like you pulled out all the stops for dinner. I thought it was just going to be the two of us," he said, glancing at the third place setting.

"Well, dear." She avoided making eye contact, bustling around the table continuing to fuss even though everything was in place. "Presley is coming to dinner."

Dax crossed his arms. "Oh no, Mother, really?"

"What? She's been a good friend of ours for years."

"Friend of yours, then. She's not my friend."

His mother gave him her trademark steely glare. "Dax, you're thirty. Time for you to settle down."

"When I'm ready to settle down, it will be with a person I've chosen and not someone you have chosen for me."

"She's excited to see you. How could I not include her in your welcome-home dinner?"

Dax watched his mother pat her upswept hair, a style that wouldn't have moved even in a hurricane. "Why can't we just have dinner together? I haven't seen you in years, either."

"That's not my fault." She fingered the pearls at her neck, a gesture that always indicated her displeasure.

They stood across the table from each other, their eyes locked in a silent battle of wills. "I'm not here to fight, Mother," he said flatly.

"And I'm just trying to help," she replied.

"You don't need to fix me up. That's not the help I need."

The doorbell rang, cutting the argument short. His mother gave him a triumphant smile.

"Dax, get the door and please do give Presley a proper welcome."

His mother had decided that Presley Beaumont would make the perfect wife for Dax when they were in high school, and for a while he hadn't seen anything wrong with her plan. Thank God he'd found his way out of Colton and learned he wouldn't be happy with a woman who never worked for anything in life and didn't give a damn about anyone other than herself.

The huge chandelier in the entryway cast tiny droplets of light on the large flowers woven into the rug beneath his feet as he made his way toward the entry. The leaded glass in the door blurred the figure behind it, but it couldn't disguise the outline of Presley's hair. He took a deep breath and opened the door with the friendliest expression he could muster.

"Well, hello, stranger." Presley threw her arms around his neck, plastering herself against him. She'd managed to find a dress in the most unnatural shade of pink he'd ever seen. It hugged every curve and showed the amount of cleavage that, he figured in her mind, he'd find attractive.

He pried himself away, trying to make as much space as possible between himself and the sickening sweet smell of cotton candy and baby powder that engulfed him. Holding his breath, he made his way back to the dining room, knowing Presley would follow him like a cat chasing a piece of string.

Presley rushed past him to greet his mother. "Miss Dorothy, it's so good to see you again!" she cooed.

"Well, don't you look pretty tonight. I guess you wanted to look extra nice for someone special," Dorothy said with an exaggerated wink that sent him straight for the liquor cabinet. "Good idea, Dax. I'll have sherry," Dorothy called over her shoulder.

"I would just love a wine cooler," Presley requested, batting her eyelashes at him.

Dax poured himself a shot of bourbon and downed it. He put up with Presley as one of his friend's younger sisters when they were kids, but he had no interest in reacquainting himself with her now. Dax figured out in high school that Presley didn't have an ounce of common sense under all that hair. And based on his mother's reports over the years, nothing had changed.

The two of them looked like mother and daughter, he thought, watching them gossip while he fixed their drinks. Both must have picked the same box of hair color, an unnatural shade of blond that looked like bleached straw. Nothing like Callie Colton's rich, dark golden curls. He finished the rest of his drink and quickly poured himself another, trying to shake the image of her shocked expression from his head.

Presley brushed her fingers against his as he handed her the wine cooler. "I'm so glad you're home. It will be just like old times."

"I hope not," Dax said under his breath, taking another large sip from his glass.

He nodded and listened with one ear while Presley babbled on about friends from school, updating him on which ones were married and who was pregnant.

She sighed dreamily, resting her hand on his arm. "I just can't wait until it's my turn, standing under the gazebo with a handsome man at my side."

The white gazebo stood proudly at the center of the town square, where throughout the years it recorded the history of the town. From summer band concerts and parades to civil rights marches, the beloved structure became a favorite location for family events and weddings, one of the rare places in Colton that hosted celebrations by both Black and White. As time passed, the legend grew that marriages that took place in the gazebo would be long, happy, and fruitful. Most young girls in Colton dreamed of standing under the dome to say their vows.

"Don't you two make a handsome couple," Dorothy observed with an approving gaze as she set a large plate of ham on the table.

Presley giggled again. Frowning, Dax looked down at his empty glass. The bourbon couldn't disguise the bitter taste in his mouth anymore.

He untangled himself from Presley and moved to pull out his mother's chair as he'd been taught. He went to take his usual seat when his mother shook her head.

"Oh no," Dorothy exclaimed, "you sit at the head of the table. You're the man of the house now."

Dax frowned, moving to the captain's chair. As much as Dorothy ruled her roost, she was still a traditional Southern woman. It would never occur to her that she could sit at the head of the table after her husband passed away.

"There," his mother said with a satisfied smile, "now you can have Presley at your side." She gave them an approving look, clasping her hands to her chest as Presley took her seat. "My handsome young man, you're all I have left now that your father's gone."

Dax narrowed his eyes. "You have another son, Mother," he insisted, his temper rising, heart pounding, echoing into a steady drumbeat in his head. It was the same tune that played every time they talked about his brother. *Why does she want to pretend he doesn't even exist?*

Dorothy pursed her lips as if she had just eaten a lemon. "Reid has never been a dutiful son," she replied.

"Maybe because you sent him away before he even had a chance to try," he shot back between clenched teeth. He got up to pour himself another glass of bourbon when his mother fingered her pearls again. This was exactly why he wouldn't ever live in this house again, and exactly why he'd dreaded coming tonight. He loved his mother, but her company was miserable. Maybe because *she* was miserable.

He returned to the table and with a smile that didn't reach her eyes, his mother took a small sip of her sherry and set the glass down, moving it a fraction of an inch before looking at Dax again. "Well, he's not here now, and let's not ruin your homecoming by talking about Reid. Let's talk about the Founders Day dance at the club. It's one of my favorite events of the year, and I can't wait to see the two of you on the dance floor together."

Dax looked from his mother to Presley, who flipped her hair over her shoulder and winked at him.

"I'm not planning on going to the dance," he said.

Presley's face fell. "But I was counting on having you as my escort. I turned everybody else down when your mama said you were coming home."

"Dax, you really can't let Presley down," his mother added.

Dax knew what his mother was really saying is that he couldn't let *her* down. Appearances meant everything to his mother, and she'd probably already bragged to all her friends about how her precious son would be at the dance.

"How are things going on the town council?" he asked his mother, trying to change the subject.

"Everything is running smoothly with a few small exceptions."

"I'm going to take over the library. Isn't that excitin'?" Presley announced.

"What?" Dax snapped to attention.

"Proper English, dear; you don't want to sound like you came from a trailer park," Dorothy answered, adjusting the string of pearls at her neck.

Presley straightened her shoulders. "Yes, ma'am."

"Once we get rid of that Colton girl, we can make sure the library is run properly," his mother continued.

"What are you talking about?" Dax narrowed his eyes at his mother, his stomach knotting.

"That girl is unsuitable to run the library," his mother said, stabbing her fork into a piece of ham.

Dax smashed his anger. "Uncle Robert told me Callie has a master's degree in library science. I can't imagine anyone more suitable."

His mother sniffed, and Presley flipped her hair with a huff. A dull headache began to form at the base of his skull. His mother's jaw ticked as she carefully set her fork down and steepled her hands in front of her.

"That girl—"

"Her name is Callie," Dax cut her off.

Dorothy's lips compressed and spots of color appeared on her cheeks, clashing with the artificial blush she applied every day. "The librarian," she began again.

Dax set his drink down and pushed his plate away. "Really, Mother? What is your problem with her? You've never liked her or her family."

"Well, you can't expect those kinds of people to have any class," Presley said, taking a dainty sip from her wine cooler.

"What kind of people are you talking about?" Dax demanded and then waited, because it was just a matter of time before Presley put her foot so far into her mouth, she'd choke on it.

"Well, you know." Presley shrugged her shoulders.

Because he did know.

He knew that his mother still believed the color of her skin gave her an innate superiority. But hearing it from Presley reminded him that leaving Colton had been the right decision, and it had set him on a better path in life. But now he was back, and he had a chance to help his mother confront her prejudice and catch up with the changing times and attitudes. She still believed in a South that had long since faded away into history. Dorothy Ellis lived in a small world of her own making, and Dax wanted to do what he could to guide her toward living successfully in the real one.

His mother continued her rant. "It doesn't matter how much money her father has. There are some things money can't buy. Her mother always wanted more than what she deserved."

"What does that even mean?" he asked.

"People need to keep their place."

"Times have changed, Mother, your… attitude is—"

"There is nothing wrong with my attitude," his mother bristled.

Presley watched wide-eyed, her head bobbing back and forth as if she was watching a tennis match.

Between his mother's attitude and Presley's cheap perfume, he wasn't sure he could keep what he'd eaten down. He shoved his chair back and stood up, tossed his napkin on the table. "I've lost my appetite."

He walked away, leaving his mother fuming and Presley staring at him open-mouthed. Once he made it outside, he took a deep breath, filling his lungs with the warm night air.

He climbed into his car and started the engine. His childhood home grew smaller and smaller in the rearview mirror, just like his hope for a different relationship with his mother, as he drove away. If he had any sense that his mother might have softened over the years, her behavior at dinner crushed it.

He would never be like his mother, he vowed. She had done her best to turn him into a replica of herself, but he would never be like her. Dax repeated it like a mantra as he drove back to his uncle's home.

His phone vibrated in his pocket as he pulled into Robert's driveway.

"Dax, you need to apologize to Presley for your rude behavior during dinner," his mother commanded.

"I have nothing to apologize for. You were the ones being rude." His teeth clenched so tight he thought they might break.

"You will not be disrespectful, Dax. You must remember we have a reputation to uphold."

Dax snorted a laugh. "What reputation, Mother, being snobs?"

"There is nothing wrong with having high standards." Her reply was cold and unyielding.

Dax glanced up as Uncle Robert wandered out to the porch and leaned against the railing with a beer in his hand. He raised a questioning eyebrow at Dax, clearly surprised to see him returning from dinner so early.

"When are you moving in?" his mother continued.

"I'm not. I bought the Barton Building and I'll be staying with Uncle Robert until I can move in there."

"What in the world are you thinking? I was counting on you to stay with me."

Dax pulled the phone away from his ear while his mother shouted about his obligation to be a dutiful son.

The familiar pang of guilt took up residence near his heart. "I can't do that, Mother. I have to get my business up and running. I need to be here.

"You could do that from here, in your father's office." Her voice took on a familiar cajoling tone that made him wince. "Dax, I'm not getting any younger and it's time for you to carry on the family legacy. It won't be for long—once you and Presley are married you can get a place of your own. Of course, this house is big enough that if the two of you wanted—"

"No, Mother," Dax cut her off.

The silence on the other end of the line made the hair stand up on the back of his neck. It was a tactic she'd always used, silence, making him squirm until the quiet made him give in. Those days were over. He gritted his teeth, waiting.

"I see." Her words were clipped and then the line abruptly went dead.

Dax kicked the dirt at his feet. He would suffer through a country club dinner to make amends and keep the peace for now.

"Hungry?" Uncle Robert asked when he joined him on the porch.

"Can I start with one of those?" Dax asked, nodding toward the beer in Robert's hand.

Reaching down, he picked up another bottle and tossed it to Dax with a chuckle. "Figured you'd need this when I saw you come home from dinner early."

Dax sat down next to his uncle. Leaning forward, he rested his elbows on his knees. "Why did I think anything had changed?"

"Let me guess, your mother ambushed you with Presley Beaumont."

"That and then she started bad mouthing Callie and talking about people keeping their place."

Uncle Robert's mouth turned down. "Some folks cling to old ideas because they're afraid of change or admitting they're wrong."

But that's exactly what Dax had done. Admitting he was wrong allowed him to change and become a better person.

He wasn't the only one who'd changed, though. Callie Colton's skin was just a touch darker than he remembered, a light golden brown, with blond highlights running through her tawny curls. But it was the eyes and the way they looked at him with the same wariness that hadn't changed at all.

"I want the folks around here to know I'm not the same awful kid who used to make everyone's life miserable."

The two men sat in silence, rocking and drinking.

"Uncle Robert, thanks for coming home to Colton and kicking my ass."

Robert studied him for a long time. "Coming back to Colton in time to set you straight was one of the best decisions I ever made."

Dax rubbed his hands over the crease of the neatly pressed khakis he'd worn to appease his mother. His uncle's confession humbled him. "You don't regret leaving the firm?" Uncle Robert had taken an early retirement from the CIA to return home, and Dax always wondered if he regretted giving up living a life of travel and intrigue.

"Who says I left?" Robert replied with a glint in his eye.

Dax knew better than to ask any questions. He may have been one of the only people besides his father who knew that Robert worked for the CIA, and even he didn't know the exact nature of what his uncle did for "the firm." It was Robert's mentorship that had led Dax to his career with the military and, in many ways, brought him back home. He had to travel around the world and back again to realize that of all the ugly things he had seen and done, his past in his hometown wasn't the worst.

If his uncle could find contentment in a small town after seeing everything the world had to offer, so could he. Small towns like Colton were struggling to survive, and he was shocked by how little governance and support his mother and the town council were providing. Small minds and small-town politics still ruled in Colton.

Buying the Barton Building was the first step toward helping revitalize his community.

He stared out at the field of corn in the fading light. "I knew it wasn't going to be easy to come home. I thought my mother would be different, that my memory was harsher than the reality."

"Not everyone around here is like your mother. There's plenty of good people who want to make a difference. The problem is your mother and the people who think like her have stacked the deck."

"The way she talked about Callie tonight...." He shook his head. "I don't get it, why is she so hateful?"

Robert pulled a cigar out of the front pocket of his overalls. He struck a match and held it, watching it burn for a moment before he lit the cigar and took a couple of puffs. "I have to confess, when your dad started dating Dorothy, I was surprised. He used to talk about wanting to change the world and challenge the status quo. Then he started hanging out at the country club with her, and instead of becoming a teacher, he went to law school. When they came back to Colton with Reid after your father graduated, he was so different. Quiet. Somber. I never understood what hold she had over him, but if your mama said jump, well...." Robert's expression grew dark; he grimaced and looked away.

"Hey, you can't go back and change the history that's already been written."

Robert gave him a wry smile. "That's true. You'll write your own history going forward, not your mother."

"I just hope my story has a happier ending than my parents'."

CHAPTER FOUR

CALLIE JUMPED every time the door to the library opened. She rubbed her eyes, trying to focus on the book in her hand, but they burned from lack of sleep and the words began to blur again. Days of being on edge, watching for Dax around every corner, and sleepless nights filled with nightmares had worn her down. She glanced at the clock again and helped the last patrons who were looking for a new book for their weekend's entertainment. She logged in returned books, becoming lost in the rhythm of work, and didn't notice when Dax came in.

"Hello, Callie."

Startled, she looked up at him.

He cleared his throat. "Hello," he repeated.

The years had added more lines to his face, and a day's growth of stubble covered his jaw. The planes of his face were harder and leaner than she remembered, but she saw a kindness reflected in his eyes that she didn't recognize, and it caused her throat to dry up.

"What do you want?" she asked.

Dax held his hands up and took a step back. "I didn't mean to scare you. I'm not here to cause any trouble, I promise."

"I'm not scared, you... you just startled me."

The memory of the last time she saw Dax washed over her.

Summer after summer, she avoided him, always vigilant. Except for that last summer when Mae convinced her to take one final swim at Turtle Pond. They always tried to go early in the day when they could have the pond to themselves, but the waning summer days meant everyone was trying to make every last minute count before the leaves turned to red and gold. Dax and his friends were already there by the time they arrived. She and Mae had laid their towels out on a large flat rock on the other side of the pond. Dax kept eyeing her while he wrestled with his friends in the water, cheered on by Presley and her friends. It was only a matter of time before Dax made his way over to them.

"Good afternoon, ladies," he sneered.

Callie put her head down in the futile hope that if she ignored him, he would go away.

"What do you want, Dax?" Mae flopped over onto her back, resting on her elbows. "It's the last day of summer. Maybe you can give yourself a holiday from being such an ass."

Dax smirked. "I just wanted to check on one thing."

Before Mae could say anything, he reached down, scooped Callie up and threw her into the water. It happened so fast, Callie didn't even have a chance to scream before the water closed over her. Her arm hit the edge of the rock outcropping with a crack as she went down, the searing pain making her gasp, filling her lungs with water instead of air. She kicked her legs, pushing herself to the surface to tread water with one arm while the other hung at her side. She came up sputtering and coughing to see Mae pushing Dax. Her words were muffled by the water in her ears, but she could see Dax throw his head back and laugh.

"I just wanted to see if all dogs knew how to swim," he said as he made his way back to his friends laughing and pointing on the other side of the pond.

All dogs know how to swim. Callie shook off the memory and asked, "How can I help you?" trying to sound as cool and professional as possible.

"I came in to get a library card and...." Dax cleared his throat. "I wanted to apologize for... everything, I'm ashamed for the things I said and did. I regret everything. That day at the pond, I...."

She jerked back. Had he read her thoughts?

His voice dropped, deepening. "I'm ashamed, and I know you have no reason to ever forgive me, but I am asking for forgiveness. I hate who I was, and I hate what I did to you."

How many years had she waited to hear those words? She shook her head. She'd never expected an apology because she knew she'd never get one. And now, here was Dax standing in front of her, apologizing. She didn't know how much she needed to hear those simple words until they hung in the air between them.

But she wasn't ready to forgive, not yet. She moved behind the checkout counter, watching him warily as she pulled up the library card form on the computer. There were no traces of the boy she knew. The youthful features were gone, replaced with a strong jaw and observant eyes, taking in everything around him. She wasn't blind. Dax Ellis had grown into a handsome man. If he were anyone other than her childhood tormentor, she might find him attractive, but he was, and she needed to be on her guard.

Dax stepped back from the counter. "I can come back another time," he said. "This might not be the most convenient time to get a card."

He lives here now, Callie reminded herself. *You're going to run into him no matter what, so you'd better get used to it.* She forced herself to look her childhood nemesis in the eye.

"No. Let's just get it done."

Mae burst into the library. "Dax Ellis, you have a lot of nerve showing up here."

Dax held up both hands. "I just came to get a library card."

Mae narrowed her eyes. "Fine, I'll just wait until you're finished."

She turned to Callie with a raised eyebrow, silently asking *Are you okay?* She nodded, and Callie cleared her throat, turning her attention back to him.

"I'll just need your address." She bit her lip. "I guess I don't need any ID or proof of residence."

"I don't want you to break any rules for me," Dax said with his lips turned up, reaching for his wallet. "Here's my driver's license—"

"I'm sure it's okay. Special rules for special people," Mae's voice dripped with sarcasm.

Callie gave Mae a look and shook her head.

"My address has changed, though," Dax added, giving her the address of one of the buildings across the street.

"That's the Barton Building," Callie said.

He nodded. "I'm going to be converting the top two floors into apartments."

"You mean to tell me you aren't going to be living with your mama?" Mae asked with a raised eyebrow.

Callie ignored her cousin. "I'm happy to see someone else investing in the town," she said. "These old buildings should be saved. They've been boarded up for too many years."

"I agree," he said, putting his wallet away. "I would love to see the town square full of shops again."

Mae snorted. "You'd better check with your mama first. She doesn't seem too interested in anyone making any changes."

"Mae, please," Callie said.

Her cousin meant well, but she wasn't helping.

Callie finished putting the rest of the information into the computer and printed out a new library card, which she then placed in a plastic sleeve and ran through the small laminating machine before handing it to Dax.

"Careful, it's hot," she warned.

His fingers grazed hers, and she jerked her hand back. The card fell to the counter, and they both reached for it, their hands bumping again.

"Sorry," they both said in unison.

Mae picked up the card, handing it to Dax with a pointed look. Callie's cheeks heated, and she turned away from his gaze. She prayed Dax wasn't a big reader.

"Thank you," he said.

Callie waited for him to leave, but he just stood there watching her, his gaze unwavering. The boy was now a man. A man who looked at her in a way that made her feel like a woman and not a scared little girl. The air around them stilled as she struggled to understand these new and conflicting feelings. Dax still made her nervous—that wasn't going to change anytime soon—but he wasn't throwing rocks at her this time, and his apology seemed sincere.

Mae cleared her throat and Callie felt the heat rising in her cheeks, catching a hint of amusement from Dax as he turned away. She could pray day and night, and all of it would be in vain. She had a feeling he would be visiting the library on a regular basis.

The minute the door closed, Mae whirled around. "What in the world was that all about?"

"You heard him, he wanted a library card," Callie said, grabbing a stack of books and started shelving, so distracted she didn't notice that she was putting a book on gardening in the automotive section. She always wanted to be as calm and badass as the heroine of her Barista Mystery series, Isobel Chase, but she didn't even come close, the way she behaved today.

Mae followed her around the library as she moved from shelf to shelf. "What did he say?"

"He said he wanted a library card." Callie shrugged.

Mae rolled her eyes. "You know what I mean."

"You were here, Mae. You heard everything just like I did." It was what he didn't say that troubled her more, the way he looked at her, with a tenderness and concern she never thought she would ever see from him.

Callie glanced at the clock on the wall. "I'll lock up and we can grab dinner, okay?"

Mae studied her for a minute before finally nodding her head. Callie knew the interrogation would continue through dinner. She gathered up her things and turned out the lights, following Mae out into the fading light of the day. The scent of the roses surrounding the gazebo wafted over her as they made their way across the park toward the red neon sign of the Catfish Café.

As they walked across the park, Mae paused, looking at the old Barton Building Dax now owned. "I wonder how much he's going to rent the apartments for?"

Callie looked at her cousin in surprise. "You would consider moving into an apartment with Dax?"

"I wouldn't be living with Dax, just in his building. Why not?" Mae shrugged. "I'm too old to be living at home, and I don't want to buy a house. Maybe I'll take a look when he's finished the remodel."

"I doubt your folks would be happy about that idea."

Mae frowned. "Probably not, but at least I stayed home and didn't leave like Beth."

"Have you heard from your sister lately?"

"No." Mae sighed. "Miss high-and-mighty is too busy being an NFL wife in Atlanta to spend any time with us common folks."

Mae acted like she didn't care, but Callie knew that she missed her older sister. Beth always had one goal, and that was to get out of Colton and never come back. She always had dreams of living a high-society life in a big city, and they came true when her college boyfriend proposed on the same day he was drafted by the Atlanta Phoenix.

"Maybe she'll come home for Easter," Callie offered as they walked into the only café in Colton.

"I doubt it. I don't care, but it's not fair to my parents."

Callie knew Mae was lying—she loved her sister and missed her.

Callie slid into the red vinyl booth, running her hands over the worn gray-and-white speckled Formica table. Tillie appeared with a pitcher of sweet tea, the reddish-brown color matching her hair. She filled their glasses without asking and then stood by with her hand on her hip. Neither Callie nor Mae picked up the grease-stained menus in front of them, having long ago memorized everything the Catfish Café had to offer.

"Evening," they said in unison.

"Evening, ladies. Are y'all having the usual tonight?"

"Yes, ma'am," they said in unison again.

Tillie put her hand on her hip, her lips quirked. "Are you sure you girls aren't twins?"

"No, ma'am," they answered together again and started laughing.

Tillie walked away and Mae leaned forward, resting her elbows on the table. "Now, are you ready to talk about what was going on with Dax back there and why you have those dark circles under your eyes?"

"Seriously, Mae, he just wanted a library card." Callie took a sip of her tea. Sugar and caffeine weren't going to help with her insomnia, but she drank it anyway, savoring the sweet drink.

"Well, I don't like the idea of him sniffing around the library or you after all the trouble he caused." Mae leaned closer. "You be careful around those sexy eyes."

Callie's eyes watered as she choked on her tea, sputtering and coughing. "Dax Ellis is not sexy."

"Oh, honey." Tillie appeared at their table with two plates of fried chicken, macaroni and cheese, and green salad. "I'm an old woman and even I know that man is sex on a stick." Mae burst out laughing while Callie blushed to her roots. Tillie patted Callie's shoulder. "You get a pass, honey, after everything that boy did to you."

Too embarrassed to respond, Callie stared at her plate. Was he hot? She couldn't deny that the gangly arms and legs of boyhood had transformed into solid muscle, and she'd had a hard time looking away from those dark brown eyes. Eyes that used to make her tremble but now made her heart flutter. Yes, Dax had returned to Colton a drop-dead sexy man, and that made him more dangerous.

"He came in here and apologized." Tillie snorted a laugh. "Insisted on paying me back for every tip he stole with interest," she said before heading to another table to take their order.

Callie shook her head. "I don't believe it. What is he up to?"

"Maybe he has changed. He's certainly not the same scrawny boy anymore." Mae fanned herself. "Good Lord, those muscles."

Callie frowned. "Stop it, Mae."

Mae bit her lip trying to fight a grin. "I'm just saying he is fine."

"Yeah, the stuff of nightmares."

Mae narrowed her eyes. "You're having nightmares again?"

"I don't want to talk about it," Callie mumbled, toying with the food on her plate.

Mae cocked her head, watching her for a minute before she picked up her own fork with a sigh. "Okay fine, let's talk about the bookstore."

That subject was just as bad as talking about Dax.

"I don't know if there's ever going to be one."

"You know you could…."

Mae didn't have to finish. Callie knew what she was suggesting, and she shook her head. She lived off her own income; the money from her trust fund was used only for special projects. She'd put a lot of effort into becoming Callie Colton, leaving poor little rich girl Callie Fischer behind, and she didn't want to remind anyone that she was the daughter of a well-known music producer with enough money to buy Colton a million times over.

"You can't buy community," her grandfather would say. "You have to earn your place, contribute and participate in making where you live better for everyone." Her eyes misted over for a minute as she tried to find the blessing in his memory and not just the pain of missing him.

It wasn't easy dealing with a woman who had a grudge and the sheriff in her back pocket. But why? Dorothy Ellis resisted change like a cat avoided water and did everything she could to give preferential treatment to her friends, making it hard for anyone else. The whole town knew it, and no one liked it, but this was the Deep South, and speaking out could still get you into a heap of trouble or even worse. Even in this day and age you heard stories of people run out of towns, and even the county, for "causing trouble."

"I can't believe the way she's got Sheriff Crosby wrapped around her finger." Mae's dark brown eyes flashed. "How many bogus citations did he come up with for the last contractor?"

"Twenty," Callie sighed. "I paid all the fines, but I couldn't convince him to finish the job. He said it wasn't worth all of the trouble."

So far, between Dax's mother and the sheriff, they'd run off seven contractors from two counties.

"I'll never understand how she became the queen bee around here."

Callie thought for a moment. "Grandpa was one of the only people who ever really stood up to her and now that he's gone…."

"And she hated that. She doesn't like anyone who she thinks doesn't 'know their place.'" Mae crooked her fingers in the air. "The fact that you're rich pisses her off even more. I know you think standing up to her will make it worse, but I think you're wrong. That woman is so stuck up she'd drown in a rainstorm. She needs someone to show her what's right."

"You're right, but I'm trying to follow my grandparents' example and not fight hate with hate; that doesn't solve anything."

"We all miss them; they were such good people." Mae gave her a sympathetic look.

"I think about Grandma and Grandpa every day," Callie whispered. Would the pain of losing them ever lessen?

"They would be so proud of what you're doing with the bookstore."

Callie smiled. "Grandpa would have been there every day helping."

"Have you thought of a name yet? Maybe we can come up with something that will honor our grandparents and piss off the dragon lady at the same time." Mae smirked.

"I was thinking of something simpler. How about The Bookworm?"

"Ugh, that is so boring."

"Okay, smarty-pants, what's your big idea?"

Mae tapped her chin. "Hmm, how about The Book Nook?"

Callie wrinkled her nose.

"Okay fine, that's not much better than The Bookworm."

Callie stared out of the window across the park toward the papered-over window of the bookstore, and suddenly she sat up straighter. "We're being too fancy." There were four streets that created the town square: Magnolia, Pine, Main, and Spring streets, where the library and the bookstore were. "What do you think of The Spring Street Book and Coffee Co?"

A slow grin spread over Mae's face. "I love it."

"Sounds good to me," Tillie called out from behind the counter, while a few of the other customers sitting close by nodded their approval.

"We have a name. Now let's focus on the important stuff." Mae leaned forward with a mischievous twinkle in her eye. "Any luck finding the hot barista I requested?"

Callie laughed. "As soon as I'm confident I can get the work finished, I'll place an ad. You can even help write it if you want."

"Wanted: hot barista for small-town bookstore coffee shop. Six five, broad shoulders, nice abs." Mae ticked off her requirements.

"Don't forget the man bun," she teased.

The two of them came up with more and more ridiculous requirements for their dream barista until their laughter drew Tillie back to their table to add her own suggestions. By the end of dinner, Callie leaned back with a relaxed expression, feeling content. As they wandered back across the park, she dared to be hopeful she might be able to sleep that night.

But she jerked to a stop when the library came into view. "No!" she yelled, breaking into a run. Her periwinkle-blue bike rested against the front window where she left it, only now it was nothing but a bent and twisted piece of metal. She fell to her knees, running her hands over the broken metal. The vintage cruiser had been one of the last gifts her grandparents gave her before they died. What was left of the wicker basket barely clung to the handlebars; the remnants of the basket fell into her hands. Her grandmother had insisted that she needed a basket for the bike and had emptied out one she used for knitting so Callie could use it. The basket had been ripped away from the hairpins her grandmother pulled out of her bun and carefully wove through the wicker to attach it to the handlebars. Callie still stopped to pick wildflowers to fill the basket the way she used to when she was little to bring home to her grandmother. Now her grandmother was gone, and the basket was splintered into pieces just like her heart.

"Come on, I'll put everything in the back of my car. Let's get out of here." Mae grasped her hands, pulled her to her feet and into her arms.

Together they put the twisted and broken pieces in the back of her Jeep. She sat in Mae's passenger seat while her tears fell. She didn't make a sound, unable to find a voice for her sorrow. It was just an object, but it kept her connected to her grandparents every day she rode it. Now it was gone. Grief was a funny thing. You thought you'd done all the grieving you could do, and then it came back with a force that took your breath away.

CHAPTER FIVE

ROCKS PINGED against the metal of the old green tractor as the scarlet-red Jeep skidded to a stop. Dax watched Mae Colton from Uncle Robert's porch as she jumped out and marched up the stairs with her eyes blazing. "Uncle Robert." She nodded without stopping.

"Evenin', Miss Mae." Robert tipped his baseball cap as Callie's cousin made a beeline for Dax.

She shoved him with both hands. "Dax Ellis, I don't know what kind of game you think you're playing, but you will not hurt Callie."

Dax held up his hands. "I swear, I'm just trying to start over."

"Trashing her bike and giving her nightmares isn't starting over, Dax."

"Wait, her bike? Nightmares?"

"What happened to Callie's bike?" Uncle Robert asked.

"When we came back from having dinner at the Catfish, it looked like someone," Mae said with a pointed look at Dax, "had run over Callie's bike. The frame was all twisted and bent." She turned to Robert, her voice breaking. "You know how much that bike meant to her."

Uncle Robert nodded, his lips pressed into a thin line. "I know you want to blame him, but Dax was here with me last night."

Mae crossed her arms and glared at Dax as if she were wishing he was nothing but a pile of ash at her feet. "Her grandparents gave her that bike."

"How long has she been having nightmares?" he asked, dreading the answer, but he needed to know.

"Ever since you came back," she said fiercely.

Dax held his breath, air bottled in his lungs.

"You have no idea how badly you hurt her, do you?" Mae asked.

"I was horrible, and I know it. But I guess I didn't understand just how much harm I caused. I hate that she's having nightmares because of me."

Dax pointed at his uncle. "Did you know about this?"

Uncle Robert ran his hand over his shaggy hair. "I didn't realize Callie was having nightmares again." His voice was low and gruff.

He slapped his hat back on, pulling it low over his eyes, and stepped off the porch heading toward the cornfield. Dax tracked his uncle until he disappeared into the green stalks.

"Is this fucking *Field of Dreams*?" Mae muttered under her breath.

Dax stared at where his uncle disappeared. "As long as I live, I'll never figure that man out."

Mae snorted. The two sat in silence, watching the corn sway in the breeze. In another week or two the stalks would dwarf him.

Eventually, Dax turned to Mae. "I didn't have anything to do with the bike. I want you to know that I'll never do anything to Callie or anyone else. I'm not the terrible person I used to be."

Mae propped her foot up on the chair, resting her chin on her hands folded on top of her knee. "The thing is, the damage has already been done."

"If I could go back and change the past, I would. Not a day goes by that I don't regret... everything."

"Good, you should regret it." She tilted her head toward him. "You made life miserable for a lot of folks before you went away. And your mama picked up where you left off."

"I feel terrible about that too. I didn't know how badly my mother's been behaving, I guess I didn't want to know."

"Parents can be embarrassing."

"What can I do for Callie?"

"Well... lookin' at Callie the way you were yesterday isn't going to help. Especially if your mama catches you looking at her like a lovesick puppy the way I did."

Dax cleared his throat and took a long drink. Mae got up and leaned against the porch railing. With a flash of red, the cardinal announced his arrival.

Dax pointed to the bucket of peanuts. "You'll make a friend for life if you give him some."

Mae plucked out a peanut and made a show of holding it up for a moment so the bird could see the treat before she threw it just a few feet in front of the porch. Another burst of red feathers and the cardinal grabbed the peanut, cocking its head to study them for a minute before flying away.

Mae laughed as she watched her new friend dip and swoop through the sky. "Cocky little bastard." She turned her focus back to Dax. "And what about you?"

"What about me?"

"You're not the same arrogant ass you used to be, so what happened?"

It was a relief to know that at least one person besides his uncle could see the difference. Dax ducked his head. One compliment wasn't going to change everything—he still had a lot of people he needed to make amends with—so this was the first few feet of a marathon, not a sprint.

"How about some sweet tea?" he offered.

Mae nodded, and he made his way into the house. He slumped against the counter, taking a minute to compose himself. At least Mae was willing to talk to him, but Callie—he might be the one who gave her nightmares, but who the hell would trash her bike? He straightened up and pulled a pitcher of tea from the refrigerator and grabbed two glasses and brought everything back to where Mae waited.

She took the glass he offered and took a sip, nodding with appreciation.

Dax reclaimed his spot in the rocking chair next to her and took a few sips before he began. "After high school, Uncle Robert pulled some strings and got me into Virginia Tech." He stopped rocking. "Those first few months were a shock, but I discovered I liked computer programming, and eventually one of my instructors recommended me for a special program."

"Special program?" Mae asked.

He cleared his throat. "Yeah, it's not something I can really talk about."

"Can I ask you a question?" Mae leaned forward conspiratorially. "For as long as I can remember, the rumor around here has been that Uncle Robert is ex-CIA."

Dax schooled his features into a blank expression.

Mae's eyes grew round. "Oh."

Dax set his drink down. "I can't say anything about that."

Mae cocked her head, studying him. "I didn't expect you to be so… thoughtful." She shook her head. "No, that's not right, maybe nice… no, that's not it either. I guess I thought you would still be an arrogant little shit."

"I grew up. I had a chance to travel and see more of the world and learn about other people and cultures."

"We've all grown up, but it's more than that. You're not angry anymore."

"I don't remember being angry." His mother had been constantly berating his father and showed cold indifference toward his brother. Was that what he felt: anger? "I guess I was angry, about a lot of things," he confessed.

"But why? You were the golden boy."

"That's why. I didn't want to be the person my mother wanted me to be. I hated that she doted on me but sent my brother away." He was about to admit a truth to Mae that he had not admitted to himself. "I always had this fear that if I didn't make her happy, she would send me away, like she did to Reid."

Mae sucked in her breath. "That's heavy stuff, Dax."

"Yeah, I guess it is," he said, with a shaky laugh.

"Honestly, I forget that you even have a brother. Where is Reid now?"

"He's been living in Chicago, working in the DA's office." Dax got up and leaned against the railing. He'd tried over the years to get closer to his brother, but Reid could never spare the time, or he didn't want to. Since their father's death, he'd become even more distant. "I hope I can persuade him to come home for a visit now that I'm here."

Mae frowned. "You're still not close?"

"I'd like to be, but Reid is so closed off now. I'm going to keep trying though, just like I'm going to keep trying with Callie."

Mae shifted in her seat. "I'm still not sure how I feel about that. Callie is my best friend, and she's had enough hurt in her life." Mae got up and grabbed another peanut, throwing it to their patient friend. "It's been hard since her grandparents died. Why she chose to live here, I'll never understand. Don't get me wrong, I love having her here, but let's face it, there are some parts of this country where people would prefer that people stick with their own kind, on both sides, and when you're mixed, it makes it harder. Some of my own relatives don't accept Callie. It's not easy. Especially…."

"Especially after the way I treated her," Dax finished for her. "I hate that she's having nightmares because of me. I swear to you, Mae, I'll do anything to make things up to her."

Mae raised an eyebrow. "Anything? Then how about you get your mama to lay off?"

Dax clenched the railing. "I'll try, but I can't make any promises. I don't know that anyone has ever been able to tell my mother what to do." *Not even my father*, he thought. Dax could count on one hand the number of times his father ever stood up to his mother. The worst fight he ever witnessed between them came on the day his brother was sent away.

"You'd be right about that," Uncle Robert said, stepping back up onto the porch. "As long as I've known her, she wanted what she wanted when she wanted it." Robert reached into the bucket of peanuts to scatter a handful in the yard. The cardinal swooped back in, hopping from nut to nut with excitement. "She was always so busy wantin', she didn't take the time to appreciate what she had. My sister-in-law is a hard woman and I hate to say, a bigot. She comes by it honestly. Her family has always held tight to their belief that they were from the superior race." His gaze landed on Dax. "I know it hurts to hear it, but I ain't gonna pretend she's anything different. It's not about getting her to change—you're going to have to change how you deal with her. It ain't gonna be easy. Are you prepared for that?"

"I am," Dax replied as if he were making a solemn vow.

Mae clinked her glass against his in a show of support.

"So…." She avoided eye contact, twirling her glass between her palms. "About those apartments you're going to have in the Barton Building. I was wondering… well, I'd be interested in renting one."

Uncle Robert chuckled and wandered off again with a wave, muttering something about pigs having finally flown.

"You'd be interested in living in my building?"

"I'm twenty-eight years old, and I think it's about time I found a place of my own. I've been working for State Senator Weems for four years now and, assuming he wins reelection, I'll have a job for another four. I don't love the hour commute to Jackson every day, but I don't want to live in the city. I guess I'm a country girl at heart."

"I can appreciate that." He nodded. "Let's talk about rent."

An hour and a handshake later, Dax had his first tenant. But he still hadn't figured out how to make peace with Callie.

THE DIRTY panes dulled the sunlight shining through the large arched windows on the top floor of the Barton Building. Dax turned in a slow circle, trying to visualize a finished space, and for the first time, he wondered if he'd taken on too much. After just a few passes with the broom, the room filled with so much dust he could barely breathe. The broom clattered to the floor and he went over to one of the windows. The ancient metal handle screamed in protest as he wrenched it open. He leaned out, coughing as his lungs exchanged dust for the clean, sweet summer air.

The top floor of his building gave Dax an eagle's-nest view of the town square. A few people were wandering through the park, some sat on the steps of the gazebo eating their lunch while a group of mothers spread out blankets, setting up a picnic lunch while their children played nearby. His gaze strayed toward the library, where the Jewels were sitting on the bench outside. Pearl's hands gestured wildly as Opal's and Ruby's shoulders shook with laughter.

Did anyone say or do anything to make Callie laugh today?

The papered-over window of Callie's bookstore caught his eye, and he counted the other empty storefronts in the square. Aside from the library, bank, and barbershop, almost every other space sat empty. Without more businesses moving in, the town would die.

He planned on doing his part to keep the town alive by investing in high-speed internet, not just because he needed it for his own business, but it would benefit others in town as well.

He leaned out a little farther and craned his neck, squinting toward the steps of the town hall. His mother was pointing toward the library while the sheriff nodded.

Dax frowned. He had a feeling whatever they were discussing wouldn't be good for Callie. He was debating going down and trying to intercede when he saw the sheriff reach up and pat his mother on the shoulder. His hand lingered for just a moment, but it was enough to make Dax even more suspicious that something was going on between the two of them.

His phone vibrated in his pocket.

He looked down at the caller ID. He was tempted to send the call straight to voice mail, but the calls would just keep coming. "Hello."

"Dax," the voice on the other end of the line squealed, "where are you? You were supposed to pick me up thirty minutes ago for Pamela Sue's party."

His dull headache suddenly became blinding. "Presley, I told you I was not going to take you."

"But your mother said," Presley began to whine.

"My mother does not control my social calendar, Presley."

There was a long pause. "That's okay," Presley continued. "We can have more fun if it's just the two of us."

There was no way he was going anywhere with Presley alone. He could practically smell her perfume over the phone. Her attempt to sound alluring and seductive had the same effect as nails on a blackboard.

"We aren't going to be spending any time alone either. This isn't high school, Presley. I didn't come back to Colton to pick up where we left off. The last thing I want is for things to be the way they were before. Goodbye, Presley," he said, hanging up and sliding the phone into his pocket.

He picked up the broom and started sweeping again. He was just starting to see the potential of the old floorboards when he noticed his mother standing in the doorway, a scowl on her face.

"I have been wandering around this derelict building for ten minutes looking for you. Didn't you hear me call?"

Dax rested the broom against the exposed brick wall. "You could have shouted."

"A lady never shouts." His mother pursed her lips and looked around. "This building should have been condemned. I never should have allowed you to waste your money on this."

"We're long past you allowing me to do anything."

His mother waved her hand dismissively. "Presley just called and she's very upset."

As always when his mother didn't like the direction a conversation was headed, she changed the subject. Only this time she picked another argument she wasn't going to win. How could she be so unaware that he was no longer willing to blindly follow her?

"You need to stop encouraging her, Mother. I have no intention of dating Presley, and I'm never going to marry her."

Their eyes locked. Her lip curled up just a bit, enough to let him know that his mother still believed she was in control. "I expect you to join the Beaumont family at our table at the country club this weekend. It's been so long since I've been able to show you off to my friends."

"I'll come for one dinner, but I'm not going to go every Saturday the way we used to."

His mother turned on her heel and walked out. When the front door slammed, he rested his chin on the broom handle, his gaze straying toward the library. He'd endure another dinner at the country club if it gave him a chance to convince his mother to change her attitude toward Callie. There was no logical reason for her to treat her with so much disdain. He'd caused her enough grief; this was one more thing he could do to make amends.

He wandered back over to the window. The day was fading into early-evening twilight as Callie stepped out to the sidewalk, locking the door behind her. She ran her fingers over the cream and gold lettering on the window as she walked down the sidewalk toward home. She should have been riding her bike, but according to Mae it was damaged beyond repair. He remembered Callie and Mae as little girls riding their bikes down the dirt roads, laughing, with pink and purple streamers fanned out from their handlebars. He wished he could go back and ride alongside them, laughing with them instead of throwing rocks and calling names.

I'm not the same person I was then.

He'd traveled around the world, served his country, and learned how to be a better friend. He'd found new brothers. No one could replace Reid, but these were men he trusted with his life and his moral compass.

CHAPTER SIX

CALLIE POURED melted butter over the warm cake and then carefully tapped the mesh strainer against the palm of her hand as a fine dusting of powdered sugar snowed down on the 7UP cake. She sneezed as the tiny particles of sugar tickled her nose. She placed the cake in the center of the table and looked around, satisfied with her efforts. Was the book club popular because of the books or the homemade sweets she baked for every meeting?

Would Grandma be pleased? Her eyes misted for just a moment before she adjusted the pressed glass platter that was her grandmother's favorite and took a deep breath. She'd like to think she'd done a good job honoring her grandmother's legacy.

The book club wasn't her invention. Callie's grandmother had started it many years ago. The Jewels insisted that she carry on her grandmother's tradition and keep the book club going after her grandmother's passing. The three sisters, Pearl, Opal, and Ruby, were her grandmother's best friends. Tradition meant a lot to Callie. When you grew up without anything to keep you grounded, even the smallest tradition took on greater importance. Her grandparents gave her a warm and loving home filled with the laughter and love she craved. And so, for the last two years on the first Tuesday of the month, members of the Colton Book Club gathered in her living room to discuss the monthly selection while they drank tea and devoured sweets. The Jewels were regular members, along with Tillie from the Catfish Café, Mae, Mae's mother, and Emma Walker. To Callie's surprise, Robert Ellis had joined the group a few months ago.

She added a vase of yellow roses to the table as a finishing touch before the doorbell rang. She opened the door with a warm smile to greet the Jewels, who were always the first to land on her doorstep. The three sisters all wore their hair short, and when they stood together, they created an ombré effect with the varying shades of gray from oldest to youngest.

"Evening, Miss Callie." Opal, the oldest of the sisters, greeted her with a hug.

Pearl nudged her sister out of the way to get her hug, followed by Ruby, who grasped Callie's hands with an anxious glance over her shoulder. "There's trouble comin' up your front walk, Miss Callie," she said in a hushed voice.

Callie peered over the youngest Jewel's shoulder, her eyes growing wide as Robert came down the front walk followed by Dax. The blue-and-white checked oxford shirt he wore stretched across his broad shoulders as he carried the book club selection in one hand and a bouquet of lilies in the other. She moved back as his imposing frame filled her doorway. The Jewels clustered around her, Ruby and Pearl on each side and Opal standing in front of her like warrior queens with their arms folded.

"Evenin', ladies." He nodded.

Opal harrumphed, followed in order by Pearl and Ruby. Robert cleared his throat and moved around Dax. He gingerly lifted Opal and set her to one side, ignoring her angry growl and swipe at his hands, to give Callie a peck on the cheek. An uncomfortable silence settled around them until Robert nudged his nephew.

"Give her the flowers, boy, before you kill 'em," he ordered.

Callie glanced down at the bouquet of white lilies. Dax had his hand clenched so tightly around the stems he looked like he was trying to strangle them.

"T-thank you," she stammered. She snatched the flowers out of his hand and retreated to the kitchen, where she pulled a vase off the shelf while she eyed the garbage can. Did he think flowers were going to make any difference? Dax showing up in the library was one thing, but having him in her home was something else. Uncle Robert coming by to vouch for him after her bike was destroyed didn't mean she could trust him or that she was interested in anything to do with Dax Ellis.

"I see you have a new member," Mae announced as she walked into the kitchen.

Callie shoved the last of the lilies into the vase. "I can't believe he thinks it's okay to show up here like this. What kind of game do you think he's playing?"

"What if it isn't a game?"

Callie paused, the last flower hovering in midair for a second before she crammed it into the vase along with the others. "Of course it's a game. He's going to start teasing again, and then…. It's going to start all over again."

"He's not a boy anymore. He's different, Callie," Mae reassured her.

"How do you know and why are you taking his side?"

Mae held her hands up. "I'm not taking sides. I talked to him, and I believe him when he says he's changed."

"You talked to him?" Callie almost shouted. "We have to go; they're waiting for us but, we are going to talk about this later."

Robert and Dax were quietly talking in the corner while the Jewels lined up on the couch, staring at the intruder.

Emma Walker was perched on the edge of her seat, her large blue eyes darting around the room. Mae's mother had arrived and was standing next to Emma with her arms crossed, tapping her foot. Mae rushed to her mother's side and whispered something in her ear that made her mother drop her arms and take her seat, her eyes never leaving their target. Callie sat the flowers on the coffee table, her gaze met Emma's, and she tried to give her friend a reassuring smile. She took her seat and folded her hands in her lap.

"Well, shall we begin?" she said.

CALLIE HANDED Mae another plate to dry.

"That may have been the worst book club meeting we've ever had." Mae shook her head as she placed the clean plate back into the cupboard.

"Definitely." She closed her eyes and let her hands sink into the warm soapy water. "He can't hurt me the way he used to." Saying it out loud made it more real. For her own well-being, she had to believe it.

"It's hard to let go of the past, isn't it?" Mae turned and rested her hip on the counter. "I didn't mean to make you feel like I was betraying you somehow for talking to Dax."

Callie pulled her hands out of the soapy water and dried them off on her apron so she could pull her cousin into a hug. "You don't have anything to apologize for. I don't know what I would have done if you hadn't insisted that we be best friends my first summer here. You were just as bossy that summer when we were five as you are now," she teased.

Mae cocked her head. "It's too bad."

"What?"

"That the hottest guy to walk through your front door in months is Dax Ellis."

"Really, Mae!" She reached into the sink to flick soapy water at her cousin.

Mae jumped back. "Those broad shoulders are a sight to behold. And don't think I didn't notice the way he couldn't take his eyes off you during the whole meeting. You know—" Mae tapped her chin thoughtfully "—you could go on a date every once in a while."

Callie pressed her lips together and scrubbed harder at an invisible spot on an already clean plate. Dates were usually a disaster for her, especially if her date knew who she really was. And she hated to admit that ever since Dax had come back into her life, she'd been thinking about her lack of a love life a lot more. Every time his eyes met hers during the meeting, her heart beat a little faster, and not just from fear.

"It was awkward for Dax, and it didn't help that I could barely string two words together. I'm sure he was uncomfortable, especially with the Jewels glaring at him the whole time."

Mae snorted. "Emma was so shocked she didn't say a word."

The shy pharmacist rarely said a word on a good day. With Dax in the room, she only managed to speak in a whisper.

"And you—" She pointed at Mae. "—you could have helped smooth things over with your mama."

"She's just being protective of her girls."

"I guess it's going to take time for all of us to get used to Dax being back."

Mae hesitated. "We had a good talk the other day and I'm willing to give him a chance, but that mother of his? Hell no!"

"And just what were you doing having a good talk with Dax?"

"Don't get mad."

Callie raised an eyebrow. Most of the time if Mae said those words, it meant she did something Callie didn't approve of.

"I went over to Uncle Robert's and confronted him after your bike was ruined," Mae added.

"Mae Theodora Colton, how could you? He's going to think I'm completely helpless. I don't need you butting in." Her cousin always meant well. Mae would make a great mother someday—her protective streak was wider than the Mississippi.

"I know, I know, I shouldn't have but I was just so... mad."

Callie let the water drain out of the sink. "So, what did he say?" she asked after a moment.

"That he's changed and he's trying to work things out with his mom and his brother."

"Have you ever seen his brother?" Callie asked.

"Reid?" Mae's brow creased. "I don't think so. He was sent away to boarding school the first summer you came here."

"I wonder why he was sent away and not Dax. He was the one who could have used the discipline of military school."

"We had a good talk, Callie, and I hate to admit it, but I like him."

The rational part of Callie knew it shouldn't bother her that Mae liked Dax, but it did. A small seed of jealousy sprouted in the pit of her stomach. "If you like him so much, maybe you should ask him out," she muttered.

Mae threw her head back and laughed until her eyes glistened. "He's not my type, and I'm not the one he couldn't take his eyes off of tonight."

"It doesn't make sense. He hates me."

"You can't help who you're attracted to." Mae shrugged. "He was a stupid little boy who was scared he'd be sent away like his brother if he couldn't make his mama happy."

"Did he tell you that?"

Mae nodded solemnly. "It doesn't excuse what he did, but it does explain a lot."

Callie bowed her head, and a curtain of curls hid her face. "I'm just not ready yet."

"That's okay, sweetie, just promise me something." Mae waited until Callie's gaze met hers. "Promise me that if Dax Ellis asks you out, you'll think about saying yes."

"Why?"

"Because I think you'd like him if you got to know him—"

"No."

"—and you two actually have a lot in common. You both love Colton. You both want to preserve the legacy of this town."

"I want to preserve my grandparents' legacy."

"Which is this town."

Callie's jaw firmed. "I can't."

"Never let the fear of striking out keep you from kissing a cute boy."

Callie reluctantly smiled. "You know I don't like baseball."

"Never underestimate the wisdom of Babe Ruth."

"I'm pretty sure that's not what he said."

"It's still a pretty good quote."

"Oh, what are men compared to rocks and mountains," Callie replied.

"Jane Austen is boring as hell."

"Never underestimate the wisdom of Jane Austen."

Mae shook her head, trying her best to give Callie a stern glare, but they both burst out laughing.

After Mae left, Callie stood in her little living room, staring at the chair Dax had occupied during the book club. She still couldn't get over having Dax Ellis in her house, eating her 7UP cake.

Since that drunk driver had killed her grandparents, there were times that their absence hurt more than others; this was one of those times. She pulled out her phone and her thumb hovered over the name at the bottom of her short favorites list. Even though she knew it was foolish, she hit the call button and waited.

"Callie, darling, we're just on our way out the door," her mother answered on the fourth ring.

"Oh." She waited. This is where her mother would promise to call later, only she always forgot.

"Darling, I know I owe you a phone call. I know I didn't call you back last week, you know how crazy it is when your father and I are traveling."

"That was a month ago," Callie said quietly.

"Was it? Oh, my goodness." Mom laughed. "Your father and I have been so busy I've lost track of time."

"The thing is, you never remember to return my calls, Mom."

"You know how crazy your dad's schedule can be. He's just finishing up a new album and then we have an awards show next week. You can't get mad every time I forget to return a phone call."

"It's more than losing track of time. It would be nice if we could have more time together than a five-minute call every now and then. I miss Grandma and Grandpa so much, and sometimes it's hard being here without them."

She held her breath. In the past she would just accept her parents' excuses for their neglect, but Dax's reappearance had triggered so many childhood memories and reopened the wound in her heart. If she was supposed to believe that Dax could change his ways, shouldn't she believe that her parents might take the time to be present in her life?

"What are you talking about? Please tell me you're finally ready to give up the idea of making that backwater town your home. Colton is dying, and you can't save it," her mother said.

"What happened that made you hate it so much? You haven't been here since Grandma and Grandpa's funeral and even then, you only stayed for a few hours."

"You know your dad had a concert we needed to get to that night."

"Yeah, I know."

There was always another album that needed to be made or concert that they had to go to. "Listen, darling, your father is waiting. I've got to go. We'll talk again soon."

"Bye," Callie whispered to the silence.

Why did her mother do anything she could to avoid Colton? It hurt her grandparents terribly that their daughter had refused to visit. When Callie came for her summer visits, she was delivered by private jet and accompanied by a nanny.

That was all the time thinking about her childhood and things that couldn't be undone she was going to allow herself. She grabbed her laptop and went out to the porch swing, her favorite spot no matter what time of year. She opened the file on her desktop and tapped her lips, planning her next gift for the town.

She hated the term *trust fund baby* but that's what she was. Instead of living off the money her parents put aside for her, she used it to fund various projects that would help the town she loved.

Her phone buzzed and she looked down in surprise at a text from Dax.

"Callie, I hope it's okay, I asked Mae for your number. I was wondering if I could buy you a cup of coffee?"

Dax Ellis wanted to meet her for coffee. Callie blew out a long breath while she stared at her phone. The devil on her shoulder told her to tell him to go to hell, but she brushed it aside. She was curious where Dax had been all this time. There were worse ways to get over a bad experience from the past than facing it over a cup of coffee.

Her fingers hovered for just a second before she typed *"Yes."*

CHAPTER SEVEN

EACH SWIPE of the rag revealed a little more of the mahogany surface of the old desk that had been left behind in the Barton Building. Once the surface was cleaned and polished, Dax pushed it closer to the front windows. He couldn't depend on the ancient wiring, and until he could get the solar panels installed on the roof and all the electrical replaced, he'd need the natural light.

He glanced across the park toward the library. He hadn't seen Callie since going to the book club meeting. If looks could kill, the Jewels could be the greatest secret weapon the Army ever owned.

It shocked the hell out of him when she agreed to meet him for coffee. He thought back to the day before, when her gray eyes looked at him with a combination of curiosity and wariness as she watched him over the rim of her cup. He cringed, remembering all the cruel things he'd said about her eyes.

"Black people can't have blue eyes. What happened to you? Were you some kind of a freak experiment?"

He drew in a sharp breath. Those childhood taunts had made him feel so superior before he knew just how much damage a word could do compared to a bullet. Bullets could kill in an instant; cruel words were a slow death, each letter inflicting pain. Over coffee he learned that she had a blog and wrote book reviews along with her work at the library, but it wasn't enough. He didn't want to learn about Callie—he wanted to get to know her. He wanted to ask questions during long walks or over dinner. *I want to take her on a proper date.*

He pushed away from his makeshift desk and paced the room. Why did Callie have to be the one he couldn't stop thinking about? His pacing slowed as a memory shimmered in the corners of his mind. He was sitting at the dining room table with his brother and parents.

"Reid, sit up straight and take your elbows off the table," his mother admonished before turning to Dax. *"How was your day?"* She asked the same question every night.

She never asked Reid about his day.

"I saw the Coltons' granddaughter at the library, and she has the prettiest eyes I've ever seen."

His chest tightened, remembering his excitement at sharing the news with his mother.

His father cleared his throat and loosened his tie, his eyes darting between Dax and his mother. Why was he so nervous?

His mother narrowed her eyes, "Richard Colton's granddaughter?" she hissed.

"Yes, ma'am," he answered unaware of his mother's growing displeasure. "She's here for the summer."

"I see."

Two words that, as he relived the moment, he realized meant so much. His father hadn't said anything, but the color drained from his face at the mention of Callie's name. There was a tenseness between his parents after that night. Just a few days later, Reid was sent to boarding school.

He connected Callie's arrival in Colton with his brother's departure.

"I blamed her," he said to himself.

The realization was a gut punch.

Even though he'd said those words to Mae, he was still coming to terms with just how much his brother being sent away affected him. He needed to talk to Reid. What did his brother remember about that night?

His phone vibrated in his pocket. Distracted, he answered without looking at the caller ID. "Ellis," he snapped.

"I guess I picked a bad time to see how the homecoming is going."

"It's good to hear your voice, Winters," Dax said, because it was. Jacob Winters had been his best friend for years.

"My paperwork just came through, and I'm headed your way."

Dax looked up at the cracks in the ceiling and the crumbling plaster medallions. "You may not be so enthusiastic when you see how much work there is."

"Not worried about it," Jacob answered easily.

Dax had proposed the idea of Jacob moving to Colton when they both retired, and, to his surprise, Jacob took him up on it. Settling in the Mississippi Delta would be a big change for his friend—hopefully, a welcome one. "Good," Dax said. "It's been a little hectic since I got back, but the good news is that there's enough work for you to set up

Winters Construction, and I already have one project set up for you. It's going to be good to have you here. I could use a friend."

"You never had trouble making friends before."

"Yeah, well… I wasn't the most popular guy when I left here."

"Sounds like there's a story you haven't told me yet."

"You're right." Dax swallowed. "I just hope we're still friends after I've told it."

"I've had your back for six years. I'm not going to stop now."

"I appreciate that."

"Look for me in about forty-eight hours," Jacob said. "But anything else you want to tell me first?"

Yes, I want to tell you I was an asshole who terrorized a little girl, but I'm afraid you'll hate me when you find out. "Nope," he lied.

Uncle Robert ambled in, fanning himself, just as Dax finished his conversation. "Whew, it's gonna be a scorcher today."

"I'd forgotten how heavy the air can get here."

Robert dropped his hat on the desk. "No, you just didn't want to remember."

"That was my friend Jacob I've been telling you about. He's headed this way. I hope you don't mind if we both bunk with you for a while."

"You and your friends are always welcome at my place, you know that."

"Did you let him know that there might be some work for him at the bookstore Callie's been trying to open?"

Dax nodded. "I did, but I don't understand why it's been so hard for her to get it finished."

"Your mother's managed to run off every contractor within a fifty-mile radius."

"Hell," he muttered.

Dorothy Ellis was a hard, shiny diamond. The woman could cut through anything before it cut through her.

"Well, Jacob doesn't scare easily."

Uncle Robert laughed. "I'm gonna get a lawn chair and an ice chest full of beer because it looks like the Fourth of July is coming early this year, and I don't want to miss the fireworks."

His stomach curled in dread thinking about the battle that was coming with his mother. Avoiding a confrontation that had been a long time coming was part of the reason he'd stayed away from Colton for longer than he should have. But his Mississippi roots ran deep, and he had to come home and soothe his soul. Despite the trouble he'd caused growing up and his difficult relationship with his mother, he'd come to appreciate the sense of community a small town offered. It's what he'd loved about being in the Army—being part of a team. He hoped he could get Reid to become part of the team as well, but his brother wouldn't even come back for the holidays.

"Have you heard from Reid lately?" he asked.

"I tried to call a few weeks ago, but he didn't have much time to talk."

"Or he just didn't want to."

Robert tugged on his cap. "He'll come around. He's just not ready yet."

"I've been thinking about him a lot since I've been home. I haven't seen him for more than a couple of hours in years. He treats me more like an acquaintance than a brother. I want to see if I can change that. I'd like for us to be close again.

"Just keep trying."

"I plan to. Hopefully, one day he'll forgive me too."

Uncle Robert cocked his head. "Forgive you for what?"

"I should have stood up for him when Mother… she never had anything nice to say about him."

"That wasn't your fault. Reid knows that."

Dax wished he could believe his uncle. "Does he?"

Robert looked away. "Don't give up on him."

"Would you tell me if you knew why they sent Reid away?" he asked.

"Your father and I argued about that more than once. I don't know why they did it. All I know was that your mother insisted. There's always been rumors." He rubbed his hand over his jaw. "I caught my brother out with Callie's mother one time, but then Callie's mama ran away to Seattle and your dad got your mother pregnant. They had a quickie wedding, and she went with him for his last year of law school. She never really bonded with your brother. Maybe they were just too young…."

"Dad and Callie's mother?" Dax leaned forward. "Is that why Mom hates the Coltons so much?"

"I'm sure it had something to do with it."

"Ever since I came back, I'm uncovering more secrets than answers."

"You've been working hard to make things right. The answers are out there—give it time." Robert pushed himself off the desk and glanced toward the front window. "I've got a hankering for some of Tillie's pecan pie. Let's head over. Maybe the world will make more sense with coffee and pie in our bellies."

They just missed the lunch rush at the Catfish Café, but there were still quite a few people lingering over their coffee and pie. The sheriff sat at the counter, reading the paper, and the Jewels were ensconced in a booth by the front window. The sheriff acknowledged Dax and Robert with a wary look and a brief nod.

"Good afternoon, ladies. Don't y'all look fine today." Robert beamed at the Jewels and tipped his hat as they walked by.

Opal and Pearl both nodded with grim faces, but Ruby's stern expression was softened by the light in her eyes when she looked up at Robert. Dax paused for just a second. Was the Jewels' presence the reason for his uncle's sudden craving?

They slid into a booth in the back of the restaurant and Tillie appeared at the table with a coffeepot in one hand and a slice of pie in the other, placing them on the table in front of Robert. Today she wore an orange gingham shirt that would have matched her hair color before it faded to a softer hue. She must have a different gingham shirt for every day of the week, since for as long as Dax could remember she had never worn anything but a gingham shirt with jeans and white sneakers.

His greeting died on his lips when he saw the sharpness in her gaze.

"We were all pretty upset to hear about what happened to Callie's bike," she said as a greeting.

"He was with me that night," Robert said, quietly, over the rim of his coffee cup. "Stop glowering and give the boy some coffee and pie, Tillie."

Her fingers flexed on the handle of the coffeepot, and for a moment Dax wondered if she was going to pour the coffee over Robert and smash the carafe over his head. Instead, she turned on her heel to grab a cup off the counter. She pursed her lips and poured Dax a cup.

"Don't forget the pie," Uncle Robert called out when she turned away.

Of all the missions Robert undertook for his country, this may have been the most dangerous one of all. No one ever told Tillie what to do.

A minute later, a large slice of pie slid onto the table.

"I shouldn't have jumped to conclusions. Old habits are hard to break, I guess." Tillie put a hand on her hip, but her expression had gentled. "I'm glad the two of you are trying to find out who destroyed Miss Callie's bike," she announced loudly enough that everyone in the café had no doubt Tillie believed in his innocence. "It's not like this one is going to do anything about it," she continued, jerking her thumb toward the sheriff as she walked away.

Dax sputtered and choked on his coffee. Sheriff Crosby stood, purple rising from his collar to his face as he slammed down a handful of change on the counter and stormed out.

The whole café breathed a sigh of relief when the sheriff left, and the normal buzz of conversation resumed.

"No one makes better pecan pie than Tillie Reynolds," Robert said, lifting another forkful to his mouth with a sly grin.

Dax took a forkful of the sugary, gooey sweetness and popped it into his mouth. He closed his eyes, savoring the memory of the same flavor from his childhood.

"We spent a lot of time at this table before I left for college."

"We did." Robert nodded. "I miss those days."

"I find it hard to believe you miss trying to keep your degenerate nephew out of trouble."

Robert slowly set his fork down and leaned forward, his elbows on the table. "Spending time with my nephew, who I like to think of as the son I never had, is a memory I will always treasure."

Dax froze. "Thanks, Uncle Robert." He managed to get the words past the lump in his throat. "You've been a better uncle than—"

Robert held up his hand. "Don't say it."

They finished off their pie in companionable silence. Dax noticed his uncle glanced toward the Jewels every once in a while, and Ruby was sneaking looks at their table as well. Dax opened his mouth, a teasing comment on the tip of his tongue, but he snapped it closed again. He had no right to tease anyone about their love life.

As if the thought alone was enough to summon her, a flutter of pink caught his eye as Callie walked toward the café. She stopped at the front door and reached for the handle but jerked back when their eyes met.

She frowned and backed away. Dax wanted to rush out to call her back, but that wouldn't help. He forced himself to stay put, waving Tillie over instead.

"Would you mind putting together whatever Callie usually orders and asking the Jewels to take it over to her?"

Tillie wrinkled her forehead, obviously perplexed by his request.

"I don't want her to miss her lunch because I'm here," he said, pointing to Callie's back retreating from the door.

Tillie's eyebrows shot up. "I'll take care of it."

"It will get better, son, I promise," Uncle Robert said.

It was going to be a long road to redemption. Dax hoped he could manage the miles ahead.

CHAPTER EIGHT

THE LOW, powerful roar of a motorcycle echoed through the town square. A minute later, Callie and Mae looked up in unison as the library door flew open. Callie's eyes grew wide while Mae's hand flew to her chest.

A giant lumberjack, at least six feet tall and wearing a gray plaid shirt, dark denim jeans, and a pair of work boots, filled the doorway. He stroked his auburn-brown beard, looking from Callie to Mae with his dark blue eyes.

"C-can I help you?" she asked.

The man smiled and held out his hand. "One of you must be Callie Colton," he said.

Callie gingerly returned his handshake. "Have we met before?"

"Dax Ellis sent me. My name's Jacob Winters. He told me that a pretty lady needed a carpenter." He looked from Callie to Mae again. "I'd be happy to help more than one pretty lady if she needed assistance." He winked at Mae.

Mae took a step back, her eyes growing wide.

This knight in shining armor routine from Dax was starting to get on her nerves. "Mr. Winters, I appreciate your offer, but I can't accept."

"Nope," Jacob interrupted, "your friend made it very clear that this was supposed to be my first stop when I got into town."

"Dax isn't my friend," Callie said, quietly. Mae reached out and gave her arm a gentle squeeze.

Jacob looked around the library with curious eyes. "This is a nice space you have here. I noticed the sign on the door for the bookstore on the window next door. Is that the place you need help with?" he asked, ignoring her statement.

"Yes, but—"

"Look, why don't we pretend I never mentioned that Dax sent me here? I'm just a contractor looking to bid on a project."

Even if she could do that, she would still be accepting help from Dax. Stubbornness warred with practicality. Dorothy Ellis spread the word around town that she'd make sure anyone who worked on the bookstore wouldn't be hired in Colton or anywhere else in the county. It was ridiculous, but she had enough influence to make life difficult for anyone who defied her. There weren't many trades left in Colton, and Callie didn't blame anyone for not wanting to take on the dragon lady.

"Mr. Winters, I can't accept. If you do any work for me, you won't get work anywhere else."

Jacob crossed his arms. "First off, you'll have to start calling me Jacob if we're going to be working together. I don't know what's going on, but between this job and working with Dax on his building, I have plenty to do."

How could she explain small-town politics and Dorothy Ellis? Before she could try, Mae jumped in.

"Dax's mama runs this town, and she hates Callie, so if you're going to help her, you'll be on her shit list too, and I guarantee you won't get any other work around here."

Leave it too Mae to cut to the chase.

"I've never been one for playing by the rules. I'm not worried." He glanced toward the storefront next door. "How about we take a look at your project? Do you have permission from the landlord to make the changes you want?"

"I own the building so that's not a problem, and I have all of the permits. I just need someone to do the work."

"Callie's grandfather owned all of the buildings on this side of the square. This has always been the Black side of the town," Mae said with pride.

"The Black side of town?"

Mae smirked. "You're in the South now. Even the cemeteries are segregated. There are more unwritten rules in small Southern towns than cotton in the fields." Mae gestured to Callie. "We are the Black Coltons, descendants of the slaves from the Colton Plantation. Your friend Dax gets to claim General Absolem Madden Colton as a relative." Mae stepped close enough that she had to crane her neck to make her next point. "There are Black Coltons and White Coltons, and one of the rules"—she emphasized *rules* with air quotes—"is that the two don't mix."

Jacob frowned.

"A lot of things have changed, and they're changing every day," Callie added.

"Dax filled me in on some of this stuff. If you think you're going to scare me away with your rules, you are going to have to try harder. I've fought insurgents in hellholes you can't imagine." He pointed at Mae. "And you may be fierce, but you don't scare me, pixie."

"Tell me he did not just call me a pixie," Mae sputtered.

Callie shot Jacob a look when he laughed and then tried to cover it unsuccessfully with a cough. Callie took Mae's hand and dragged her toward the door. "Let's give Mr. Winters a tour of the space, and he can decide if this is a project he wants to take on."

Callie had just unlocked the door to the bookstore when Mae poked her in the ribs, jerking her head toward the end of the block. Mrs. Dorothy Ellis barreled toward them, head held high. Sunlight glinted off her perfectly coiffed blond hair. Her beige heels clicked on the pavement with determination.

"Shouldn't you be in the library, Callie?" she sniffed. "What if a customer came in while you were out here loitering in the street?"

Mae drew in a sharp breath. Callie caught her eye. Her lips pressed into a thin line, a silent warning to keep her mouth shut. With an apologetic look to Jacob, Callie turned her attention back to Mrs. Ellis.

"Good afternoon, Mrs. Ellis. I can clearly see if any patrons want to use the library." Callie looked at her watch. "As a matter of fact, I have another forty-five minutes until story time. That leaves me just enough time to consult with my new contractor."

Jacob nodded. "Good afternoon."

Dorothy looked him up and down without returning his greeting.

"It's bad enough that you insist on having inappropriate books in the library. Selling them is a disgrace."

Jacob snorted and rolled his eyes.

Mrs. Ellis narrowed her eyes. "And you are?"

"Jacob Winters, ma'am."

She looked down at his outstretched hand. "You aren't from here, Mr. Winters." It was a statement more than a question.

"No, ma'am, I'm not. But my friend is from here and he invited me to come down. He seems to think this is a nice place to live."

Dorothy peered at the vintage black-and-silver Harley Davidson parked on the street next to them. "Are you in a gang, Mr. Winters? We don't appreciate your kind around here. We have enough trouble as it is," she finished with a pointed look at Callie.

Jacob looked as though he was thoroughly enjoying the exchange. He lifted an eyebrow and crossed his arms. Didn't he understand he was poking the dragon and any minute now she would spew fire?

"And who is this friend?" Dorothy asked, back ramrod straight.

"That would be me," Dax announced, walking up behind his mother.

Callie's heart fluttered. Was it from the way Dax was looking at her or from the way his mother looked at him with a glint of triumph in her eye? Was this the moment when Dax disappointed her and turned back into the mean and spiteful boy?

Mae moved closer to Callie. Instead of greeting Dax, Jacob moved to her other side, bracketing her. She felt both trapped and supported, and Dax may have been speaking to his mother, but his gaze never left hers. Callie held her ground, even though what she really wanted to do was run back into the library and lock the door.

"Dax, you know this person?" Mrs. Ellis demanded, slipping her hand through the crook of his arm.

How many times had Callie seen them walking down the street just like that? Dorothy, her arm linked with her son's, their heads held high, the queen of Colton and the crown prince. Callie shuddered. Everyone kept telling her Dax had changed, but time stood still when she saw him in this familiar pose.

"Jacob, glad to see you made it okay." Dax nodded, pulling his arm out of his mother's grasp and reaching out to shake Jacob's hand.

Callie noticed a few of her story-time regulars heading across the park toward the library, their parents in tow. "I should get back to the library," she said edging away from the tension between mother and son.

"Yes, you should," Dorothy snapped.

Dax started to speak, but Callie gave a slight shake of her head. She didn't need or want Dax defending her. Whatever game he was playing, she didn't want any part of it. She went back into the library with Mae hot on her heels.

"She's lucky my mother raised me to be a lady," Mae said as soon as Callie shut the door.

They watched Dax and his mother through the window. Their voices were muffled, but the animosity was impossible to miss. Jacob stood by watching, at one point he glanced toward Callie and Mae and winked.

"Cheeky," Mae muttered, pulling back from the window with flushed cheeks.

Callie didn't want to like anyone who was friends with Dax, but Jacob Winters had an easygoing manner that made her feel comfortable around the big, burly man. She frowned as she picked up the pile of books she'd selected for story time.

"What's wrong?" Mae asked.

"I can't accept Jacob's offer."

"Why not?"

"One"—she ticked off on her fingers—"he's a friend of Dax. Two, it would be accepting help from Dax, and three, Dorothy Ellis will make life hell for all of us."

"One, who cares who he's friends with if he can get the job done? Two, stop being silly. If you're paying him, you're not getting any help from anyone. And three, he's hot," she finished with a grin.

The door burst open with the chatter of excited children. Callie glanced outside. There was no trace of Jacob, Dax, or his mother. Thank goodness for small miracles. Dax sending his friend to help and then arguing with his mother— He was such a mama's boy growing up, and now?

Callie pushed her jumbled thoughts aside and greeted the children with hugs and welcomed their excited chatter. Now wasn't the time to try to understand Dax, and as far as she was concerned there never would be a good time for that. Mae picked her way through the children arranging themselves on the braided rug, smiling and nodding at the parents as she passed.

"Time for me to make my exit before these little munchkins eat me alive," she said, under her breath.

Mae always made her intentions clear when it came to children. She would proudly take on the role of Auntie Mae, but she had no desire to have any of her own. Callie wanted nothing more than to have her own family someday, two children at least and more if possible. Her children would have siblings to play with and they would never be alone with a nanny or housekeeper.

She looked over the eager faces of the children in front of her. The children's story hour was definitely her favorite part of the job. At the end of the hour, all the children and their parents had left but the littlest, Travon. He climbed into her lap asking for "just one more" until he fell asleep in her arms.

At some point during story hour, Dax had slipped quietly back in, listening at the back of the room to her read. He waited patiently while Travon's mother checked out the books Callie recommended, all the while cradling the sleeping boy until she transferred him into his mother's arms. Travon's mother mouthed her thanks, and Dax opened the door for them so she could slip out without waking her son.

"You're good with kids," he said.

"Thank you," Callie said, gathering the books from story hour.

"I'm sorry about my mother back there."

"Why? It's not your fault."

Silence stretched between them. "I read your review of that new spy thriller, and I was wondering if I could check it out?" he said, clearly wanting to change the subject.

"It's checked out, but I have another book from that author you might like."

"Great."

She went over to one of the shelves and pulled out the book and handed it to him.

"This doesn't seem like the kind of book you would like," she said, watching him frown at the cover.

"I usually don't like this genre, but your review made it sound so good."

Callie plucked the book from his hands and reached for a different book. "You strike me as more of a historical fiction kind of guy; give this one a try."

This time his lips turned up at the cover. The book was about a family living in a logging town on the Oregon frontier. "I have to confess I've read it twice."

"So did I," she confessed.

With each tentative conversation she realized that they had more in common than she ever thought they would.

"I like reading about the past, it gives me perspective on the future."

"You're right."

"Callie, I would really like it if we could put the past behind us and be friends."

She looked down at his outstretched hand. *Friends.* Dax Ellis wanted to be friends. As Callie shook his hand, she wondered what other unexpected surprises a friendship with Dax was going to bring, and just how much hell she was going to catch when his mother found out.

JACOB POKED his head in the door. "Do you have a key I can have so that way I won't have to bother you?"

Callie pulled the key ring out of her pocket and slipped one of the keys off, holding it out to Jacob. "Thank you."

"I'll start making an inventory of any additional supplies you'll need."

"Thank you, Jacob. I really appreciate you taking this project on."

"Thank Dax, he's the one who convinced me to come down here," he said with a wave.

"I didn't convince him to come down here just to help with the bookstore. Jacob is my best friend, and I thought he might be happy here. He was looking for a place to start a construction company, and Colton needs new businesses. I just thought it was a good idea."

Was that a tinge of embarrassment she saw in his eyes? This was a different man than the boy she knew before. He was more cautious and careful than the brash boy she remembered. It made her curious to know more.

"You don't have to explain, Dax. You did a nice thing. Thank you."

"Thanks, Callie, I appreciate it."

They spend a little more time together. Dax checked out two books before he left.

That night when she walked home, she didn't worry about Dax jumping out to scare her the way he used to when they were kids. Callie found herself wondering what it would be like to take a walk with Dax instead.

CHAPTER NINE

DAX WAITED on Uncle Robert's front porch for Jacob to arrive. He still couldn't get over his mother's behavior. Her rudeness to Callie was intolerable, but watching her condescending attitude toward Jacob brought his anger to a boiling point.

Soon the dull roar of Jacob's Harley could be heard in the distance. A moment later a flash of black and silver brought his friend into the driveway. He dismounted and made his way to the porch. He pulled his pack off his back, let it drop to the floor, and stood in front of Dax with his hands on his hips.

"Do you want to tell me what the hell that was back there now or after we've had a couple of beers?"

He forced himself to look his friend in the eye, something that should never be difficult to do. They trusted each other with their lives, and yet he hadn't been able to share this part of his life with him. "That was terrible, my mother's behavior was inexcusable. You should have had a better welcome than that."

"I don't give a shit about that. What in the world is going on between you and the librarian?"

"It's complicated. Let's get you settled first and then I'll try to explain."

Dax led him into the cabin for a brief tour. Jacob craned his neck, looking at the exposed trusses where the ax marks that created them could clearly be seen. He let out a low whistle. "They don't make them like this anymore."

"Nice to meet someone who appreciates things done the old-fashioned way," Uncle Robert said, walking up to Jacob with his hand outstretched. "Robert Ellis, nice to meet you."

Jacob shook his hand. "Nice to meet a friendly Ellis."

Dax groaned.

"What happened?" Robert asked.

Dax shot his uncle a frustrated glance. "Mother was at the library."

No other explanation was needed. Uncle Robert nodded and went to the refrigerator, pulled out three beers, and headed out to the porch. Dax jerked his head and they followed him out.

"Listen, about my mother," Dax started.

Jacob cut him off. "Maybe you should start with why Callie Colton is so scared of you and your mother."

"Appreciate those protective instincts," Dax acknowledged. A hint of jealousy mingled with approval at the way Jacob instinctively had moved to Callie's side during the confrontation.

"I don't think I was needed with that friend of hers," Jacob said ruefully.

"You must have met Mae," Robert guessed.

"He did," Dax confirmed.

Robert stopped rocking. "She's Callie's best friend and fiercest protector, but sometimes she uses her toughness as a cover."

"Yes, sir," Jacob answered.

Dax saw the flash of red out of the corner of his eye. Growing bolder this time, his feathered friend swooped in, landing on the porch, hopping up and down the railing. Black eyes watched carefully, judging every movement as Dax reached into the bucket of peanuts. He held up the treat for a moment before tossing it into the air.

"I bullied Callie when we were kids," Dax said bluntly. There was no way to sugarcoat it and no reason to.

Jacob set his beer down and rested his elbows on his knees, waiting.

"It was worse than bullying." Dax grimaced. "I threw rocks at her, called her names. I… I would have done worse if I'd had the chance."

Jacob's jaw ticked, but he didn't say anything. Dax took a deep breath and continued.

"It wasn't just Callie. I was an ass to everyone in this town. Growing up, my mother was constantly telling me how superior we were to everyone else in town, and I—" His gut clenched. "—I bought into it. I was just like my mom, until Uncle Robert moved back to Colton and set me straight. Thank God he did."

For a moment no one said anything. Uncle Robert was looking away, expression blank, but Dax could still feel the shame of the past. He despised who he'd been. He hated remembering that version of himself.

Jacob cleared his throat. "I don't know the person you just described to me. I only know the man who has been an honest and loyal friend. But I do have one question."

"What?"

"When did you fall in love with Callie?"

Dax stared at his friend, wide-eyed. Uncle Robert slapped his knee and barked out a laugh. There was no way in hell he was going to tell anyone about the dreams he'd been having about her.

"Okay, maybe love is too strong of a word, but you definitely have a crush on her, and I want to know what you're going to do about it," Jacob said.

"I don't know," he finally admitted.

"Well, you'd better come up with a better plan than making moon eyes and arguing with your mother." Jacob took another swig. "And Callie sure didn't appreciate you trying to pay for everything either."

Uncle Robert snorted. Dax threw him a sharp look. Years of always having a plan and strategizing, all the tactical training he'd received, completely failed him now. He had absolutely no idea what to do.

"You called for backup, and that's a good start. You're going to have to win over her friends and family first," Jacob said.

"Working on it."

"But doing things behind her back isn't going to win her over. You need to talk to *her*."

"She doesn't want to be anywhere near me."

"I think she's just as conflicted as you are." Jacob sipped his beer. "Now, what the hell is going on with your mother? Is she always that mean?"

"She's gotten worse since I've been gone, but she's always been hard to please."

"Some people are born already dissatisfied with life," Robert said. "Your mother has been like this as long as I've known her. Your mama can call a rose beautiful and complain that it has too much perfume all in the same breath. I never understood why my brother chose to marry her."

Dax grimaced. "But it's worse now than I remember."

Uncle Robert shifted in his seat. "She didn't take very well to Callie moving here."

It struck Dax then that he was going to have to make a choice. His family or his principles, and he knew already, his principles would win. It was time to be the man he should be.

"I'm just not sure where to start. I've got the Barton Building and my consulting business to get up and running. Now I need to start working on becoming a part of the community."

"Well, you could start with a haircut," Jacob laughed. "You look like shit."

Dax grinned. "You're one to talk. Exactly what are you trying to hide in that beard?"

Jacob ran his hands over his unruly mane. "Hey, this is a work of art."

Dax tugged on the curls at the nape of his neck. "I haven't had time to drive over to Greenwood for a haircut."

"I don't understand. I drove by a barbershop when I came into town."

"Hank's is for—" Dax struggled to explain one of those strange unwritten rules of the South—that White men drove to the next town to get their hair cut while generations of Colton's African-American community received their first and last haircuts at Hank's. "If you're Black you get your hair cut at Hank's; and if you're White you drive over to Greenwood. It's always been that way."

Jacob stared at him with a raised eyebrow. "You're serious."

"It's ridiculous, I know," Dax agreed.

"I've watched movies and read books set in the South, but for some reason I didn't think it was real. Be honest with me: is this really about an old racist rule, or are you afraid you'll get kicked out on your ass because of how badly you behaved before?"

"Maybe a little of both?" Dax said, even as he privately admitted that he was being a coward. He did need a haircut. And he shouldn't continue to follow those unwritten rules of the South anymore. Dax rose. "I'll let you get settled in here while I head back into town."

"Where are you going?" his uncle asked, as Dax set his half-full beer bottle down.

"To get that haircut."

All the conversation stopped when Dax walked into Hank's Barbershop. The angry glares were reflected back at him in the wall of mirrors along one side of the room. The space was small, and it took only two steps to cross the pale blue and brown linoleum tiles to the center of the room. The scent of Lilac Vegetal and Barbasol filled the air.

"Evening." Dax nodded to the two men who sat hunched over a chessboard in the corner. Hank stood behind a man reading a newspaper, his scissors hovered in midair for a moment before he continued his work with a curt nod.

Dax ran his hand through his hair. "I was hoping I could get a haircut if you don't mind."

Nate Colton paused, his hand hovering over his knight, staring at Dax. His teammate, Sam, sucked in his breath.

"Don't think we didn't see you talking to Callie Colton," a deep voice behind the paper said. "Are you planning on causing trouble?"

Dax cleared his throat. "No, sir."

The paper slowly lowered, revealing the face of Joseph Colton, Mae's father.

Nate set his rook down with force, frowning at Dax. Sam's eyes darted between the two of them. Joseph folded the paper as Hank turned on his clippers and began to shave the back of his neck. The buzz of the clippers filled the silence.

Four pairs of eyes bored into him. Dax forced himself to look each man in the eye and not flinch. Clearly, his reputation as the town bully was still alive and well.

"I know none of you have any reason to trust me, but I want you all to know that I'm sorry for all the trouble I caused," Dax said quietly. "Mr. Thompson, I'm sorry I broke the pole," he said to Hank as he gestured to the blue and red pole continuing its slow, lazy turn outside.

He turned to Nate, the only official member of Colton's fire department. "Mr. Colton, I'm sorry I lit those firecrackers under your front porch.

"And Mr. Riley," he continued, "I'm the one who yanked all the wires out of that house you were working on."

Sam's eyes grew wide. "That was you?"

Dax nodded and forced himself to face Mae's father. "Mr. Colton." He cleared his throat. "I'm sorry for everything I ever did to Mae and Callie. I was a punk. And spoiled. And wrong.

Joseph continued to study him. Just when Dax was about to give up, Joseph stood and motioned for Dax to sit. "You better hope Hank knows how to cut a White boy's hair," he said.

Dax fought the smile that threatened to break free. It was too soon to celebrate. He sat in the worn, brown leather chair while Hank made a great show of shaking out the cape. Dax didn't say a word when he wrapped the paper around his neck just a little tighter than he needed to. It was worth the discomfort to sit with these men.

"When was the last time you had a White boy in that chair, Hank?" Sam called out.

Hank paused. His face clouded. He rested his hands on the back of the chair and met Dax's gaze in the mirror. "There was a group of Freedom Riders, six young men—four Black and two White—heading into Greenwood the next day to sit at the lunch counter. Callie's grandfather asked my father to make sure they were clean-shaven and their hair neat and tidy." His voice grew gruff. "We made sure they looked like gentlemen so they could be treated like animals."

The silence of memory settled around them. Hank continued to stare at Dax in the mirror for a moment before he rested a heavy hand on his shoulder. "Maybe we all need to talk about the past more so we can make a better future."

"That's why I moved back here. I want to do my part to help Colton be a town people want to invest in."

"How are you going to do that?" Nate jeered.

Dax didn't let the criticism get a rise out of him. "Colton needs access to modern infrastructure—high-speed internet and cell service—but it also needs change in other ways, and I want to be part of that change. It's time we need to face some ugly truths about Colton's past—and my past—so that we... *I* can be a better person."

Sam and Hank nodded with approval.

"Word around town is that you bought the Barton Building," Joseph said.

"Yes, sir, I'm working on restoring it. I'm going to convert the main floor into my office and the upper floors into apartments." Dax stared straight ahead, afraid if he moved, he'd lose an ear to Hank's scissors, but he spoke to the men at the chessboard. "I've got a buddy helping me, but we could use another hand. I know you recently retired, Mr. Johnson, but is there any chance you'd be interested in the job?"

Sam Johnson's eyebrows lifted. He looked intrigued. "I may not move as fast as I used to, but you're not going to find a better electrician around. I did all the work for Miss Callie at the library and the bookstore. Your mama's threats don't mean anything to me."

"That's because you're retired, fool, and checkmate," Nate announced, capturing Sam's king.

Sam studied the chessboard in dismay. "I'm still the best," he grumbled.

"How are things at the station, Nate?" Dax asked.

"Well, as long as we don't have a fire, I guess everything's okay. Your mama has the town council convinced the fire department can run on outdated equipment and one tired old man," Nate replied, resetting the chessboard.

All four of the men nodded.

"Who's on the town council these days?" Dax asked. He'd noticed the poor condition of the firehouse.

"Your mother, the sheriff, and Clyde Walker," Joseph said.

"Shouldn't one of you be on the council?"

All four men snorted and rolled their eyes.

"We've all tried. Your mother finds an excuse to make sure the council doesn't have any Black folks on it," Hank said, pulling out his clippers.

It was amazing that the town functioned at all with his mother's interference. Hank whisked the cape off Dax's shoulders, and soft bristles brushed along the back of his neck as the barber flicked away any stray hairs that remained. Dax stood and reached for his wallet, but the older man waved him off.

"A first haircut at Hank's is always on the house." He pointed a finger at Dax. "If you do anything to hurt Miss Callie, I'd best not see you round here for a second one."

Sam shoved Nate's shoulder, the two silently laughing.

"I'm here to do right by Callie and everybody else." He looked around the room. "I'm sorry about my mother. I didn't know... I just want to make sure I apologize to everyone for anything I may have done that hurt them." What else could he say?

Nate walked over to stand in from of him "Look at me, boy," the older man said quietly. "It took a lot of guts to walk in here, and I know you've been going around town trying to make amends. At some point, you're not going to have any apologies left to make, and you've got no reason to apologize for your mother's behavior."

Dax's eyes stung. He swallowed hard. He hadn't done enough to earn Nate's compassion. "Colton is home. I'm going to do everything I can to help the town grow and make it a better place."

Joseph snorted a laugh. "Funny, Callie said the exact same thing when she came back."

"Callie is a smart woman. I admire everything she's been doing with the library and the bookstore."

Joseph raised an eyebrow. "That had better be all you admire."

Nate and Sam exchanged a look while Hank paused his sweeping to lean on his broom with a grin.

"Let me tell you something." Joseph pointed his finger at Dax. "You behave yourself around Callie. She may not be my daughter, but I love her like she was one of my own. If you hurt her again, I'll make sure there's nothing left of you but haint."

He had no doubt that Joseph Colton would follow through on his promise to turn him into nothing more than a ghost if he made a wrong move with Callie.

"Sir, I—"

Hank slapped him on the back. "Quit while you're ahead, son," he whispered in his ear.

"I would expect nothing less," Dax pushed on, determined to finish what he was going to say, "and if you don't, I know my uncle will." He then held his breath, hoping it would be enough to receive a pardon.

Sam's hand hovered over the chessboard. All eyes were trained on Joseph, waiting for his judgment. Finally, Joseph nodded. "Well, all right then."

The whole room took a collective breath and life began again.

Sam asked about his progress on the Barton Building and offered to come by the next day and take a look at the electrical work. Nate said he would be by as well to make sure everything was up to fire code. Dax paused on his way out and peeked in the mirror, running his hand over his new haircut. He felt lighter than he had in a long time. If Callie's uncle and the other men in the barbershop were willing to give him a chance, maybe with time she would too.

CHAPTER TEN

"HELLO," CALLIE called into the empty main floor of the Barton Building. She had knocked twice, but there was no answer. The door was slightly ajar and Dax's truck was parked in front, so she knew he had to be somewhere inside.

"Hello," she called out again a little louder.

A loud crash followed by a muttered curse echoed from upstairs. She heard footsteps above and a moment later Dax appeared on the stairs, covered in dust. His eyes grew wide for a moment. He started patting the dust off his jeans and gray Lucas Monroe concert T-shirt as he descended, creating a cloud of dust around him. He came toward her, breaking into a slow smile, but slowed his advance when she took a step back.

"Hi, I didn't hear you. I was trying to get some work done upstairs. I'm afraid I'm not much of a carpenter."

"I came to tell you that I will be paying for any work Jacob Winters does for me. I told him I'd pay him every two weeks, and he's refused twice now. You can't buy my forgiveness, Dax."

"I—Okay," he agreed.

Callie blinked at him for a moment. She had been prepared to argue with him, so his concession threw her off-kilter and she wasn't sure what to do next. "Well… thank you."

An awkward silence descended over them. Sunlight filtered through the windows, casting shadows across his face. That must have been what made him look so handsome; there was no other reason Callie could think of.

"Would you like a tour?"

He pointed toward the oak staircase. Curiosity won the battle over the tiny sliver of unease she couldn't help feeling around him. She had always wondered what this building looked like inside, and she was curious to know what Dax had planned.

"Sure."

"This is going to be my office." Dax swept his arm around the open space on the main floor. The cobwebs and dust had been swept away, and Callie admired the beautiful old desk by the window.

"Colton doesn't have fiber optic. How are you planning to run all of this equipment?" she asked pointing to the stack of monitors along one wall.

"I have some temporary servers up, and if everything goes the way I plan, Colton will have fiber optics in the next six months or so. I just signed the contract last week to extend the line from Greenwood."

Callie raised an eyebrow. "That's a pretty expensive undertaking."

"It's worth it if it will help keep this town alive, don't you think?"

"I do."

She had been making plans to do the same thing.

He gestured toward the stairs. "Would you like to see the rest?"

Callie nodded.

"The second floor will be divided into four apartments," he said as they paused on the second-floor landing.

They arrived at the third floor and the open loft space. The same exposed brick walls from downstairs were showcased with exposed wood beams and large arched windows along three sides of the room.

"This is beautiful," Callie said, crossing the refinished hardwood floors to look out of one of the windows. "It's like being in a tree house. You can see the whole town from here."

"Wait until you see it first thing in the morning when the light floods the space. I hate to put up any kind of window covering, but if I don't, I'm afraid I'll be waking up at dawn every day."

"But what a beautiful thing to wake up to, the sky turning from purple to pink to blue every morning, don't you think?" She smiled at him.

Dax was looking at her in a way that made her stomach do another one of those flip-flops. It was a feeling she hadn't had very many times before. There was the boy in high school she'd had a crush on for a year who never even realized she existed. And a couple of short-lived relationships in college. Her shyness and preference to spend her evenings cuddled up with a good book or writing rather than hanging out at parties quickly ended most relationships before they ever really had time to take hold of her heart. She didn't want to like the dimple that formed every time Dax smiled at her or the way his eyes crinkled at the corners when he laughed. She pressed her hand to her stomach and took another step back.

"I wish more of these old buildings could be rehabbed like this," she said.

"That's my plan. I'd like to invest in other buildings in town and offer up the space at a reduced rent for local businesses. Small towns die every day. I don't want Colton to be one of them."

He spoke about Colton with a passion she didn't expect.

"But you left and you didn't come back. I thought you hated it here."

"I didn't hate Colton," he said. "I just didn't like who I was here... before."

"No one liked who you were before," she said quietly.

He was silent a moment. "That's something I don't think I'll ever stop regretting. I hope that my actions will show that I've changed."

Callie studied him, finding only sincerity in his gaze.

"Time has a way of making you appreciate things in a different way. Living in big cities and seeing a lot of the world made me appreciate Colton much more. Nowhere else ever felt like home the way Colton does." He moved a step closer. "Can I ask you a question?"

She nodded.

"Why did you come back?"

"The only people who ever loved me were here."

He wouldn't understand. No one really did, not even Mae. How could she explain? Before she had a chance, another voice called from below.

"Hello, anybody here?"

Callie followed Dax downstairs, where they found Presley's brother.

"Ash, it's good to see you." Dax shook his hand.

"Ashton," Callie quietly acknowledged.

Ashton and Dax had been thick as thieves when they were kids. He wasn't as mean as Dax, but he wasn't friendly either. Because he was the manager of the only bank in town, Callie had no choice but to deal with him from time to time.

Ashton looked at the two of them with wide eyes, clearly surprised to see them together.

"It's... I... It's funny to find you both here." Ashton rubbed the back of his neck. "Callie, I was going to stop by the library tomorrow. We have a bit of an awkward situation here." He laughed, nervously.

"Exactly what kind of situation do we have?" Dax asked.

"You see—" Ashton's eyes darted between the two of them. "—it's really quite funny when you think about it." He laughed again.

"Spit it out, Ash," Dax said, with an exasperated sigh.

"You both came in and requested a cashier's check for the same thing."

Callie drew in a sharp breath.

Ashton winced. "Aw hell, I should have kept my mouth shut."

Dax turned to her. "For the fire department?"

She'd made it very clear that her donations to the town were to be anonymous. He handled all her transactions personally so that the other bank employees wouldn't catch on. The news would be all over town if anyone else knew.

"Nate's been asking for new equipment for years now, and the town council keeps denying the request. He can't do his job with an old broken-down truck that barely functions."

"I know," Dax stopped her. "Or at least I just found out when I was at the barbershop the other day."

"You went to the barbershop?"

"I told you I'm not the same person I was," he said quietly.

Heat flooded her face. This new Dax was almost as upsetting as the old one. She didn't know how to stay angry at this version of Dax.

Ashton cleared his throat. "We still have two checks for the same thing. Callie, for what it's worth, I agree with you that the town council is a joke. Nate needs a new truck. Hell, the whole firehouse needs to be remodeled."

"Ash, you can cancel my check," Dax said. "Callie deserves the credit."

"Callie won't get the credit. She makes all of her donations anonymously," Ashton blurted out, then his face fell when he realized what he'd just done. "Oh hell, Callie, I'm so sorry."

"Just stop." She closed her eyes, shaking her head.

"I think I'd better go before I make an even bigger mess of this," Ashton said, backing away. "Just let me know what y'all have decided."

As soon as the door clicked shut, she opened her eyes to find Dax watching her. How did he keep worming his way into the nice, quiet life she'd built for herself, and why were the colors of her world just a bit brighter with Dax around?

"I won't tell," he said, reaching out to briefly touch her hand.

"I believe you."

"When I said before that I hope my actions will show that I've changed, well, maybe you can help me out with that."

"What in the world could I do to help?"

"You're already helping the town. What if we combined our efforts and created a fund for more projects? You've been doing the work; you can tell me what the town needs."

"You and I working together?" Callie shook her head.

"Please don't say no, just think about it."

"I wasn't. I just can't believe that after all this time we're going to be… partners."

Dax looked at her thoughtfully. "If we combine our efforts, we can do a lot of good here."

His eyes were doing that crinkly thing again, and her wariness ebbed away, replaced with something she didn't want to identify.

"I'd still like to remain anonymous."

"We can do that."

"I'm not sure. Ashton doesn't seem to be very good at keeping secrets."

"I'll talk to Ashton. He means well, and he's got a much better head on his shoulders than his sister."

"That's not a very nice thing to say about the person you're supposed to marry."

"My mother thinks Presley and I should get married." He took a step closer, and his gaze held hers. "I do not."

Dax jerked his head up.

"Hell," he muttered.

Callie followed his gaze to find the Jewels on the sidewalk, staring through the window at them, triple expressions of concern on their faces. She smiled and waved, trying to reassure them, but Opal opened the door and poked her head in.

"Miss Callie, is everything okay?" she asked, glaring at Dax.

"You best come with us." Pearl crowded in behind her sister.

Ruby glanced nervously down the sidewalk. "Trouble is on the way," she said, gesturing for Callie to come to them.

A flash of pale lavender in the distance caught her eye. "Does this place have a back door?" she asked.

"Yes, why?"

"Because your mama is headed this way," Opal hissed.

Dax pointed to a door behind the stairs. "You don't have to—"

"No, but she should," Pearl said with panic in her eyes.

"Go, girl, now!" Ruby pushed her toward the door.

The four of them dashed into the alley.

"Miss Callie, what in the world were you doing in there?" Opal's voice was laced with concern.

"He didn't force you to go in there, did he?" Pearl followed.

"That was a narrow escape." Ruby twisted her hands, glancing over her shoulder again.

Callie gave the Jewels a reassuring smile. "I'm fine. I just had some business to discuss with Dax."

Her grandmother's best friends clustered around her.

"What kind of business could you be havin' with that boy?" Opal sniffed.

"You better hope his mama doesn't see you doin' business together," Pearl said, crossing her arms.

Ruby raised an eyebrow and crossed her arms just like her older sister.

Nothing she could say would convince the Jewels that she was okay being around Dax; there wasn't anything she could say to herself either. Callie had believed she would always hate Dax. Now… she didn't hate him, but she didn't exactly like him either.

It didn't matter if they shared some of the same goals for Colton. He needed to stay on his side of the town square, and she would stay on hers.

"Come on, ladies, my lunch hour is over. I just received a shipment of books and there's a new Beverly Jenkins romance I put aside for you. Let's head back to the library and you can see if there's anything else you want to check out."

Pearl's eyes sparkled. "Oh, I hope it's spicy," she said, rubbing her hands together.

Opal and Pearl made a beeline across the park while Ruby held back, linking her arm with Callie's.

"You're a grown woman, and I know you can take care of yourself, but please be careful. You're playing with fire, baby girl."

Callie looked at her grandmother's friend in a new light. "It sounds like you're speaking from experience."

Ruby frowned. "I'm an old lady now. My time for regrets has passed, but you're young, and I don't want you to be disillusioned by love the way I was."

"Miss Ruby, you've been keeping secrets from me."

"Some secrets are hiding in plain sight and some are best kept hidden away." Ruby stopped and took Callie's hands in hers.

"Now my sisters are gonna break that door down if we don't catch up. Lordy, Pearl will be up all night reading Ms. Beverly's book, moaning through all the spicy parts, and none of us will get any sleep."

She opened the door and ushered the Jewels in. Opal and Pearl went straight to the boxes that sat on the table in the center of the room.

Callie leaned against the checkout desk and laughed quietly, watching the Jewels dig through the boxes, sorting the books by genre and making a pile for themselves…. *This is why I came home.* She put her hand over her heart and went over to her desk, where she pretended to sort through a stack of papers, quickly shoving the envelope she found in the book return that morning in her desk along with the others. There was no point in reading it; she knew it would be just like the others.

"You okay, honey?" Opal hovered next to her.

Callie looked down at the rest of the papers clenched in her hand and carefully set them down, smoothing out the crumpled edges. "I'm fine, Ms. Opal. I'm just worried about—"

"That Ellis boy. I know. We all are."

"No, ma'am, I was worried that his friend Jacob doesn't have the supplies he needs to finish the bookstore. I may have to order more lumber from the yard over in Greenwood," she lied.

Opal wrinkled her forehead. "Oh, well, I still think you need to be on your toes with that boy. His mama is bad enough as it is. Now that her precious boy is home, she has backup."

Callie frowned. Opal was wrong. She'd seen Dax stand up to his mother since he'd returned. He was trying, but it couldn't be easy to undo years of pressure to be the dutiful son. She knew from her own experience that loving your parents but hating their actions was a hard tightrope to walk.

Dax wasn't the one sending the notes. It was easy to hold on to the old narrative about him, the self-centered bully, to protect herself from the way he made her heart beat faster. She had to decide if she wanted to keep her heart in the shadows with memories of the boy she knew or come into the light and let the man in.

CHAPTER ELEVEN

JACOB'S SHOUTING pierced the air, interrupting a quiet Thursday afternoon. "Put that down right now!"

Callie raced next door just as Dax ran down the sidewalk and crowded into the doorway of the bookstore behind her. Tiny particles of drywall dust floated in the air. Broken pieces of drywall lay along one wall. Jacob and Mae stood toe to toe. Mae held a drill at her side.

"I don't need your help," Jacob said, between clenched teeth.

Callie started to move toward them, but Dax put his hand on her shoulder and cleared his throat. Jacob turned, glaring at him. He looked from Dax to Callie and back at Mae. With a heavy sigh he stepped back.

"She's in my way!" he said, pointing at Mae.

"I'm helping!" Mae shot back.

"Don't you have a job? Why are you always hanging out here anyway?"

"I have a great job that allows me to take time off to help my friends," Mae replied.

Jacob crossed his arms. "Darlin', right now you and I are not friends."

"Mae, I know you want to help, but maybe there's something else Jacob would rather have you work on," Callie gently suggested.

"Yes, please." Jacob growled.

"But I want to help," Mae said stubbornly.

"But I can't work when I have to keep an eye on you."

Mae's hands went to her hips. "No one asked you to keep an eye on me."

"You need someone to watch you. You're making holes in the walls faster than I can patch them up."

"It took me a few tries to figure out where the studs were," Mae said, shrugging.

Callie bit her lip, trying not to laugh. She glanced over at Dax and saw his lip twitch.

"What is so funny?" Mae asked.

Mae had been coming by every chance she had since Jacob started, with the excuse of wanting to check on the progress of the bookstore. Callie suspected Mae was checking out Jacob more than any work being done.

Callie stepped over a broken piece of drywall to move between them. Mae poked her head around her to stick her tongue out at Jacob.

"Mae Colton, you stop that this minute!" Callie had never seen her cousin behave so childishly.

"Jacob, why don't you take a break?" Dax offered.

Jacob's jaw ticked. "I don't need—"

A knock on the door interrupted him. "Excuse me, folks." Sheriff Crosby walked in tipping his hat. The older man's eyes lit up when he noticed Dax. "Well, well, Dax Ellis," he exclaimed. "I'm surprised to see you here of all places."

"Sheriff Crosby." Dax shook his hand.

The sheriff hitched up his belt and turned to Callie. "Callie, I'm afraid we've had a complaint about unsafe working conditions and permit violations. We're going to have to shut this project down while we investigate."

"I didn't realize this was something the sheriff would handle," Dax said.

Jacob stepped forward. "I'm the contractor on this project, and I can assure you that Miss Colton has all of the correct permits."

"I'm sure Callie—"

"That's Miss Colton," Dax said.

The sheriff cleared his throat. "I meant, I'm sure Miss Colton thinks she has everything in order, but the town council will have to check and make sure."

"You've got to be kidding me," Dax said, disgusted.

Callie turned to him. "I may not have done it when I was a girl, but I can speak for myself now."

He stared at her for a moment and then gave her a brief nod.

"None of you are helping," Callie added in a hushed whisper. She hated that no one believed she could stand up for herself. Yes, she was shy and quiet, but that didn't mean she was helpless.

"Sheriff Crosby, since we have been through this before, I can't say I'm surprised that you're here." Callie put her hand up when he started to speak. "I contacted the county inspector two weeks ago when Mr.

Winters started working. He will be here tomorrow for an inspection and to double-check to make sure all of our permits are in order."

Callie pulled a file out of her bag and handed over a piece of paper. "In the meantime, the county inspector emailed me this in case you showed up before he could get here. As you can see, once again, the inspector has stated that you do not have the authority to shut down a construction site or do an inspection without his approval."

As the sheriff's face turned from bright pink to purple, Callie took a small step back and then stopped. She wasn't going to let the sheriff think she would back down. Dax stepped behind her. He made no move to touch her, but Callie could feel his warmth at her back. Having Dax behind her would have scared her in the past, but not today. She appreciated his support and worried about the repercussions at the same time. The sheriff stared at Dax, working his jaw, clearly unhappy with Dax taking her side.

The sheriff glared at her for a moment before turning on his heel and walking out. The windows rattled as he slammed the door, leaving the rest of them in strained silence.

Mae nodded with approval at Callie. "Well, that was interesting, and also good thinking, Callie."

"I'm surprised it took him this long to try and shut us down," Callie answered, feeling pretty good herself. It was nice to score a victory, even if a small one.

"When did you come up with the idea to reach out to the inspector?" Mae sked.

"I didn't. After the last contractor was run off, the inspector suggested it. I think he's just as tired of coming out here as I am."

"How many times has this happened?" Jacob asked, frowning.

"Seven."

"Seven!" Dax's voice rose. "This is ridiculous. I'm going to speak with my mother—"

"Dax, wait, please don't!" Callie called after him, but he didn't pause, and just kept walking out.

"Callie, he's on a mission now." Jacob put his hand on her arm, holding her back from chasing after him. "He's sick and tired of his mother's interference, not just with you but everyone in town."

"And do you think I'm not?" she demanded, aware that challenging the status quo would only bring more phone calls with complaints to any county official Dorothy could cajole and sweet talk into slowing down construction on her bookstore. "He's just going to make it worse."

Mae looked up at Jacob. "You've never lived in a small town before, have you?"

"What am I missing here?" he asked.

"Small-town politics can be even more complex than anything you see in a big city. Everybody knows everybody here, most of us are related in one way or another. Nothing happens around here without Ms. Dorothy Ellis's approval. No one wants to deal with the trouble that woman can cause. Sometimes you have to pick your battles rather than wage an all-out war," Mae explained.

Jacob glanced at Callie, and she knew from his expression that Dax had told him some version of what happened when they were children.

"Listen, both of you," Callie said firmly. "I can handle this."

Both Mae and Jacob gave her a skeptical look.

"How?" Mae demanded. "What can you do when that *Gone with the Wind* bitch is still flouncing around this town as if she owns it?"

"Mae, this isn't the time or the place." Callie gave her cousin a sharp look. She turned to Jacob. "If you can try to get as much work as possible finished before they come up with another reason to shut us down again, I would appreciate it."

"I'm going to get this finished no matter what." He looked at Mae. "And I don't need any help."

Mae put her hands on her hips. "You're not the boss of me, Mr. Winters."

Before Mae could say another word, Jacob pulled her toward him until they were nose to nose. "I think you could do with some bossing around, Miss Colton," he said against her lips. Just as quickly as he grabbed her, he turned on his heel and stormed out leaving Mae wide-eyed with her mouth open.

"Oh honey, I think you just met your match." Callie fanned herself. "Come on, let's go. I've got to get back to the library. I'm sure Jacob will be back when he's had a minute to cool off. And Mae, arguing with Jacob isn't going to help. Let him do his job."

Mae sighed. "Fine."

Callie had never seen her cousin like this before. Mae needed a strong-willed partner who wouldn't let her bulldoze her way through life, and she liked Jacob.

Callie put her arm around Mae's shoulder. "Don't worry, the bookstore is going to get finished eventually."

"Forget about the bookstore. Ms. Ellis isn't going to stand by and watch you make eyes at her precious son."

Callie opened her mouth and snapped it shut again.

Mae raised an eyebrow. "What are you going to do about that?"

"I was not making eyes. We're getting to know each other as the people we are now, that's all."

"That's good."

Mae went over to the café to get them some lunch. As Callie walked back into the library, she saw the envelope. She glanced around the room. Everything was just as she'd left it, and there was no one else around. She rushed over to check the bathroom and closet just in case and then returned to her desk, snatching it with trembling hands.

Callie looked down at her name written in clear block handwriting that she didn't recognize, other than it matched the other notes that had been left behind. She hesitated before opening it.

NO ONE WANTS YOU HERE, YOU FILTHY MUTT!

She shoved the message back in the envelope and put it in the back of her desk drawer with the others. The envelopes had started arriving months before Dax arrived, so she knew he wasn't the one sending them, but each one used the exact same words he'd used when they were kids. Dax wasn't the only one who called her those names, but he was definitely the ringleader. There were a few people around who could be behind them, but why? She tried to keep to herself and help the town she had grown to love—what had she done to inspire so much hate?

A small noise made her jump and she glanced over her shoulder, but the room was empty. Her pulse was racing but she tried to slow her breathing. In the beginning, she'd tried to ignore the notes, but with each one she became more nervous and angry. She'd even installed an extra lock on her door, in a town where no one locked their doors.

She should tell Mae about the letters, but her cousin hovered enough as it was and she would tell her parents, and they would worry as well.

Dax might not be behind the notes, but she suspected whoever was sending them wanted her to think they were coming from him. A flash of blond caught her eye as Presley Beaumont flounced past the window. Callie shook her head. Presley wasn't capable of putting together a scheme like this; the woman could barely walk and chew gum at the same time.

Mae came back and plunked a cup of sweet tea on the counter. "Ugh, I swear you could smell the stench of Presley's perfume from halfway across the park, and what in the world do you think she's hiding in all that hair?"

Callie laughed and took a long drink of the sweet liquid, welcoming the rush of energy from the sugar after the stress of her confrontation with the sheriff. "You could say the same thing about me," she said, fluffing her curls. "Maybe I should follow your lead and go short."

"Don't you dare." Mae waggled her finger at her. "Close-cropped is not your style."

True, Mae rocked the modern, edgy look in a way Callie never could. She'd always loved floral prints and pale colors while Mae preferred tailored suits. Even when she was dressed casually in her skinny jeans, a fitted T-shirt, and black motorcycle jacket, Mae maintained her hard edge.

Mae gave Callie a sly look over the rim of her drink. "It was pretty cool the way Dax was so protective of you at the bookstore."

"I'm sure he was more embarrassed for his mother's behavior than being protective."

"Nope, he was definitely going all caveman over you." Mae cocked her head. "It was pretty sweet actually."

Callie nodded. "You spend so many years thinking of a person as only one thing and then you learn they are so much more. I only ever thought of Dax as a bully, and now I see him as a...."

"A man?"

"Okay, missy, you've got the gender pronouns down."

"Just trying to help." Mae shrugged.

And that was the essence of Mae; she was a fixer at heart.

"The thing is, what other prospects do you have? Let's face it, you haven't met anyone else you've been attracted to as much as Dax in a long time."

Mae had a point. The few people her age drove to Greenwood or Jackson to hang out at a bar or go to a club, but that wasn't Callie's scene. She hated loud, crowded places with overly confident guys trying out bad pick-up lines. Lately the person she was interested in getting to know better was the person she'd avoided for so long.

"Don't try to distract me from talking about whatever that was that happened between you and Jacob. I've never seen you lose your cool like that. You better hope your mama doesn't hear about you sticking your tongue out, acting like a child."

"We finally get a man who is sex on a stick living in this sleepy little town, and he turns out to be so stubborn."

"Um, pot meet kettle."

"It's different when I'm stubborn."

"How is it any different?"

"I don't know; it just is."

"That's not fair, Mae. Jacob has been wonderful about helping out, and he's doing a great job. The store is going to be ready much sooner than I could have hoped."

Mae looked down, her cheeks turning a deep shade of pink. "I just want to help, to be productive instead of sitting behind a desk. Senator Weems is a good man but he's a unicorn, a Democrat in Mississippi, and we can't accomplish anything. I just want to feel like I'm making a difference." She spread her hands wide. "I thought Jacob and I would work well together. I had a picture in my head that didn't match the reality."

"Maybe you should try a different approach," Callie offered.

"Okay, I admit I can be a bull in a china shop."

"I wish I had your gumption."

Mae raised her eyebrows. "Gumption? What are we, in a Katharine Hepburn movie?"

"You know how much I love Katharine Hepburn, but I love you more and I want you to be happy."

"We both deserve to be happy and settled in our lives. I want us to be the moms sitting on the steps of the gazebo while our kids play in the park." Mae pointed to where a similar scene unfolded across the street. "Well, you'll be the mom. I'll be the cool auntie." She grinned.

They moved toward the window and watched the three little boys and two girls running in circles around the gazebo while their mothers sat on the steps, chatting. "They do remind me of us," Callie said wistfully, pointing to the two little girls covered in dirt and grass stains who were grinning at each other while holding hands and skipping around the gazebo.

Callie had no right to tease Mae about being stubborn.

CHAPTER TWELVE

"IF YOU keep going, you're going to pound it through to the other side," Jacob said.

Dax and Jacob had been working on the second floor of the building all week. Jacob helped out whenever he wasn't working on the bookstore for Callie. Working together they managed to cut the to-do list in half in less than a month, but today Dax was attacking the work, his hammer thundering against the wall.

"What's got you so worked up anyway?" Jacob asked.

"This building, my mother, Callie… everything, I guess," Dax answered. There were no rules for being attracted to the girl you used to bully, and no book on how to win her over either. If there were, Dax would have checked it out of the library just so he'd have an excuse to see Callie again.

The hammer suddenly slipped and Dax let out a string of curse words as he hopped around on one foot.

"Why don't you take a break?" Jacob suggested.

Dax looked up at the tangle of exposed wires and wooden support beams, finally ready to admit he was in over his head with… everything. Sam had come by as promised and installed a new electrical panel, and he would be back to help install fixtures and outlets once they had the drywall up.

"We need another person to help with the framing," he muttered.

"And a plumber and another carpenter." Jacob ticked the trades off on his fingers. "But that's not what's bothering you."

Dax slid down the wall to the floor, resting his hands on his knees.

"I want to ask Callie on a date, but I don't know if she would agree to that."

"Time. You've got to give her time to see you as a potential boyfriend instead of a bully."

"I don't know if I'm ever going to be able to convince anyone around here of that. My mother isn't helping things either."

"You're twisting yourself into knots trying to show everyone around here that you're not the same as when you left. Give it time."

Dax couldn't shake the feeling that without having Callie as a part of his life, his homecoming wouldn't be complete; he wouldn't be complete.

Jacob stood and held his hammer out to him. "Come on, the sooner we get the work done the sooner we can move in. I don't mind your uncle's cabin, but I'm ready to settle in for the long haul."

Dax took the hammer and pulled himself up. "Thanks, man, I couldn't have done this without you." They were making good progress on the building. The solar panels were going up on the roof in the next week, and it wouldn't be too much longer before both he and Jacob could move in.

"I do like Callie, though," Jacob said. "She's smart, kind, beautiful." At Dax's frown Jacob held up his hands. "I'm not interested in her. It's just that you two do have a lot in common. You both love this town. You both feel like outsiders."

"That's enough analyzing me. What about you? When are you going to find someone who's good for you?"

"Nope. I'm not interested in taking care of anyone anymore, and I don't want anyone thinking they have to take care of me. I'm happy just as I am."

"Never say never, my friend—did you ever think you'd be putting down roots in a small town?"

Jacob laughed. "The crazy thing is, I like it here." His gaze roamed over the loft. "I can see myself being happy here. This is a place I can call home, and I haven't had that in a very long time."

"I never thought I'd hear you say something like that."

Jacob shrugged. "Honestly, neither did I."

"I thought I knew what I was doing coming home, but I've never been so... unsure of myself. It's been over a month, and I still have no clue what I'm doing. I just want to get it right."

"You're doing fine, Dax. As much as I like it here, I won't lie, this little town isn't perfect. And your mom, well... she's a piece of work that's for sure, but you're trying to figure it out and you have good intentions."

"Can you let Callie know that?" Dax gave his friend a wry smile.

"You think she doesn't see that you're trying? Come on, Dax, think about it: you bullied her every summer, then you're gone for years and when you come back, you're trying to kill her with kindness. It's a little Dr. Jekyll and Mr. Hyde, don't you think?"

"I'm not that bad, am I?" Dax wandered over to the window overlooking the park and the library.

"You could just ask her out on a date," Jacob said, coming to stand beside him.

"I have a hard time believing she would say yes."

"You're so hard on yourself."

"And you're not?" Dax shot back only to be met with a raised finger from his friend. "Thought so." He smirked.

A movement caught his eye. He craned his neck to watch Callie step out onto the sidewalk with a young boy carrying a stack of books. She leaned over to say something and laughed with his mother for a moment before kneeling and giving the boy a hug. He'd heard of women saying they wanted children so bad their ovaries hurt—what was the equivalent for men? Wanting a kid so bad your balls hurt? Whatever it was, Dax realized he was ready to settle down in more ways than just moving home. He was ready for a family of his own.

Callie stood and waved as the mother and son made their way down the sidewalk. He started to wave and then let his hand fall back to his side. He didn't want to look too eager.

"I give up," Jacob muttered at his side.

"What am I supposed to do?" Dax growled.

"Just ask her out already." Jacob threw up his hands and walked away.

A minute later the buzz of the generator filled the air and the steady thump of the nail gun picked up again.

Dax caught sight of a flash of yellow and looked up to find Callie standing in the doorway. She was wearing a yellow dress with ruffles that caressed her shoulders. The afternoon light gave her skin a warm, golden glow. Her gaze swept the room, coming to rest on him. He took a step toward her and nearly tripped over a two-by-four. Fortunately, he caught himself before he fell.

Dax gave Callie a sheepish look. "It's one of those days."

"I was rude, I shouldn't have interrupted you," she said.

"No, it's fine," he said.

"I… I was hoping you could help me." Her eyes darted toward Jacob. "Could I talk to you for just a minute?"

"I need to check on something," Jacob said with a sly smile as he backed out of the room.

She took a step into the room and then another, stopped, and turned in a slow circle. "You've made a lot of progress."

Dax tried to slow the beating of his heart back to a normal rate, but his excitement at having Callie on his doorstep couldn't be contained. He moved closer, making sure to avoid any more obstacles that might make him fall flat on his face. "What can I help you with?" he asked, knowing that whatever she needed, he would figure out a way to give it to her.

"The fire truck is going to be delivered later today and I was wondering…." She glanced past his shoulder. "I thought you might have a view of the firehouse and maybe I could watch the delivery from here."

"Don't you want to be at the firehouse?"

"It's an anonymous gift."

"Ah."

"It might look suspicious if I just happened to be standing in front of the station when a new fire truck is delivered."

Dax nodded. "You're right." He gestured toward one of the windows on the other wall. "You should have a good view from this side."

She followed him over and they both peered out of the large arched window that overlooked the opposite corner of the park. The light filtering through her curls created a luminous halo. He leaned forward just enough to catch her scent. He didn't know anything about flowers, but she smelled like sunshine.

"You were right—you can see everything." Callie put her hand against the glass and wiped away a small circle of dust. She peered out and turned to Dax with a shy smile. "This is perfect. Are you sure you don't mind if I come back and watch from here?"

The leaves outside twisted and turned in the soft breeze just like his heart. "Please come back." Dax winced. He sounded as if he was begging. "I don't want you to miss this moment. Nate is going to be really happy. You did a nice thing, Callie."

Pink spread over her cheeks. "Thank you."

"What time is the delivery?" he asked, walking her back downstairs.

"In about two hours, late afternoon they said."

"Great, just come on up when you're ready, no need to knock."

Callie nodded and Dax watched as she made her way back across the park to the library. She stopped to smell one of the roses surrounding the gazebo on the way, her slender hand carefully cupping the blossom. Dax couldn't help grinning when he met Jacob on the second floor.

"Is it a date?" Jacob asked.

"Do me a favor? Clean up as much as you can upstairs. I've got an errand to run and then, Jacob—can you make yourself scarce later today?"

Jacob broke into a grin.

"Don't, okay. Just don't," Dax warned.

With a quick salute, Jacob headed back upstairs. *It's not a date*, Dax reminded himself over and over again while making the quick drive to the grocery store for the supplies he needed. That didn't mean he couldn't try to make a good impression. If he could get through this without making an ass out of himself, he might have a shot at asking Callie out on a real date. He made one more stop at Uncle Robert's, thankful that he could quickly grab what he needed and disappear before his uncle returned. Dax could put up with Jacob giving him a hard time, but that was his limit. He didn't need Uncle Robert to join in the ribbing.

True to his word, Jacob was nowhere to be found when Dax returned to the Barton Building. He took the stairs two at a time, arriving on the top floor out of breath. Jacob had stacked the lumber in the corner and swept all the sawdust. The tools were all put off to one side with the extension cords coiled neatly in a pile. He pulled out his phone and sent a quick text.

Thanks, I owe you one.

His phone chimed a second later.

Yes, you do. Whatever it is you're up to, I hope it ends well.

Dax checked his watch. He had just enough time to get everything ready. He kept his eye out for Callie while he worked and when he saw a flutter of yellow heading toward the building he raced back downstairs, reaching the door just before Callie did.

He opened the door for her just as a slight breeze lifted one of the ruffles off her shoulder and his mind went blank.

Callie looked up at him without any fear in her gray eyes. "Thank you again for letting me watch from upstairs. The trucking company called. He should be pulling up in about fifteen minutes."

He realized he was blocking the entrance and jumped aside to let her in. "Come on in."

"Thanks again for letting me watch from here."

"It's no trouble. I want to do nice things for you. I mean, I just wanted to make it nice for you." He gave himself a mental kick. "I'll stop talking now."

They reached the top floor and he stood to the side to let Callie in. The late afternoon sunlight streaming through the windows reinforced why Dax wanted to make the top floor his home. Even though the floorboards were still covered with a light film of dust, they showed their potential and the exposed brick walls glowed red, russet, and brown. Dax hung back, watching Callie make her way toward the window and put her hand on the glass.

"You cleaned all of the windows," she exclaimed, stopping short when she noticed the makeshift table he'd made from sawhorses and a sheet of plywood. "Did you do this for me?"

"I wanted you to be able to see the look on Nate's face when the truck arrived," he said gesturing toward the binoculars on the table.

She picked up the bottle of champagne and looked at him with a raised eyebrow.

"Just because it's an anonymous gift doesn't mean you shouldn't celebrate."

"Thank you, this is really thoughtful."

"Would it be okay if I watched with you?"

Callie scooted over to make room. "No, I don't mind at all."

Dax perched on the windowsill across from her and they both looked out the window, waiting for the truck to arrive.

A few minutes later, he caught a flash of red outside the window. "The truck is coming," he said, thankful for an excuse to change the subject.

He reached above her and opened the large casement window; the hinges groaned in protest as it swung open. Dax handed her the binoculars.

"It just pulled up to the firehouse," she exclaimed.

Callie looked at him; her eyes shining with excitement. She leaned a little too far out in her eagerness to see what was happening, and Dax grabbed her around the waist to steady her. "Careful," he said.

"He just came out," she continued her play-by-play in an excited whisper. "He's shaking his head and now the driver is giving him the letter."

"Letter?"

"I wrote a letter saying the truck is from a donor, the family of a former fireman who started a foundation to help underfunded small-town fire departments. Oh look, the driver is taking it off the truck," she exclaimed.

Her excitement was infectious; from their viewpoint Dax could see that Hank and Sam had joined Nate. They were smiling and slapping Nate on the back. A small crowd formed around the station as the truck was unloaded. The Jewels were there along with Uncle Robert and Jacob. Tillie, with her apron on, stood in front of the café, nodding her head with approval. When the delivery driver handed the keys to Nate, a small cheer went up from the crowd. Dax noticed Nate wipe his eyes. Callie pulled the binoculars away to wipe her own eyes.

"He's so happy."

The look of joy on Callie's face matched Nate's.

She was more cautious than shy, he realized. There was a quiet confidence about her. Callie had grown into a woman of beauty and grace. Her inner qualities attracted him as much as her outer beauty.

"How many anonymous donations have you made?" he asked, taking advantage of her distraction while she continued to watch Nate show off the new truck to the town folk that gathered around.

"Well, I buy all the books for the library, of course—that's not a donation, really—and the school didn't have any computers," she said distractedly, craning her neck out the window. "What the town really needs is a doctor. The clinic's been closed for a year now. Greenwood isn't far, but it would be better to have a clinic here for emergencies. I've been trying to figure out a way to get another fireman hired, and an EMT who could work with Nate, so he wouldn't have to rely on volunteers. But I can't donate that, and the town council won't approve the funds."

Dax had made his own donation to thank Nate after he came and did a safety inspection on the building and made suggestions on improvements. "Do they have money in the budget?"

Callie wrinkled her nose. "They have enough money to do whatever your mother wants done." She lowered the binoculars and looked at him. "That wasn't very kind."

"It's embarrassing, the way she behaves. It's… wrong."

"Parents aren't always who we want them to be."

"You sound like you speak from experience."

"It's silly to think they're ever going to change. If they haven't done it by now, I doubt they ever will."

Dax nodded. "I'm beginning to understand that with my mother, I'm trying to be optimistic but…."

Callie looked at him with understanding in her eyes. "Every time she does something that shows she's not going to change, you lose a little hope."

"Callie, I don't want you to feel that way about me. I have changed and if you can give me a chance, I'd like to prove it to you."

She bowed her head for a moment and then looked up at him. "I… I like you, Dax, and I have to be honest, that scares me sometimes. It isn't easy to let go of something that you've held onto for a long time, and not liking you is something I've been doing for a long time."

"I understand."

"I'm not saying no, Dax." She reached over and touched his hand. "I'm just saying… I want to let go, but I'm just not sure how."

Dax gently placed his other hand on top of hers. "That's more than I deserve, thank you."

"Just give me some time," Callie requested.

"Callie Colton, you are a woman worth waiting for."

CHAPTER THIRTEEN

FOR THE first time since Dax had returned, Callie thought life was settling down just a bit. It wasn't as quiet as it was before, not with the sounds of construction and Jacob's motorcycle echoing through the town square, but her days had settled into a pleasant routine, and she was delighted by the progress on her bookstore.

Callie looked up from her desk as the tall, lanky figure of Mae's father caught her eye.

"How's my favorite niece?" Joseph asked, opening his arms wide as he walked into the library.

Callie came around the checkout desk and walked into his warm embrace. Her eyes misted for just a moment. His hugs reminded her so much of her grandfather. She pulled back and asked, "What brings you to the library today?"

"You." Joseph searched her face. "Ella and I are worried about you. It's been too long since you've joined us at our Sunday table."

"I should have called, I've been... distracted lately."

"How are things going with the bookstore?"

"We're finally making good progress. We've gotten all the inspections completed, and Jacob is working on the finishing touches."

"And how are you doing having Dax Ellis back in town?"

Callie sighed. "I don't know, some days are better than others."

"Come on, baby girl, let's sit down and talk for a bit." Joseph led her over to the large oak table in the center of the room. He settled into one of the chairs and crossed his arms on the table. "I know it's been unsettling having that boy move back here."

"We've talked a few times and I appreciate that he's trying. I admire him for turning his life around, but his mother is still so terrible. Dax was always such a mama's boy when we were young, and now he's... defending me, taking my side against her, and it makes me nervous. This isn't going to end well."

She'd never thought to ask her uncle before but now was the time. "Do you know why his mother hates our family so much?"

Joseph sat back and pulled his hands into his lap. "There's a lot of history between the two sides of the Colton families. Some things are better left alone."

"I don't understand. Mom won't even talk about her life here."

Joseph leaned forward and covered her hand with his. "Your mother always had her sights set on bigger and better things than spending her life in the Mississippi Delta. She followed her dreams to Seattle and she's never looked back."

"You miss her, don't you."

"Your mom and I were as close as you and Mae were growing up. Your mom is the one who introduced me to Ella."

Callie smiled. "I didn't know that."

"We were so close growing up, and I was sad to see her go, but we all have to make our own choices in life and decide what will make us happy."

"She's so disappointed that I decided to make Colton my home."

"I always knew I would come back to Colton when I finished college, and she couldn't get out fast enough." Joseph's face fell. "She left in a hurry and hurt a lot of people when she didn't say goodbye. It hurt me that, as close as we were, she didn't confide in me.... I hoped she would make different choices." He squeezed Callie's hand. "But she gave us you, and no one could ask for a greater gift. Don't pay any mind to Dorothy Ellis—her bark is worse than her bite. That boy over there—" Joseph pointed across the square. "—he's grown into a fine young man, and he's not going to put up with his mama's foolishness."

He got up and came around the table to pull Callie into a hug. "I wish I understood why your parents haven't done right by you. All the money in the world doesn't take the place of having loving parents. I know it's not the same, but Ella and I will always be here for you."

"I wish they were still here."

"We all do, honey. There isn't a day that goes by that I don't think of them. They would be so proud of you, just like Ella and I are."

"Will you be honest with me?"

"About what?"

"Do you think they would be upset if I were friends with Dax or maybe... went out on a date with him? I just wish they were here to tell me what I should do."

Joseph threw his head back and laughed. "Oh, Callie, even if they were here, they wouldn't do that. Being a good parent or grandparent means giving your children the tools to figure things out for themselves, even if it means making some mistakes along the way."

"That's not what I wanted you to say, you know," she grumbled.

Joseph kissed the top of her head. "I know, baby girl."

He gave her one more pat on the back and slipped out of the door as a few more patrons came in, robbing Callie of the chance to dwell on their conversation.

Dark clouds edged the evening sky when the last person selected their book and Callie could close the library and start her walk home. She'd looked at a few vintage bicycles online but hadn't found anything that she wanted to buy. It wasn't the bike; it was the fact that her grandfather found the old cruiser and restored it for her. Nothing could replace the love that came with that gift. She could use the sleek silver sports car her parents surprised her with after graduation, but it only made her look like more of an outsider in this small town.

Gravel crunched under her flats, kicking up small puffs of dust. Walking didn't take that much longer than riding anyway. She glanced up at the sky at the first low rumble of thunder, cursing herself for not paying attention to the rapidly approaching dark clouds before she set out. A slight breeze ruffled her hair and her nose twitched as the air became heavy with moisture. The clouds above cast a dark shadow, bringing an eerie, unnatural twilight. Just as she reached the halfway point, another low rumble of thunder brought the first splatter of raindrops.

Within minutes her favorite dress was drenched and clinging to her legs. She clutched her tote bag to her chest, trying to protect the books and her laptop from the rain. With her head down, she put all her focus on getting home as quickly as possible. With each footstep the raindrops got bigger. She was so focused on trying to avoid the worst of the rapidly forming puddles, she didn't notice the truck pulling up alongside her.

"Callie, stop. Let me give you a ride."

Dax pulled ahead of her, the red brake lights came on as the truck jerked to a stop, and Dax came bounding out. "It's coming down hard," he said.

She struggled with her bag and nearly slipped on the wet and muddy gravel.

Dax grabbed her around the waist before she fell, hands warm through the damp fabric. "Callie, you're getting soaked through. Come on, let's get you into the truck."

"Thank you," she shivered. "I thought I could beat the storm."

"This is only going to get worse. Let's get you home before lightning strikes."

She let him help her into his truck, and then she buckled her seat belt. *Which would be more dangerous: the lightning or Dax?* Maybe they were both the same thing. A bright flash accompanied another rumble of thunder.

He climbed in, smelling like sandalwood and musk. She closed her eyes and held her breath. A thousand butterflies had taken up residence in her stomach. She tried to stop the tremors that ran through her body. Was it from being out in the rain or so close to Dax? When she opened her eyes, she looked down and realized the rain had made her dress transparent. The delicate floral lace pattern of her bra was clearly outlined underneath the pale pink floral dress. She blushed to the roots of her hair and hunched her shoulders, trying to hide herself while Dax buckled in next to her.

He reached for the knob on the radio and began to scroll through the stations. She couldn't tear her eyes away from the corded muscles on his arms or his long fingers as he fiddled with the dial. "I can find another station," he said, turning down the radio.

"It's okay. I… I like Lucas Monroe."

Dax raised an eyebrow.

"What, brown girls can't like country music?" she said. She lifted her chin. "I also like Thomas Rhett and I love Dolly Parton. Miss Dolly tells us the stories that we might not want, but we need to hear," she finished with a solemn nod.

"I didn't… That's not…." He sighed and rested his arms on the steering wheel. "I served with Lucas. I'm glad you like his music."

He started down the road; the windshield wipers swished back and forth, fighting a losing battle against the deluge. Southern storms were known for being brief but fierce; a thirty-minute storm in Colton could do as much damage as a day of rain back home in Seattle. Callie didn't miss the days and even weeks of constant rain, but Seattle storms were rarely accompanied by thunder and lightning. Another bolt of lightning split the sky in two. She wrapped her arms around herself.

Callie looked down at the damp upholstery on the bench seat. "I'm getting everything wet."

"Small price to pay to rescue a damsel in distress."

"Thanks again for not telling anyone about the new fire truck and letting me watch from your place."

Within minutes Dax pulled into her driveway. He turned off the engine and the rain created a dull roar around them. He turned toward her; his gaze locked with hers. "I told you, you can trust me," he said in a calm, quiet voice. "As a matter of fact, I was thinking we should talk about our plans so that we don't step on each other's toes again."

"Do you have another project for the town in mind?"

"I want to do everything I can, not just to make up for how terrible I was as a boy. This is my home, and I can do my bit to be a part of the community and help Colton grow. I'd like to look at some ways to help more small businesses open up in town. I'd like to know what kinds of goods and services you think Colton could use."

"We could talk about that," she agreed.

The cab of the truck suddenly became too small. She needed to get away so she could breathe again.

"I should go," she said, jerking the door handle open.

"I'll walk you up." Dax jumped out of the truck and escorted her to her front door.

They faced each other on her porch. She looked into his brown eyes and her heart hammered at the intensity in his expression. For a minute the rain disappeared, and it was just the two of them. His face was suddenly so close to hers, she could see the tiny drops of water that clung to his eyelashes and his lips. Without thinking, Callie opened the door, reached for Dax, pulling him inside. Another flash of lightning illuminated the sky, bringing another deluge. His wet T-shirt hugged his muscular chest, and little raindrops slid down his jaw.

"Just a minute." She ran to the bathroom and came back with a large towel, shoving it at him.

Dax took it from her, but instead of using it on himself, he reached over and began to wipe her face. Callie closed her eyes. She felt his breath on her cheek and then his lips brush against her damp skin at the corner of her mouth. She wasn't sure if he shifted or if she was the one who gave that fraction of an inch that brought them together. The only thing she did know was that she had never been kissed like that before.

Sloppy kisses from timid boys in high school and the college boys who wanted to show off their skills were all forgotten when his lips met hers.

She gasped from the wonder of it, and his tongue slipped inside. He reached up, caressing the back of her neck. Her knees would have given out if he hadn't pulled her closer, and suddenly she found herself pressing against him, wanting more.

She cupped his cheek, reveling in the feel of his whiskers against her fingertips. He moaned, and the knowledge that she had the power to make him do that went straight to her head. She placed her hands on his chest and could feel his heart beating in time with hers. He started to pull away, but she grasped his shirt and held on. He covered her hands with his and pried them away but continued to hold them, his gaze searching her face.

"I know I shouldn't, but I couldn't help myself. I'm—"

Callie closed her eyes. "Don't say you're sorry. Just don't."

He ran his thumb along her cheekbone, wiping away a tear or a raindrop; she wasn't sure. He pressed his forehead against hers.

"I should... I need to go."

Callie swallowed and nodded. The right thing would be for him to leave. There was a time when the safe thing for her was to run away from the boy, but that time had passed, and she wanted to stand with the man holding her so gently now.

"I'm not afraid," she whispered to herself as much as Dax.

A moment later she heard the truck start up; she opened her eyes and watched the taillights disappear. Callie reached up, touching the place where Dax had kissed her. Despite being soaked through, she felt warmth wash over her. Slowly, she closed the door then moved through the house, turning on a few lights and making sure her laptop and her phone were plugged in just in case the power went out, as it often did when the rain hit hard.

She lit a few candles, and their warm vanilla fragrance filled the air. After a hot shower, she wrapped herself in her favorite kimono with a cherry blossom pattern on a yellow background. She'd bought it on a trip to San Francisco. She ran the tie through her fingers. Her father had offered to take her with him when she was in high school. She'd been so excited, thinking that she would actually get to spend time with him, but when they landed and she saw two black Escalades waiting at the bottom of the stairway, she knew.

That was the moment she gave up on the little hope she had left in her parents' ability to change, and she stopped asking them to participate in any aspect of her life after that day. There was no point in wanting them to come to her school assemblies or parent-teacher conferences. She wasn't going to get affirmation and love; she could rely only on herself.

That trip also became a turning point. After the tour guide took her on a tour of Chinatown, she brought Callie to the City Lights bookstore, where she fell in love. She bought her first Moleskine journal and a Sandra Brown book, and she was hooked. She wrote a short story that night about a boy who threw rocks at little girls.

Her phone pinged with a text message.

"I'm just checking to make sure you're okay."

"I'm fine, thank you for giving me a ride home."

Calle watched the three dots in the bubble appear, disappear, and then appear again.

"I lied. I'm not checking to make sure you're okay, I'm checking to make sure you don't regret kissing me."

Callie leaned back against the headboard. Did she regret kissing Dax?

"No, I don't regret kissing you."

The bubbles did their dance again.

"Would you consider letting me do it again?"

A smile played on her lips. She must have worried him while she took her time trying to craft a response.

"I'm getting cocky again, I shouldn't have asked that."

"It's okay I was just thinking."

"Do you want to share?"

A loud crash of thunder was followed by a flash of lightning and the power went out. Callie drew the covers up to her chin.

"Did your power just go out?" he texted.

"Yes."

"Ours too. Are you okay, do you need anything?"

"Nope, I'm good."

"Are you going to tell me what you were thinking about?"

"I was thinking that in a million years I never thought I would be lying in bed in the dark texting Dax Ellis during a thunderstorm."

"That's not fair and that's not what you were thinking."

"Why isn't it fair?"

"Because now I'm picturing you in bed."

Callie chuckled. *"Don't be cheeky."*

Dax sent a sad face emoji. *"Clearly I need to work on my flirting skills."* Followed by, *"Do you want to picture where I am?"*

"I'm guessing you're on Uncle Robert's front porch watching the storm."

"You're good at this. I missed rainstorms like this when I was away. Are you going to tell me what you were really thinking about before?"

Callie sighed. *"I was thinking about how much has changed since you've been here, about how I've changed, and I was trying to decide how I feel about it... about you."*

"I wonder the same thing about you. I think about what projects we can work on together for the town and how much I look forward to sharing my ideas with you."

"We need to get the clinic up and running again, any chance you know of a good doctor who would be willing to move to a small town?"

"No, but together I know we can find someone."

"It's getting late, we can talk about it some more tomorrow."

"Good night, Callie."

"Good night, Dax."

The thunder and lightning began to drift away. She sighed, burrowing deeper under the covers, wondering if she was heading into a different kind of storm.

Chapter Fourteen

Dax was just getting ready to head over to the library when he heard the sound of breaking glass echo across the town square. He ran outside where he could see the jagged edges of what was left of the library window glinting in the sunlight.

Jacob came running down the stairs. "What was that?"

"The library," Dax shouted over his shoulder as he took off running across the park. Callie stood at the window; her shaking hands and pale face stopped Dax in his tracks.

Jacob was right behind him. "We have some plywood at the bookstore we can use to board this up. I'll take care of it."

"Callie, stop, you'll cut yourself," Dax said as she reached down to pick up a large piece of glass.

She jerked up and red oozed from her hand where the glass had sliced into her skin. Dax grasped her hand. The glass fell to the floor and shattered again. He cradled her hand in his, pressing against the cut to stop the bleeding. Callie flinched and tried to pull away, but he continued to put pressure on the wound.

"Hold still. You might need stitches."

"How about you let me be the judge of that?" Nate said, carefully stepping over the broken glass. He pried Callie's hand away from Dax. "You were right to put pressure on it," he said as he examined her palm. "Callie, do you have an emergency kit?"

She just stared down at her hand, her lip trembling.

"Where is it?" Dax asked.

"In-in the bathroom."

Dax located the kit and rushed back to her side.

Nate nodded and turned his attention back to Callie. "I don't think you need stitches, but I want to make sure this wound is cleaned."

Dax started pulling out the supplies. Callie jumped as Jacob started hammering plywood over the open window frame. Nate worked quickly, cleaning the wound while Dax hovered anxiously over them.

"Callie, can you tell us what happened?" he asked as he applied antibiotic ointment and began to wrap her hand in gauze.

"I… I was in the back." She began to tremble. "I didn't see anything. I just heard the crash." She pointed at the boarded-up window. "Grandpa had that glass painted," she said as a single tear escaped and rolled down her cheek.

Dax couldn't help wrapping his arms around Callie. He expected her to pull away, but she turned and buried her face in his shoulder. Nate raised his eyebrows and cleared his throat.

"I guess you don't need anything else from me."

"Thanks, Nate." Dax nodded.

Callie sniffed and pulled out of his arms, wiping her eyes. "Thank you, Nate." She turned to Dax. "I'm okay."

Nate grunted and walked out just as Jacob walked in.

"I'll start making calls and get a new window ordered."

"Thank you, Jacob, but you don't have to—"

Jacob frowned down at her and crossed his arms. "Darlin', do you really think I'm going to let you take care of this?" He poked his chest. "I'm your contractor—let me do my job."

"What the fuck!" Mae walked in. "Are you okay?"

Callie held out her bandaged hand. "I cut myself cleaning up the glass."

"Oh, honey." Mae looked down at the faint pink seeping through the gauze.

"This is why we need to get the clinic up and running again," Dax said. "When was the last time you had a tetanus shot?"

Callie wrinkled her forehead. "I'm not sure. I'll just drive into Greenwood—"

"You're not driving forty-five minutes with your hand like that," Dax said.

"No, she won't, I'll drive her," Mae announced. Gathering up Callie's things, she ushered her out the door.

With the window boarded, the light in the library became dull and the air heavy. Jacob picked up the broom and started sweeping the rest of the shattered glass.

"We need to set up security cameras," Dax said when they finished cleaning up.

"I can start the wiring while I work on the window repair, and I'll add it to the bookstore as well."

Dax nodded. "I'll get the equipment ordered, but we have a couple of things we need to do first."

"Afternoon, Dax," Sheriff Crosby called out with a nod as he and Jacob entered the sheriff's office five minutes later. He waved them over to where he sat with his feet up on the gray-green steel desk. Not much had changed since the courthouse was remodeled sometime in the '50s. Four jail cells still lined the back wall, and two smaller desks for deputies sat side by side on the other side of the room.

The sheriff folded his hands over his substantial paunch. "What can I do for you boys?"

"Someone threw a brick through the library window. I was wondering if you had any intention of investigating."

The sheriff's lips twisted into a knowing smirk that made Dax's stomach knot. "Don't worry, son, nothing you need to be concerned about."

Jacob growled, and Dax put his hand on his arm, feeling the waves of anger rolling through him. He glanced at his friend, sending a silent message: *don't do anything*. The sheriff obviously considered himself an ally.

"I also own property in town, Sheriff Crosby. I'm here as a concerned citizen. I certainly hope that you find out who is behind this before any other incidents occur." Dax tried to keep his voice calm and level even though what he really wanted to do was strangle the man.

"I don't think you'll have anything to worry about. Your mother is well respected in this town."

"I see," Jacob said, through clenched teeth. "And Callie isn't?"

"You certainly can't compare her to a true Southern woman like your mother."

"No, you can't," Dax said. The man wasn't smart enough to understand that the comparison didn't favor his mother. "Come on, Jacob, we've taken enough of Sheriff Crosby's valuable time."

Both men drew a deep breath once they stepped back outside.

"Well, that was… toxic."

"That was more than toxic." He pointed toward the jail. "That was my mother's doing."

"Do you think your mother had a hand in this?"

"She wouldn't get her hands dirty and throw the brick herself but, and I can't believe I'm saying this, I wouldn't put it past her to get someone to do it for her. This is my fault."

"How is this your fault?"

"I kissed Callie last night. News travels fast in a small town and if someone saw us, I'm sure my mother's heard about it my now."

"Well, we're going to have to figure it out because the more time you spend with Callie, the more these incidents could escalate."

Dax's stomach knotted with dread. Jacob was right: the pattern was clear. His phone vibrated in his pocket.

Callie's getting a few stitches. She's okay. We need to talk.

He held out the phone to Jacob.

"She's a good friend."

Suddenly Jacob stiffened. Dax followed his gaze; the Jewels were barreling across the park toward them.

All three of their faces were twisted with rage.

"Callie told us you'd changed." Opal pointed a shaking finger at Dax.

"You hurt our girl," Pearl followed.

Ruby opened her mouth, but no words came out as her face crumpled and she began to cry. Opal and Pearl surrounded their youngest sister, murmuring words of comfort while Dax stood by helplessly.

"Ladies," Jacob said, "I give you my word that Dax had nothing to do with this." They all glared at him as Jacob added, "We're going to find out who did this, I promise."

Opal pressed her lips into a thin line. Her sisters remained silent by her side. They spoke in birth order and, apparently, they held their judgmental silence in the same way. The three turned away, only Ruby glanced back looking sad and disappointed.

"This is my fault," Dax said again.

"Bullshit. This didn't happen because of you, so get over yourself. You're not that special."

Dax found himself smiling even though he wanted to wallow in self-pity for just a little bit longer.

When they returned to Uncle Robert's, Dax went in and began to throw clothes into his bag.

Jacob and Robert crowded the doorway. "Do you want to fill us in on what's going on?" Robert asked.

"I'm moving into the Barton Building."

"That place ain't fit to live in yet," Uncle Robert said.

Jacob pulled out his duffel and began packing alongside Dax. "Surveillance," he said, with an understanding nod.

Dax paused. "You don't have to come—it's not going to be very comfortable."

Jacob shrugged as he balled up another shirt and shoved it into his bag. "It won't be as bad as that cave we had to camp out in for two weeks, remember?"

They both started laughing. He was thankful to have his best friend, someone he considered a brother, at his side. He paused; he missed his biological brother as well. They had been so close before he was sent away, or at least as close as their mother would allow them to be. They'd sneak off into the woods, building secret forts and chasing frogs at Willow Pond. He'd pushed those memories away, but since he had returned to Colton, every moment of his childhood flashed through his mind.

Robert came in with some binoculars, one with a night scope. "Here, these will help."

"Thanks," Dax said, taking the equipment and shoving it into his bag.

"You let me know if you boys need anything. It's been nice having you around."

Dax put his hand on his uncle's shoulder. "We're not going far. I expect we'll still show up on your front porch a time or two."

Jacob hauled his duffel over his shoulder. "Ready?"

Dax nodded, feeling his psyche slip into mission mode. "Ready," he replied with a curt nod.

It didn't take long to set up in the empty space on the third floor when they got to the Barton Building. Jacob had done some rough framing for a bathroom and there was no kitchen to speak of, but they could make do with the bathroom downstairs and takeout from the Catfish Café for now.

"I'll take the day shift and can keep an eye out when I'm working up here and at the bookstore," Jacob said dropping his duffel on the floor.

Dax had already pulled out the binoculars and set them on the windowsill. He scrolled through his phone, ordering a pair of night vision goggles that would be delivered the next day.

A soft knock on the doorway made his head jerk up.

"I knocked downstairs. I stopped by Robert's and he told me you would be here." Mae stood in the doorway.

"How's Callie? Is she alone? You shouldn't have left her." The words tumbled from Dax.

Mae's eyes grew wide. "Whoa, calm down." She glanced toward Jacob. "Your friend here is a little wound up."

"He's concerned," Jacob said. "We're all concerned. How is she?"

Mae's shoulders dropped. "I tried to get Callie to go home, but she insisted on going back to the library. My mom and the Jewels are with her."

"Thanks for taking her to the hospital, you're a good friend," Jacob said.

A rosy pink glow spread over Mae's cheeks. "Yes, well...." She turned to Dax. "These incidents keep escalating. Even before you got here, stuff happened. She stopped driving her car into town because the tires were slashed once, and then someone keyed it another time."

"Did she report it?" Dax asked.

"Who would she report it to, the sheriff?" Mae scowled. "We both know that would be worthless."

"Anything else?" Jacob asked.

Mae shook her head. "Not that I know about but... I'm not sure Callie would tell me if there were."

"Do you think she has said anything to anyone? What about her parents?" Jacob asked.

"Her parents would just arrange for security, and the last thing Callie would want is a bodyguard following her around; she had enough of that growing up."

"Why would Callie have bodyguards when she was a kid?" Jacob asked.

"Callie's dad is a well-known producer, and the owner of Columbia City Records," Dax said.

"Her parents love the concerts and the parties, but Callie chose to live here because she doesn't want to be in the spotlight. She hates the attention."

Jacob nodded. "Understood."

Thank goodness Callie had Mae as her friend and protector. But that still didn't help the fact that someone wanted Callie out of Colton. Badly.

Dax had Mae sit and go through all the incidents she knew about, and then he made her go through them again while he created a timeline on his computer.

"That's all I know, I don't have anything more I can tell you," Mae said.

Jacob put his hand on her shoulder. "Thanks for letting us know."

"Well, you guys did security stuff in the Army, right? I mean I figured you would—" She shrugged. "—I don't know... know stuff."

These were just the incidents Mae knew. Were there others Callie hadn't mentioned, he wondered.

"You'll tell me if you find anything?" Mae asked.

"Of course," Dax said.

Mae paused, narrowing her eyes. "Even if it's your mother?"

"No matter who it is. I'm not going to keep anything from you or Callie. That's a promise, Mae."

After Mae left, Dax paced in the loft, stopping to look out of the window every few minutes until Jacob yelled at him to stop and just go over to the library already.

The light was dim in the room with the windows covered. The Jewels were buzzing around Callie as she sat at her desk. To his surprise, her eyes lit up when he came in, and she jumped up and rushed over to him.

"Thank you for coming, Dax. I was telling Miss Pearl that I would be just fine and closing soon. It was so kind of you to offer to walk me home." Her words were rushed as she gave him a pleading look.

"Good afternoon, ladies." He nodded in the direction of the three identical icy glares.

"Miss Callie, we...." Opal began.

"We'd be happy to take you home, honey," Pearl continued.

"You don't need him," Ruby added, in a quiet voice.

Callie went over and pulled all three women into an embrace. "Thank you so much for helping me today." She gently pushed them toward the door. "I'll be just fine, and I promise I'll call when I need more help."

Opal looked over her shoulder at Dax before she stepped out onto the sidewalk. "We'll check on you tomorrow, Miss Callie."

"Just to make sure—" Pearl hovered in the doorway.

"You're okay," Ruby finished.

Callie slumped against the doorway as soon as the Jewels left. "Thank you, they mean well, but I needed a break."

"You can use me as an excuse anytime."

"You don't really have to walk me home," she said.

"I'd be happy to." He gestured to her bandaged hand. "Are you okay?"

"It's just a couple of stitches—it's nothing to worry about."

"Is there anything else you need here or are you ready to go?"

She moved to her desk to get her bag. "No, there's nothing more I can do today."

He took her bag and slung it over his shoulder. "Let's go, then."

"You really don't mind walking me home?" she asked.

He reached up and tucked a stray curl behind her ear. Cupping her cheek, he said, "I'd walk you to Memphis and back, Miss Colton," before dropping a brief kiss of her forehead and escorting her out.

A light breeze rustled through the trees. The sunlight was just beginning to fade, creating long shadows on the road as they walked side-by-side.

They reached her doorstep, and she looked at him with a shy smile. "Would you like to come in?"

"I would, but I need to head back. Can I have a rain check?"

She nodded, and he waited when she went inside until he heard the click of the lock.

He pressed his hand to the door. He wanted nothing more than to spend more time with Callie, but he didn't want to risk putting her in any more danger. He needed to be careful until he figured out who was threatening her.

As he walked back home, he pulled out his phone, thumbing through his contacts, hovering over the one he was searching for. He took a deep breath before he hit the green icon.

"Ellis," a stern voice snapped on the other end.

"Reid, it's Dax." The silence on the other end of the line stretched uncomfortably. "I was hoping we could talk."

"Now isn't a good time." His brother's voice was clipped.

"Okay, I'll try again, and I'm going to keep trying until you'll talk to me."

There was a beat of silence. "I don't get home until late most nights, so it's better to try to call on the weekends."

"I'll call you this weekend."

He looked over his shoulder toward Callie's house. He'd needed his brother's help, if Dax's suspicions about the attacks on Callie turned out to be true.

Chapter Fifteen

Callie took her time making her way across the town square toward the library. It was one of those late spring days that confirmed winter's end and held a promise of the lazy days of summer. The sunlight had been just a bit brighter when it streamed through her bedroom window that morning, and even though she missed her bike, she didn't mind the walk into town that day. Morning dew and tiny pieces of fresh-cut grass clung to her shoes as she circled the gazebo, caressing the new delicate yellow blooms of the rosebushes surrounding the centerpiece of the town square.

She smiled as she dipped her head, breathing in the sweet perfume of a freshly opened blossom. Her circuit complete, she made her way to the library. On a day like today, her loyalties were divided between her love of books and her desire to spread out a blanket and picnic in the park.

The new plate glass window glinted in the morning sun. Callie paused for a moment, eyeing the naked glass. The sign painter would be coming later that day to replicate the design her grandfather had chosen so long ago.

With a sigh, she opened the door. Without the lettering on the windows, the library wasn't the same. It didn't feel like home. Once she collected the mail and a few books from the box below the mail slot that patrons also used for after-hour returns, Callie made herself a cup of tea and sat at her desk for a quiet moment before the start of the day.

A movement from across the park caught her eye, and she saw a shadow move in one of the large arched windows on the top floor of the Barton Building. She'd only had a few brief glimpses of Dax since the day he found her standing on shattered glass and walked her home. Part of her was hoping that he might kiss her again, but he was a perfect gentleman. She laughed softly. Dax Ellis a perfect gentleman—Dax was who she'd pictured for every villain she read about, now she imagined him as the hero. He was still in her dreams most nights. Some were still nightmares, but others were more troubling, especially the ones with Dax kissing and caressing her as they made love.

As always toward the end of the week, the library was a hub of activity. Throughout the morning, townfolk came in to pick up a new book to entertain them for the weekend. The morning rush had just died down when Dax walked in. His eyes darted toward the older man sitting at the large table looking though a book on farming. Dax acknowledged him with a nod and turned back to Callie.

"Good morning, Callie." His eyes dropped to her hand. He reached out and gently cupped it in his, running his finger over the bandage.

Heat flowed from where their hands touched, and her heart beat faster. She pulled her hand away to smooth nonexistent wrinkles from her skirt.

She looked into the brown eyes from her dreams gazing at her with a warmth that gave her butterflies. The air grew still and heavy around them as they locked.

"Is… is there something that you wanted?" she asked.

"I just wanted to see if you were able to get all of the repairs made and—" His eyes dropped to her hand again. "—make sure there wasn't anything else I could do to help."

Callie shook her head. "No, I'm okay."

Her heart began to do that strange fluttering thing that seemed to happen every time Dax came near. Why couldn't she carry a conversation as easily as the characters in her books? She wrapped her arms around herself, a habit she'd used to comfort herself. Now she imagined his strong arms around her instead. She took a step back. *It's a strange dance we are doing—one partner retreating while the other stands still.*

The door banged open, rattling the new pane of glass, and Callie rolled her eyes. "Oh Lord," she muttered under her breath.

Dorothy Ellis entered the library. She paused to brush an invisible speck of dirt from the lapel of her pale purple suit before she marched over to her son. "Dax, what on earth are you doing here?"

"I'm here to check out a book. What else would I be doing here, Mother?"

"I can't imagine that there is anything here you would be interested in."

The man at the table shoved his chair back. He pulled another book from the shelf and set it down on the table with a determined thud and a frown at Dax's mother.

"Actually, Mother, there's quite a bit here that I'm interested in," Dax said with a pointed look at Callie.

"It has come to my attention that you continue to stock the shelves of this library with inappropriate books," Dorothy said to Callie.

"Exactly what books are you referring to?" she asked.

"Those trashy Katherine Wentworth mysteries as well as that terrible Indian poet," Dorothy spat out. "How completely inappropriate."

"Do you hear yourself, Mother? You are way out of line."

Before Dorothy could reply, the man who had been sitting at the table pushed past her with two books in his hand. "I'd like to check these out, please, Miss Callie."

Callie took the books and fought back a smiled at the titles of one of the most banned books in the country alongside one of her favorite books, *The Macchiato Murders*, by Katherine Wentworth. "Of course, Mr. Lawrence."

Dax and his mother continued to argue in hushed whispers that she did her best to ignore. She guided Mr. Lawrence over to her desk and had begun to check him out when Ms. Ellis interrupted. "You didn't ask to see his identification."

"I beg your pardon?" Callie's hands hovered over the keyboard.

"You did not ask for his identification," Dorothy repeated, enunciating each word as if Callie didn't speak English.

"He has a library card."

"For all you know he could have stolen that card."

"That is enough." Dax grasped his mother's arm. "I apologize for my mother's rudeness," he said pushing her out the door.

Mr. Lawrence looked at Callie with a raised eyebrow.

Callie held up the books. "Mr. Lawrence, I appreciate your way of trying to help, but you don't have to check these out if you don't want to."

Mr. Lawrence shook his head. "No, ma'am." He took the books out of her hand, hugging them to his chest. "Anything Ms. Ellis says is inappropriate is something I want to read."

"They are both wonderful books, I hope you like them."

"You don't pay Ms. Ellis any mind." Mr. Lawrence patted Callie's hand. "I think her boy is finally gown up enough to take his momma in hand."

Thankfully, the rest of the afternoon was quiet with a steady ebb and flow of patrons. The sign painter had come and gone after carefully reproducing the original lettering in cream and gold on the window. The birds were just starting to sing their evening song when she slung her leather backpack that held her ever-present laptop over her shoulder, stepped outside, and locked up for the night.

Dax sat outside the library with his head bowed and his hands clasped. For the first time since he moved back to Colton, Callie wasn't surprised to see him. She hitched her backpack on her shoulder. "What are you doing Dax?"

He jumped up. "Callie, I'm—"

"Don't." She held her hand up. She sighed and let the backpack slide off her shoulder to rest at her feet. "You have to stop saying you're sorry and…." She swallowed. "And I have to stop wanting you to."

Dax stood up and moved in front of her taking her hands in his. Callie held her breath as his eyes searched her face, finally zeroing in on her lips. She tore her eyes away, reaching for her bag, but he grabbed it first, slinging it over his shoulder.

"I thought I could give you a ride home." He shrugged.

Callie took a deep breath and glanced up to where pale pink had begun to tint the edges of the clouds. "Thanks, but no, it's too nice of a night not to walk."

She held out her hand for her bag, but Dax pulled it out of her grasp. "You're right—it is a beautiful night. Can I walk you home again?"

For the second time Callie found herself walking side-by-side with Dax. She tried her best to ignore the curious stares from the few people they passed on their way. Even the birds were chirping louder as if they were sharing in the gossip that was sure to come. The news would be all over town that she and Dax had been walking together again before she even made it home.

"I'm not so sure this is a good idea," she said as a car swerved when the driver did a double take, looking back at the two of them with his mouth open.

Dax chuckled, and then she started laughing as well. The more she thought about the situation, the harder she laughed until tears streamed down her cheeks. Dax stood in front of her with his hands on his hips, smiling down at her, waiting for her to catch her breath.

"What are you doing, Dax?"

He frowned. "I'm walking you home."

"No, that's not what I mean. Why do you keep showing up? I... I don't think you're trying to stir up trouble on purpose, but you have to know that's what you're doing. Everyone whispers about us as it is, and now... well, it's no secret that I'm not your mother's favorite person, and... you don't like me."

Dax reached for her injured hand, frowning at the bandage before his eyes met hers. "You're wrong. I like you. When I first saw you all those years ago, I thought you were the prettiest little girl I had ever seen."

Tears pricked at the corner of her eyes. "Then why?"

"I'm just beginning to understand it myself." His voice shook. "I'm so embarrassed and ashamed. It doesn't help that my mother encouraged my behavior. I'm not making any excuses," he said in a rush. "At the end of the day, I'm the one who threw the rocks and called you all of those horrible names. Callie, I...."

She reached up and put her fingers on his lips, shaking her head. "No more, remember?"

He nodded and then, taking her good hand, he continued walking. They didn't say anything; Callie was trying to process what Dax had just told her. They reached her house too quickly and Callie wasn't ready to say good night.

"Would you like some sweet tea or a glass of wine?"

Dax hesitated for a minute. "I'd like that. It's a nice night. Do you want to sit out here?" he asked, gesturing to the porch swing.

"Just give me a minute," she said, fumbling with her keys. Callie leaned against the door once she got inside, pressing her hand against her rapidly beating heart.

"Get it together, Callie," she said, under her breath. She grabbed a sweater off the back of her rocking chair and threw it over her shoulders before she snagged a bottle of wine and two glasses. Part of her hoped Dax wouldn't be waiting for her when she opened the door. Why did she ask him to stay? She was a jumble of confusion, half wanting, half hoping for what—another kiss or more? She took a deep breath and opened the door.

Dax was sitting on the swing, his hands clasped in his lap, looking just as nervous as she was. She handed him a glass and then sat down at the opposite end of the swing, tucking one leg under her. She set her glass on the ground, opened the bottle, and poured.

Dax took a sip and then picked up the bottle, looking at the label. "This is good. I've never seen this brand around here."

"There are a few things from home I miss too much to give up; coffee and wine are high on the list. I have it shipped," she said.

"I can't blame you. I've heard about the coffee and wine scene in the Pacific Northwest. Do you miss Seattle?" Dax asked before taking another sip.

"Sometimes," she admitted. "I wouldn't mind a true winter every once in a while. It gives you an excuse to snuggle up in front of a fire and hide away from the world."

Dax leaned forward. "Anyone in particular you've been snuggling up with?"

"Mr. Ellis, that is awfully forward of you," Callie teased.

"I'm just trying to find out if I have any competition."

"This is crazy." Callie shook her head. "I still can't believe that you really like me."

He shifted a little closer. "But I do."

"I don't know if I'm ready for you to like me," she admitted.

He nodded. "Fair enough. Can I ask you one more question?"

"I guess that's only fair."

He reached over and ran his finger along the hem of her dress. "Your favorite color is yellow and you like flowers."

"That wasn't a question."

"I'm getting to that part." He smiled. "What's your favorite flower?"

"Roses."

"Yellow roses?"

"Yes." She cocked her head. "That wasn't what I thought you'd ask. Why my favorite flower?"

"Because I want to know what I should get you to make you forgive me when I get into trouble."

"Now it's my turn. How much trouble do you think it's going to cause when word gets around you've been sitting on my porch?"

Dax sighed. "The last thing I want to do is cause you any trouble. There was a time when all I wanted was my mother's approval, but over the years I've learned that's not the kind of approval I'm looking for. Since I've been home, I'm realizing a lot of things about my childhood that I never took the time to understand before."

"Like what?"

"I was so scared my mother would send me away the way she sent my brother away, I was willing to do anything to keep her happy," he admitted.

She scooted closer and slipped her hand into his. "That's a terrible fear for a child to live with."

"One day I was climbing trees and having a game of catch with my brother, and the next day he was gone."

"Do you know why he was sent away?"

"I honestly don't know." Dax closed his eyes. "I miss him. I don't really feel like I know him, and I want to. Since Dad died and my mother is, well… the way she is, Reid is my closest family connection next to Uncle Robert."

"Where is Reid now?"

"He lives in Chicago. He barely speaks to me, and he doesn't want to have anything to do with Colton. I've tried, but so far I haven't been able to convince him to come home, even for a short visit."

"Good or bad, family is important. It may be messed up, but at least your parents loved you."

"You don't think your parents love you?"

"Most of the time my parents forget I exist. They are so wrapped up in the business and each other. I'm never going to be as outgoing or glamorous as they want me to be. Sometimes I think it's easier for them to forget about me than be disappointed in me." She saw his pained expression and waggled her finger at him. "Don't you dare take pity on me. I had the most wonderful grandparents in the world. They were the only people in my life who ever loved me for me."

"That's not true," he said, tenderly caressing her cheek. "So many people here love you—can't you see that?"

"This isn't about me. We were talking about you and your brother. Don't give up," she said. "If we can be friends, anything can happen."

"Callie, I don't want to be friends with you."

Her heart sank.

Dax wrapped his arm around her, pulling her close. "If I just wanted to be your friend, I wouldn't think about doing this every time I'm around you." He lowered his head and brushed his lips against hers.

She put her hand over his and arched forward, returning the kiss. His lips were cool and firm against hers.

"I want to be so much more than your friend. I want to be the man who has earned you." He drew back to look into her eyes. "I want... you."

Callie sucked in her breath. "I want you too, but I need to go slow."

"I agree." He rose from the porch and held his hand out to her. "Let me walk you to your door and kiss you good night."

Callie allowed herself to be drawn to her feet, but once on her feet, she stood in his arms, studying his features in the light from the doorway. His mouth tipped up at one side in a way that she had to admit she found more and more attractive. There were tiny lines at the corners of his eyes, and she wondered if they came from laughter or stress. Her fingers itched to reach out and soothe them away. His jaw ticked; she had the power to make him lose control, and the knowledge made her giddy. She rested her hand on his chest, where his rapid heartbeat matched her own. She kissed the spot and smiled when she felt his body tense.

"You're beautiful," he said huskily. He reached up, tucking a stray curl behind her ear, letting his fingers brush along her jawline. He leaned forward and pressed his lips to her forehead. "Lock the door," he said, stepping away.

She understood then that he wouldn't budge from her front porch until he heard the lock. She closed the door and watched out of the peephole as he waited. As soon as he heard the click, he turned and walked away. She leaned against the door, pressing her fingers against her lips.

If she did get any sleep tonight, she knew there wouldn't be any nightmares, only sweet dreams.

CHAPTER SIXTEEN

DAX WOKE up with his mind in a jumble. As happy as he was about kissing Callie last night, he couldn't ease the knot of worry in his stomach about his mother and how she was going to react when she found out he was serious about seeing Callie. And he was serious. Callie was going to be a part of his life and his mother wasn't going to like it, and she wouldn't be quiet about it. He had no proof that she was behind the incidents that were happening, but he suspected she was.

His mother's behavior at the library was inexcusable, and it was impossible to ignore her attitude anymore. Another fight with his mother was coming. There was no way to avoid it. He wasn't willing to keep his distance from Callie to keep the peace with her. He stumbled out of the shower to find Jacob waiting for him in the half-finished kitchen, pouring himself a cup of coffee.

"Morning." He lifted his mug in greeting.

"Why are you so chipper this morning?" Dax grumbled as he reached for his own mug.

Jacob shrugged. "I don't know, I just am. I like this town of yours. I had a talk with the owner of the hardware store. He's thinking about retiring and I made an offer to buy the place."

"Wow, Billy Colton retiring? He's been behind the counter at that store for as long as I can remember."

Jacob nodded. "He turned seventy-two this year; no wife or kids, says he wants to spend the rest of his years fishing."

"I can't say I blame him." Dax refilled his cup. "I hoped you would like it here when I asked you to come down, but this is a big commitment. You haven't even experienced a Southern summer yet; are you sure you're ready?"

"I've done a lot of thinking. I can still take on some small projects on the side for you and some construction jobs here and there. I want to expand the hardware store and add a workshop where I can focus on making custom furniture."

"That's a great idea. Once people see the work you've done here, you'll have folks lining up for one of your custom pieces."

"So, how's your plan coming along?" Jacob asked.

"What plan?"

Jacob jerked his thumb in the general direction of the library.

"Oh, that plan. I'm making progress, but I'm having dinner with my mother at the country club tonight. I'm sure I'm going to get an earful about seeing Callie, but it's a good excuse to try and talk to her and understand why she hates her so much."

"You really think your mother is behind these attacks against Callie, don't you?"

"I do. She's my mother and I hate to think she could do something like this, but I have to go with my gut, and she's my prime suspect."

"If you can prove that your mother is behind all of the attacks on Callie, have you thought about having her end in jail?"

"An older white lady in a small Southern town," Dax shook his head, "that's not likely to happen. But I can confront her and let her know that I won't cover for her. It's going to be ugly."

"It's a shitty position to be in."

"I kind of feel like this is part of making amends. If this is the price I have to pay for the things I did in the past, it's a price I'm willing to pay."

"JUST LET me know what you need from me; you know I'll support you no matter what happens. Since you'll be out tonight, I'll keep an eye on things at the library while I work here," Jacob said.

"Thanks, man—I'm glad you've decided to make Colton your home, and thanks for helping me keep an eye out for trouble."

"I like Callie. I just wish her cousin would stay out of my way."

"I hate to break it to you, but she's going to be your neighbor. Mae rented one of the apartments we're going to be building downstairs."

"Great, just what I need. She's cute as hell, but I don't want someone in my life who refuses to listen."

"Maybe you're saying the wrong thing?"

"Not helpful." Jacob downed the rest of his coffee and slung his tool belt over his shoulder. "I've got work to do. I'll catch up with you later."

After Jacob left, Dax wandered toward the wall of windows that overlooked the town square. Sure enough, there was Callie walking past the gazebo, stopping to smell the roses as she did every morning on her way to open the library. Today she was wearing jeans and another one of her fluttery floral tops and a pair of red ballet flats. The morning sun created a halo around her as it filtered through her curls.

Dax leaned forward, pressing his hand against the glass. Suddenly, she turned and looked up right where he was standing. Dax pulled back. She couldn't see him through the privacy film he had installed on the windows, but he sensed that she knew he was there. He smiled down, wanting nothing more than to go to her, but he didn't want to do anything that might jeopardize the progress he'd made. She'd told him she wanted to take things slow and that's what he planned to do.

He made his way down to the main floor, running his hand along the new black metal banister that continued the modern-meets-vintage look that he'd envisioned when he first bought the old building. He sat down at his desk, and before long he was immersed in creating firewalls and encryptions that would safeguard his clients from any kind of cyberattack you could imagine. A few hours later his phone rang, bringing him out of his work trance.

"Hi, Reid, thanks for calling me back."

"I figured you wouldn't stop leaving messages until I did."

"How have you been?" he asked.

"Really, is this why you're calling? What do you want, Dax?"

"I'm hoping you'll reconsider and come for a visit. You don't have to see Mother; you can stay with me. It's been a long time, Reid, and I'd like the chance to rebuild our relationship."

"What do you really want, Dax?" His brother sighed.

"I want to get to know you better. I've... I understand a lot of things about our family that I didn't know before." He paused. "I've learned a lot about myself as well. I'd like to have my big brother in my life. I understand that you don't want to come here, and if you want me to come up to Chicago, I will, but I'm not going to give up on trying to repair the damage that's been done."

Silence stretched before Reid responded. "What does Mother have to say about all of this?"

"I didn't ask, and I don't care."

"I see." Reid cleared his throat. "I... I'll think about it."

Reid hadn't said no, and that was progress, and Dax wouldn't push, not now. "Thank you."

"I have to run. I'm due in court."

He hung up before Dax could say goodbye. It wasn't much, but that was the longest conversation he'd had with his brother in years. Dax was grateful, though, and he just needed to keep the lines of communication open.

When Dax arrived at the Colton Country Club that night, the grounds were lit with market lights strung across the perfectly manicured lawn. Guests were guided by an illuminated path leading to the grand entrance, flanked by white columns lining the front of the Colonial-style two-story building. Laughter drifted toward Dax from the dining room as he made his way inside.

Presley's brother met him at the bottom of the grand staircase. "They are in rare form tonight."

"It's good to see you, Ash. I've been meaning to reach out; we haven't had much time to catch up."

"About that day, with Callie. That was unprofessional of me, I should—"

"Don't worry about it," Dax cut him off. "You were trying to help. Callie and I both understand. As a matter of fact, you ended up helping me out in a way."

"Care to elaborate?"

"I was planning on stopping by the bank to discuss the details with you. Callie and I have agreed to work together and start a town fund."

Ashton's eyebrows rose. "Wow, that's really great. I'd like to contribute as well if y'all don't mind."

"We need to make sure Callie is on board, but I'm okay with that. There's just one thing. Callie wants any donations we make to remain anonymous; do you think you can keep this to yourself?"

"I won't make the same mistake twice."

A loud peal of laughter made them both jerk their heads toward the dining room.

"Next time I'm bringing noise-canceling headphones," Ashton muttered.

"I'm glad you're here and you and I can talk over dinner. I want to hear what you've been up to since I've been gone."

"Not much besides running the bank and coaching Little League." Ashton glanced toward the dining room, "We'd better get back in there before my sister and your mother see that you're here. I'll get an earful for keeping you from them."

"Hey, before we head in, I just wanted to apologize for when we were kids. I got you into a lot of trouble and encouraged you to do stuff… and I should have apologized years ago."

"I was a willing participant. It's nice to know that we've both grown up to be better people." More loud giggles interrupted them, and Ashton rolled his eyes. "Not everyone has learned their lesson."

Dax forced a pleasant expression as he approached the table where his mother and Presley had their heads together, gossiping.

"You're late," Dorothy greeted Dax, presenting her cheek to him.

"I thought you were going to wear your uniform." Presley pouted. "I picked this dress so we'd match." She twirled in front of him in a sequined red dress with ruffles everywhere they shouldn't be and a large cluster of feathers that looked like the remains of a bloody peacock perched on her shoulder.

No uniform would ever match that dress. Dax already wanted to leave the stifling rules and manners of the country club and Presley's gaudy outfit behind. He'd rather spend the evening on Callie's porch with her wearing one of her pretty floral dresses with ruffles that kissed her shoulders.

"Dax," his mother snapped, "be a gentleman and tell Presley how lovely she looks."

Presley wrapped herself around his arm and batted her eyelashes at him.

"You look… shiny," he said, batting away at a feather that floated free, unable to bring himself to offer anything more.

"Really, Dax, did you lose all of your manners since you've been gone?" his mother admonished.

Unable to pry himself from Presley's grasp, he awkwardly dropped into his seat, shooting an annoyed look at Ashton, whose shoulders were shaking with silent laughter.

Absolutely nothing had changed. Pale blue paint and gold damask drapes covered the walls. Round tables covered with crisp white tablecloths dotted the burgundy, blue, and gold floral carpet. Even the faces at the tables were unchanged except for the unavoidable alterations that came with the advance of time. Dorothy and Presley smiled and waved at longtime club members as they drifted through the room.

Presley's father looked up from the sheaf of papers in front of him to greet Dax. The Beaumont and Ellis families had shared the same table for generations. "It's nice to see you, Dax." Judge Beaumont shook his hand.

"Thank you, sir."

"I hear you're restoring the Barton Building—that's quite a project," Judge Beaumont said.

Presley wrinkled her nose. "Why would you want to fix up that dirty old place?"

"It's a historic building, part of the town just like the library and the gazebo." The moment he mentioned the gazebo Presley perked up, and Dax instantly regretted including it in his examples.

"I just can't wait until it's my turn to get married," Presley cooed, winking at him as his mother nodded her approval.

Rescue came from Presley's father. "Dax just got back into town. I'm sure marriage is the last thing on his mind," he said.

"Daddy!" Presley glared at her father.

Dax coughed to cover his laugh. The arrival of Mae's parents drew his attention across the room. He watched as they were seated at a table. "It's nice to see some positive changes around here," he said, quietly.

His mother's gaze followed his, frowning. She pulled her shoulders back, glaring. Clearly, his mother wasn't pleased. Dax nodded and smiled at the Colton's, relieved when they nodded back. *Progress.* Dax turned his attention back to the table and his mother's sour expression.

"Mrs. Ellis, I thought you were going to have them change the rules back so they can't come here," Presley said, with a huff.

Dorothy took a sip of her cocktail. "I tried, dear, but I was outvoted by the board."

Dax narrowed his eyes at his mother and Presley. "What's wrong with the Coltons joining the club?" he asked, knowing and dreading the answer.

"There are standards," his mother started.

Dax held his hand up. "Don't—don't you dare. There isn't anyone in this town who lives up to your standards, is there, Mother? This is the Colton Country Club, for God's sake. It's disgusting that only half of the Coltons in this town have ever been allowed to join."

His mother pursed her lips, her eyes cold and calculating. Presley sniffed and shared a conspiratorial look with Dorothy.

"It's important to have standards. We don't want people who are too loud and crude," Presley said.

Without taking her gaze away from Dax, Dorothy patted Presley's hand. "Good blood will always tell."

Ashton choked on his drink. Judge Beaumont set down the papers he had been reading and peered at his daughter over the top of his horn-rimmed glasses that were permanently perched on the end of his nose.

"Presley Beaumont, I have been neglectful as your parent. It has been easier to ignore your stupidity than take the time and energy to give you the proper discipline." The judge clasped his hands in front of him, frowning. "I accept responsibility for that. But I will not allow an ignorant racist to live under my roof. If you continue to speak before thinking, your allowance will be cut off and you will be on your own."

He turned to Dorothy. "There is a line, and you have crossed it too many times."

Presley's jaw dropped, and the feathers on her shoulder trembled along with the rest of her. Bright spots of color appeared on Dorothy's cheeks. Her eyes narrowed as she slowly took a sip from her drink, glaring at the judge. But Judge Beaumont had spent over thirty years on the bench and wasn't intimidated or impressed easily. He stood and reached for the gray seersucker jacket hanging on the back of his chair, shrugging it on the same way he donned his robes. Dax wondered if he had a gavel hidden in one of the sleeves.

He placed both hands on the table, leveling both his daughter and Dorothy with a stern gaze. "Joseph and Ella Colton are pillars of this community, and I am happy to welcome them as new members of the Colton Country Club." He glanced over to where the couple sat. "As a matter of fact, I've been meaning to arrange a golf date with Joseph. I think I'll do that now."

Dax exchanged a look of agreement with Ashton and they both stood in unison, following the judge, ignoring his mother's and Presley's outraged gasp and furious whispers.

"There'll be hell to pay," Ashton muttered under his breath.

Dax smiled as he approached Mae's parents. "It's worth it."

CHAPTER SEVENTEEN

USUALLY CALLIE loved a lazy Sunday afternoon, but today she had a hard time focusing on the book she was reading, and every scene with the hero and heroine kissing had her drifting off, picturing kissing Dax again. She wandered out to the porch and plopped down onto the swing, but an unfamiliar restlessness made her jump up again. For the umpteenth time she wondered how Dax was spending his day. She pulled out her phone, thinking about sending him a text, when her phone vibrated.

"Let's go swimming at Turtle Pond," Mae declared before Callie could say hello.

Callie glanced up at the bright blue sky. The morning coolness had already burned away, and it would only get hotter as the day went on.

"Sure."

"Great! I'll call Emma. I'll pick you up in fifteen minutes."

Thirty minutes later, Callie dipped her toes into the deep turquoise water and leaned back with a sigh.

"See, I told you this was a good idea," Mae said, lifting her foot out with a flick that sent an arc of sparkling droplets into the air.

Callie closed her eyes and let her head fall back. "You're right, this was the perfect place to spend the afternoon."

"Thanks for calling me. I needed a break," Emma added.

Callie and Mae exchanged a look. Emma Walker was the unofficial Cinderella of the town. Her father and stepmother kept her working at the family drugstore and rarely allowed her a break. When they arrived at the pond, Mae had nudged Callie as Emma pulled off her T-shirt, revealing pale bruises on her upper arm. It wasn't the first time they had seen them. Emma always claimed they were from bumping into the shelves at work, but a keen eye would notice that they aligned with her father's fingerprints.

"I'm glad you could come out with us." Callie gave Emma's hand a gentle pat.

Mae reached into the picnic basket at her side and handed them ice-cold beers. They spread their beach towels on a large flat rock that jutted out over the pond and perched on the edge, letting their feet dangle in the cool water. True to its name, a row of turtles rested on a log nearby, basking in the sun.

"I love this spot," Mae said, pulling her tank top over her head to reveal a bright, royal-blue bikini top.

Callie glanced at her cousin as she shimmied out of her cutoffs and flopped down on the beach towel, pulling out her book. She wished she felt as comfortable in her own skin. The sun quickly warmed her body and her shirt stuck to her back. She finally gave in and started to peel off her T-shirt. She applied a thick layer of sunscreen around the pale-yellow triangles that made up her own top.

"I knew that suit would look good on you."

Callie rolled her eyes and tossed the bottle of sunscreen to her cousin.

"Don't you want some?" Mae asked.

Emma shook her head. "I put some on before I left." She glanced down at her freckled arms. "I have to use the heavy-duty stuff."

She reached into her bag and pulled out a large straw hat, settling it over her pale red hair as she dipped her toes in the water alongside them. She took a sip of her beer and turned to Callie.

"So, I heard Dax walked you home last week."

"I suppose everyone knows by now."

"Dax came over and sat with my parents at the country club Friday night," Mae added.

"He's been very polite when he's come into the pharmacy," Emma added.

"I know he's changed. It's... new," Callie admitted.

"The way he looked at you during book club." Emma sighed. "I wish someone would look at me like that."

Callie rested her cheek on her knee. "I used to think that, but it's not as simple as a Hallmark movie. It's a little bit scary wanting...." She bit her lip, trying to find the right words.

"Are you still worried about his mother?"

"Not so much worried as annoyed."

"I'd be a little bit worried too, she's terrible, and when she gets together with my father and the sheriff...." Emma shuddered. "I hate it when they have meetings at our house."

"You can always come over and hang out with me," Mae offered.

They had both offered Emma a place to stay but she always refused.

"Well, I'm not going to sneak around with him," Callie declared.

"Does that mean you're going to keep seeing him?" Mae asked.

"I like him," she confessed. "He's trying to help Colton, and he cares about the people here."

"Just like you do," Emma said.

Callie scooted to the edge of the rock and dropped into the water. She sank down into the turquoise depths, and when she emerged Emma and Mae were treading water next to her.

"You don't have to drown yourself to avoid talking about your love life," Mae said.

Callie swept her arm across the water, sending an arc toward her cousin. "Okay, fine, let's talk about yours."

Callie and Emma giggled as Mae held her nose and sank under the surface. Tiny bubbles popped before she emerged, gasping for breath. They swam back to the shore. The midday sun quickly dried them as they laid out on their towels. Callie flopped on her back, admiring the sunlight filtering through the leaves of the trees overhead.

"Here's some good news," Callie announced. "Jacob is almost finished with the bookstore."

"Do you have anyone in mind to help run it?" Emma asked.

"I've placed an ad, but no one has applied yet." Callie picked up a small rock, turning it over in her hand and running her thumb over the smooth surface before throwing it into the pond and watching it skip across the water.

"I don't expect anyone around town will want to work for me, not if they're going to get harassed by Dorothy Ellis and her minions, and I don't blame them. It's not the kind of job I would expect someone to move here for, so I'm not sure what I'm going to do."

Emma sat up and wrapped her arms around her knees. "I have a suggestion. I have a cousin…." Her gaze darted between Callie and Mae. "She's not like the rest of my family, I promise. Her name is Charlotte Walker. She's been working at a café in Greenwood but… I think she's looking for a change."

Her friend's eyes lit up. "I'll have her come by the library one day next week. You'll like her, I promise."

Mae opened another beer. "Great now that we have that settled, when do you think Dax is going to ask you out on a proper date?"

"How about you tell us about your date last week instead?" Callie challenged.

Mae flopped back and threw her arm over her eyes. "Worst date ever," she groaned. "Don't ever let me go out with a lobbyist again."

"What happened?" Emma leaned forward, eager for a good story.

"I should have known he only wanted to go out with me because he had a proposal for the congressman. And then get this." Mae sat up. "That little shit had the nerve to tell me I was too educated for him."

"What?" Callie and Emma both exclaimed.

"Yeah." She smirked. "He said my English was too proper and he related better to Black girls who were more real."

"You have got to be kidding me."

Emma stared at them with her mouth open. "Is… is that a thing?"

"Unfortunately, yes." Mae sighed. "Some people don't understand that there's more than one way to be Black."

"Somewhere out there is a guy who will love you just the way you are."

"Spoken like a true romantic." Mae laughed at Callie's declaration. "What about you, Emma, any prospective beaus hanging around?"

Emma turned a bright shade of pink and shook her head. "I… I don't have time."

Callie glared at her cousin. "Don't tease her," she mouthed.

Mae shrugged. "Sorry," she mouthed back.

A loud squeal echoed across the water. The three of them jumped up. Callie shaded her eyes against the sun's glare and peered across the pond.

"Presley," Emma sighed.

"And her friends—I don't understand why they have to come here. Why can't they stay at the country club and leave the pond for us poor folks?" Mae grumbled.

"Your parents belong to the country club now too," Callie reminded her.

"Now is not the time to be logical."

"We should go." Emma edged away. "I know some of those boys. We should go," she repeated. Emma began gathering up her things, her eyes darting nervously toward the group that gathered across the pond.

"Well, hell," Mae muttered.

They all stopped picking up their things and watched Dax, Jacob, and Ashton join the group across the pond. Presley let out another ear-splitting shriek and bounced toward them, throwing her arms around Dax. Callie's breath caught when Jacob nodded toward them. Dax stiffened, his mouth turned down, while Presley wrapped both her arms around his waist, molding herself to his side. Her eyes narrowing to slits, she gave them a smug smile while Ashton lifted his hand in a halfhearted wave. Callie tore her gaze away, shoving her beach towel and book into her bag. Would it be just a matter of time before Dax fell back in with his old crowd and started calling her names again, she wondered.

"He didn't look happy to be there," Emma offered on the ride back.

"I just don't understand why after everything he's been saying he would be hanging out with that crowd."

Emma sandwiched Callie's hand in hers. "It's okay, I'd be jealous too if I saw Presley wrapped around someone I liked."

"Like a goddamn anaconda," Mae muttered.

Jealous? The air washed out of Callie's lungs, as she realized that's exactly what she was. Jealous. She closed her eyes and leaned her head back on the headrest.

They dropped Emma off, and Mae drove to Callie's house. She turned off the engine and leaned on the steering wheel. "Do you want me to come in?"

"I don't need a babysitter."

"Can I be honest? It's kind of nice to see you get your feathers ruffled." She held up her hand as Callie opened her mouth. "Hear me out. You're always so calm. It's pretty clear there's something going on between you and Dax. Don't let Presley Beaumont run you off."

Callie swallowed. She shared just about everything with Mae, but she couldn't tell her about the notes she'd been finding in the library. Presley was at the top of her list of suspects. Of course, Presley wouldn't get her hands dirty to throw a brick, she might break a nail, but that didn't mean she wouldn't have gotten one of her friends to do it. She'd bat her eyes and flip her hair, simper and whine and get some poor fool to do her bidding. That knowledge added to her discomfort seeing Dax with her today.

"This thing with Dax is new. He's not my boyfriend, he can hang out with whoever he wants to."

"You're right and I should mind my own business."

"You've always been a fixer, Mae, and I love that about you, but you need to know when to let people work out problems on their own, and this is one of those times. Whatever happens between Dax and I, if—" she held up her hand when Mae opened her mouth, "—anything happens between us, it will happen in its own time and you can't force it."

"You know I push because I love you, right?"

"I know." Callie gave Mae a hug.

Once Mae pulled away, Callie went inside and made herself a cup of tea. Seeing Dax with his old group of friends brought back memories of the last summer she saw Dax. Only this time his confident smirk was replaced with a frown. Maybe she was wrong thinking Dax had changed, but he'd shown her in so many ways that he had. Callie decided that even though she'd been taking things slow, they were still going too fast.

CHAPTER EIGHTEEN

MR. WALLACE thumped two beers down, taking Dax's money with a grunt and a raised eyebrow before he went back to polishing the bar with a rag that was more a pile of loosely connected threads than a piece of usable fabric. Other than being a little grayer on his head, not a wrinkle had been added to his rich, dark skin over the years. No one really knew how old he was, but he must be over seventy now. For as long as Dax could remember, Mr. Wallace had polished that bar while keeping his conversations with his customers to one or two words since he'd taken over the old juke joint from his father many years ago. The bar had passed from father to son for at least four generations now.

Dax nodded his thanks. Peanut shells that littered the floor crunched under his feet. Mr. Wallace's idea of snacks were piles of roasted peanuts on every table. The shells usually reached a depth of an inch or two before they were swept away. He slid one of the beers in front of Jacob.

"How old do you think this place is?" Jacob asked, eyeing the ax marks on the rafters above.

"Over a hundred years at least," Dax said, kicking at the peanut shells under his feet. The decor at the Buckthorn consisted of shiplap walls and bare oak floors; picnic tables scattered around the room created a maze leading to a bar in the back of the room. Light bulbs covered in chicken wire gave off just enough light that you could pick out a friendly face in the crowd. The smoky wheat smell of whiskey mingled with the scent of peanuts. They sat at one of the picnic tables nursing their drinks and their sunburns.

"Well, that was a dumb idea," Dax said.

"Okay, I'll admit you were right about that, but we had to try."

Mae walked in and joined them at the bar. "I don't know what you guys are up to, but you're not going to win over Callie by hanging out with Presley and her friends."

"What in the hell is that smell?" Jacob interrupted, covering his nose with the palm of his hand.

Her perfume announced her arrival long before Presley arrived at the bar.

"Well, hello there, handsome," she said squeezing Dax's arm as she perched as close to him as possible without actually sitting in his lap. Dax leaned away, trying to get away from the cloying scent of baby powder mixed with cotton candy. "You haven't called." She pouted, pressing up against him and making sure her cleavage was on full view.

"I just saw you a few days ago, Presley. Don't wait for me to call because that's not going to happen."

"But we had so much fun at Turtle Pond."

"We were there for half an hour and you wouldn't leave me alone, so we left."

Presley gaped at him like a dying fish while Dax freed himself and moved to the other side of the table. Ashton dropped down next to her, fanning his face.

"Jesus, Presley, why do you have to wear so much of that drugstore crap?"

Jacob choked on his beer laughing.

Presley glared at Mae, Jacob, and her brother. "Maybe you can find a table. Dax and I need to talk."

"I'm not going anywhere," Mae said.

"Where's your little friend tonight?" She smirked. "Looking for some other mutts to play with?"

Mae jumped up headed in Presley's direction, but Jacob caught Mae, pulling her against his chest. "Don't do it," he said in a low voice.

"Keep your filthy hands off me," Presley squealed.

"Shut up, Presley," Ashton scowled at his sister.

Presley looked Mae up and down. "What are you even doing here anyway?"

"Are you seriously asking what I'm doing here? You're lucky Mr. Wallace allows your sorry ass in this place. Do you know the history of juke joints? They were started for us—" Mae thumped her chest "—because your kind wouldn't allow us to get a drink anywhere else. You. Don't. Belong. Here."

"Come on, pixie, let me buy you a round." Jacob practically picked Mae up and whisked her toward a table.

Mae punched Jacob's arm as he led her away. "You call me a pixie one more time and I'll turn you into a haint."

"Sure thing, short stuff."

If looks could kill, Jacob would have turned into a pile of dust right then and there.

Presley flipped her hair and turned her attention back to Dax. "How can you just let her talk to me like that?"

"Because she's right," Ashton said.

"Callie thinks she's better than us because her daddy's rich, but money can't buy you class."

"Do you think you have more class than Callie?" Dax asked.

Presley giggled, completely unaware of the anger that radiated from him. "Of course. Lower-class people always want to marry well and move up, silly."

"You have got to be fucking kidding me," Ashton said.

Dax stood with enough force to make Presley lose her balance and fall off the stool and onto her rhinestone, denim-covered ass.

"Ashton, I'm going to sit with Jacob and Mae—you want to join me? I'm buying. I'd rather drink with the lower classes than an ignorant racist."

Ashton looked down at his sister, shaking his head. "Grow up, little sister. Don't come crying to me when you end up without any friends in this world."

"Ashton Beaumont, I am your kin. You should be on my side!"

"Not when you're wrong." Ashton turned and followed Dax to the table. "Hey, Dax, any chance I could rent one of those apartments in your building? It's long past time that I move out. I just didn't want to commit to getting a house. But that one—" he jerked his thumb to where Presley just walked out "—is going to be impossible to live with."

"It will be a little while before they're ready, but sure, I'd be happy to have you as a neighbor."

Ashton grinned. "Great, I'll come by tomorrow and we can talk more."

DAX WAITED two more days before he made his way to the library to see Callie. She'd been avoiding him since the day at the pond, and he was determined to set things straight. It was a dumb idea to try and see if they could get any clues about who was harassing her from Presley and her friends.

When he walked into the library, Callie was standing behind the checkout desk, frowning at an envelope she held in her hand.

"Callie, is something wrong? It isn't another notice from the inspector, is it?"

She looked at him and then back down at the envelope. "These started arriving just before you moved back."

He took the envelope out of her hand. There was nothing on the front. He pulled out the folded piece of paper and drew in a sharp breath when he opened it.

GET OUT OF COLTON OR DIE LIKE THE DOG YOU ARE

The words were neatly printed out, in handwriting Dax didn't recognize.

"How many of these have you gotten?"

Callie walked over to her desk and pulled out a handful of envelopes that matched the one that he held. Dax read each one. The one she just received was the first one with a death threat.

"Callie, why haven't you said anything? Have you told anyone about these?"

"Who am I going to tell—Sheriff Crosby? Do you honestly think he would do anything? If I tell my parents, they'll just send bodyguards. I came here to live a normal life. Having men in suits following me around everywhere isn't going to help." She slumped against the counter. "I'm not going to be scared away by some nasty notes someone keeps putting into the book return."

"Callie, this is serious." Dax shook the notes at her. "You should have told someone."

"Well, now you know."

A couple of patrons came into the library, eyeing Dax and Callie with curiosity while they browsed the shelves. Dax leaned forward. "We are not done with this conversation," he whispered.

"Doesn't Presley need you to escort her to whatever cotillion or country club dance your mother has planned?" she whispered back. "I don't need any help from you."

He pretended to browse the shelves until they were alone again.

"Callie, Mae told me about your tires being slashed and the other incidents."

"She shouldn't have."

"She did because she's really worried about you, and so am I. That's why Jacob and I were at Turtle Pond; we were trying to find out if Presley or any of her friends had anything to do with what's been happening."

"You don't get to come back and play knight in shining armor, Dax. I can take care of myself."

"I'm not saying you can't. Don't you understand? I care about you, and I don't want anything to happen to you."

"Remember what you said on my porch in the rain, you haven't earned me yet. You can't just stroll in and take charge. Whatever we are, it's still new, and we have to figure out what the boundaries are."

"I'm just trying to help."

"I know you are, and I appreciate it, but this isn't your fight."

"You can't stop me from caring about you, and I protect the people I care about."

"Even if that means going against your mother?"

Dax didn't hesitate. "Absolutely."

"I'll let you know when I need your help. Until then we have to figure out how to be friends before we can be anything else, and that takes time."

The door opened and another customer came in. Callie turned to greet her patron, and Dax knew the conversation was over for now. He went next door to the bookstore where Jacob was putting the finishing touches on the coffee bar.

"We have a problem," he announced.

CHAPTER NINETEEN

THE EVENING sunlight filtered through the large oak tree, creating a leafy lace pattern on the large tombstone. Callie's fingertips traced over the words carved into the pale gray granite.

Richard Colton, Beloved Husband
Minnie Colton, Beloved Wife
United in Life, United in Death
Those we love don't go away, they walk beside us every day.

"I miss you," Callie whispered fighting back her tears. It was always hard going to the cemetery, and yet visiting her grandparents' gravesite was important to Callie. "There's so much happening in Colton. I wish you were here so I could share it with you. I've almost got the bookstore open, and there's another new business in town." Callie could feel herself blushing. "Dax Ellis is back, and he bought the Barton Building. He's been working hard to restore it. Grandpa, you'd be so happy with how nice it looks. He's helping to make our little town shine again, just like you hoped it would. Dax has changed; he's… different. I like him." She whispered her confession.

A cardinal swooped down and flitted back and forth in front of her, tilting its head as if the little bird wanted to hear what Callie had to say.

"Ella brought a lemon cake to the library for my birthday today, but it's just not the same." She ran her hand over the blunt ends of the freshly cut grass around the gravestone, plucking a few weathered and dried rose petals. She made sure to make an extra donation to the church to keep it that way. Her gaze roved over the small but immaculate graveyard next door to the Colton Baptist Church. Her yearly donation ensured that, along with her grandparents', every grave was tended, honoring every descendant of the slaves buried in unmarked graves somewhere on the grounds of the plantation. Callie could only bring herself to visit twice a year, on the anniversary of their deaths and today, her birthday. "If you're wondering, Mom and Dad didn't call." She shifted, leaning up against the side of the gravestone, a poor substitute for the hugs her grandparents always had for her. She wrapped her arms around her knees, pressing her shoulder into the cold stone. "I've made a life for myself here, but I miss you so much. Grandma, no matter how hard I try, I can't get my 7UP cake to taste like yours." Her voice broke. "And, Grandpa, I'm trying to keep your legacy and the library going but sometimes…."

Footsteps approached.

"Good evening, Miss Callie."

"Good evening, Reverend." Callie suppressed a sigh as she turned to face the minister.

"I wanted to personally thank you for your generous donation. We sure do miss seeing you on Sundays. I hope you'll join us soon."

They had the same conversation every time she came to visit the gravesite. She grew up sitting at her grandmother's side in the front pew, but she never liked the reverend's hellfire and brimstone sermons or some of his conservative leanings. Grandpa never went to church. The truth was, he was asked to leave during the sixties. His civil rights activities were seen as troublemaking and weren't welcome. But Grandma was a beloved member of the Women's League and had been held in the highest regard in the church.

"Thank you, Reverend, as always. I appreciate the offer, but church isn't for me."

The older man knit his brows. His lips pressed into a thin line of disapproval. Her generosity was the only thing that kept him from chastising her, and they both knew it.

"I can't help being concerned. Everybody is talking about you taking up with that Ellis boy. You know there are plenty of young men at our church who would be happy to court you. Don't you think you'd be better off with your own kind?"

"What kind is that, Reverend?" Callie bristled.

"There are some fine African-American men in our community."

"Reverend, I don't want to be disrespectful, but don't you dare ask me to choose between one half of me and the other. Black or White, anyone I decide to date will be my own kind," Callie interrupted.

"I see. The door is always open at God's house," he said with a curt nod.

The reverend walked back to the little white clapboard church, the first building built by the freed Colton slaves after the Civil War.

She turned back to the gravestone. While it wasn't her place of worship, this was the right place to lay her grandparents to rest. Even though her grandfather had been shunned, he raised the money to cast a bell for the church steeple, the same bell that still rang out every Sunday. She smiled at the memory, sitting on his lap while he told the story of how he started a penny drive in the seventies so the steeple would finally have a bell. Her heart ached remembering the pride in his voice when he used to talk about the first time he heard the bell ring.

A low rumble of thunder in the distance pulled her from her memories. She glanced up at the edge of dark clouds. She placed one last kiss on the gravestone and whispered goodbye before heading home.

She ran to her front porch just before the first raindrops began to fall. Her footsteps faltered when she saw the package on her doorstep. A small box about half the size of a shoebox sat in front of her door. Yellow ribbon matched the roses printed on the wrapping paper; a small bunch of yellow roses were tucked under the bow. Callie didn't get many presents. Since she moved home, Mae and her parents insisted on bringing cake for her birthday, and she appreciated the gesture and the sweet cards they always gave her. Mae always came up with something silly. This year she gave her socks that read, "Be quiet, I'm reading," with a picture of a librarian on the side. Mae had already given her a gift, so who could have left this?

Callie reached down, picked it up and lowered herself onto the porch swing, carefully placing the box in her lap. She untied the ribbon, letting the silky smoothness run through her fingers.

With her fingertip she broke the tape along the seam, pulling away the paper, revealing a wooden box. Callie ran her hands over the pecan wood, sanded silky smooth. She turned it around in her hands, admiring the craftsmanship. Someone had put a lot of effort and care into making it. Just as she lifted the lid the air crackled around her from the incoming storm.

She gasped. Her eyes filled with tears as the memory washed over her.

She tried to be vigilant hurrying home. Her hand clutched the small brown paper bag to her chest. She didn't notice them until it was too late; the sharp pain from the rock hitting her in the back made her stumble.

Dax climbed down from the tree by the side of the road and ran up to her, blocking her path. "Hey, whatcha got there?" he sneered.

Callie glanced toward her grandparents' house. Could she run?

Ashton scrambled down after Dax and stood by his side as he gave her shoulder a hard shove. "I asked you a question. Can't you hear, ugly?" He grabbed her upper arm, halting any chance of escape.

"It's just candy," Callie muttered, her knuckles turning white as she gripped the bag.

"Thanks." Dax ripped the bag from her hands, spilling the Now and Later candies onto the dirt.

"Look what you did, ugly—you better pick them up!" Dax yanked her down to her knees. "I said pick them up." He pushed her into the dirt.

The red and yellow wrappers blurred in front of her as Callie fought back her tears. Grandpa would give her a nickel for every small chore she did around the house. At the end of every summer, Grandmother would take her to Walker's Pharmacy and let her buy some candy. Banana and watermelon Now and Later candies were her favorite. Callie had turned ten that summer and begged Grandmother to let her walk to the store by herself. She wanted to show her grandparents how grown up she was. Her fingers fumbled in the dirt, trying to gather up the small squares of candy.

"Hurry up, freak!" Ashton shouted.

"Freaks don't get candy," Dax said grabbing the pieces from her hands and shoving them in his pockets. After one last shove that sent her sprawling into the dirt, of course.

They laughed and walked away. "Thanks for the candy, mutt," he shouted over his shoulder.

Callie stayed on the ground until he was out of sight. She picked herself up, trying to brush the dirt off her hands. She swiped away her tears and made her way slowly to her grandparents' house. She told her grandmother that she ate all the candy on the way home. Callie never told her grandparents how Dax and the other kids treated her. She never wanted her grandparents to be disappointed in her the way her parents seemed to be.

She looked down at the yellow and green wrapped candy that filled the box to the brim. Banana and watermelon Now and Laters—her favorite flavors. The low rumble of thunder covered Callie's crying. Even after all these years, he'd figured out a way to hurt her.

"Callie?" Dax called out, kneeling in front of her. "I didn't mean to make you cry. I just... I remembered that day, and I wanted to do something nice for you to try to make up for what happened."

Lightning flashed closer and the wind shifted, the porch no longer offering shelter from the storm.

His arms wrapped around her. "Callie, please don't cry."

She jerked back. "Why?" She pounded his chest. "Why?" she screamed so loud she felt her vocal cords pop. "I never did anything to you!" Years of pent-up anger poured out of her while she hit him with each word.

He winced but didn't move or say anything; he just sat there taking each hit. His stoic stance only made her angrier. She couldn't physically hurt him, but she continued to strike blow after blow until she finally collapsed, sobbing on his shoulder.

Only then did he take her in his arms.

"Callie, if I could take it back, I would."

"But you can't." She looked down at the box of candy and let out a shaky laugh. "I needed that. I think that was the last of the anger I felt toward you."

"I'm sorry. I'll keep saying it until you believe me." He reached up and cupped her cheek, wiping a tear away with his thumb.

"Why? I was just a little girl. What did I do to make you hate me hate so much?"

"Nothing, you didn't do anything. I don't know why I did the things I did. I don't know why my mother egged me on, and it doesn't matter that she did. It was me. I had that inside me, and I will always be terrified that I can go to that dark place again. What can I do to show you that I care about you?"

"You have all these regrets, I get it. You say that you care about me, but you don't even know me. You show up here after all these years and you want to be friends, lovers? I don't want you to be with me because you feel guilty. I'm not the scared little girl you pushed into the dirt anymore. I'm more than the little girl you hurt."

"I see you," he said softly. "Since I've been back, I've seen the strong and brave woman you've become. All your work at the library, the donations you've been making in secret. Every day I see how much you care about this town and the people who live here. I don't want to be with you because I feel guilty about what I did. I want to be with you because you're everything I ever wanted in a woman. I want to keep you safe because if anything happened to you now, just when I have the chance to spend time with you, it would break my heart."

"I'm scared of you, not the way I was when I was a girl. I'm scared of the way you make me feel as a woman," she admitted.

"And I'm terrified of making another mistake. Before we go any further, I have one more gift for you. I'd better give it to you now since my first gift was such a disaster. If this one is too, you can tell me to go."

He turned and ran to the back of his truck and pulled back a tarp. Callie squinted through the kaleidoscope of rain and then gasped when Dax pulled out a bicycle. The lines and colors, even the basket, were just like the original. He carried it up the stairs and placed it carefully down between them. "You probably don't remember him, but my cousin Taylor knew someone who does restoration work. Mae told me how your grandparents gave this to you. I know you could have found something similar, but it wouldn't be the same, would it?"

Fresh tears ran down Callie's face. "How—?" She took a deep, shuddering breath. "How... I didn't think it could be repaired."

"I knew if it was salvageable, Taylor would know someone who could do it." Dax reached out and covered her hand as it rested on one of the handlebars. He squeezed her hand. "I know I've made a mess of this, but I wanted to do this for you. I want to do so much more for you. I don't have the right, but I like you. If I can only have your friendship, I'll learn to be satisfied with that. I'll stand by and watch some other man come along and ask you for your heart, and I'll be your friend. I'll work by your side and support any plan you have to revitalize the town. I'll get my coffee and buy all my books at your store. I'm going to find out who is trying to hurt you because I'm your friend."

He had moved to the other side of the bike and stood in front her. Callie reached up and tipped his face toward hers.

"Look at me. I need to see your eyes."

She let her hand drop and laced her fingers with his.

"You're going to catch a cold," she said. The rain fell in the same tempo as her heartbeat as they made their way into the dark house.

Once inside she hesitated, and then drew him to her bedroom. She pushed Dax down on the bed, set her gifts on the bedside table, and went into the bathroom for some towels. She draped one over his shoulders, reaching out to brush his cheek with her fingertips before wiping his face with the corner of the towel. It was just a whisper of contact, but his eyes darkened and he shivered under her touch. He reached up and took her hand, kissing her palm.

"You are the most beautiful woman I know," he said, his lips against her palm.

"You make me feel beautiful," she answered, smiling shyly. "You also make me feel important."

"You are," he said. "There is no one more important to me."

A little shiver of pleasure raced through her. Here was Dax, the boy she'd hated, with her as a man, putting her first, telling her he cared.

She let her hands drop from his, her fingertips tracing the path of the raindrops down the column of his throat before brushing across his shoulders. She reached up to outline his lips with her fingertip. He froze, his breathing shallow as she explored the contours of his mouth. His long eyelashes were spiked from the rain, framing those brown eyes with so much longing reflected in them. Slowly, gently, she moved closer until her lips hovered over his. She inhaled his scent—rain mingled with sandalwood—and her lips curled into a smile.

When their mouths finally met, her heart stuttered. This was so much more than the kisses they shared before. Her body burst into flames, and she lay back, pulling him with her, their mouths fused.

He groaned and pulled her closer until there wasn't a part of their bodies not touching. He nibbled at her bottom lip before deepening the kiss until she was left clinging to him, breathless.

She wanted this, and him. When he pulled back, his gaze searching her face, she kissed him fiercely. "I want you, too," she said. "You're not asking for more than I want to give."

He drew her back into his embrace, and while the storm raged outside, they found hope and forgiveness, in each other's arms.

CHAPTER TWENTY

IT TOOK a moment for his eyes to adjust from the bright sunlight when Dax walked into the Buckthorn, but he clearly recognized the man standing at the bar having an animated discussion with Mr. Wallace. There weren't many people in the room, but Dax knew by midday the whole town would know that Reid Ellis, that outcast son of the Ellis family, had returned. He looked out of place in his dress shirt and dark pants. His hair was shorter and his face clean-shaven, but the resemblance remained.

As Dax moved closer, his brother paused, and brown eyes that mirrored his own assessed him for a moment before he turned back to Mr. Wallace.

"Have you thought about adding just a touch of wheat to your mash bill?" Reid asked, taking another sip of the amber liquid.

Dax wasn't expecting a warm welcome, but there was still a pang in his chest when his brother didn't acknowledge him right away.

Mr. Wallace chuckled. "I've been makin' bourbon the same way my daddy and my granddaddy did—ain't never seen any reason to change it."

Reid nodded. "Tradition is important."

Mr. Wallace nodded to Dax. "You want a shot?"

"I'll just have a beer, thanks." Dax pulled out his wallet.

"Nope." Mr. Wallace shook his head. "This one is on the house." He turned to Reid. "It's good to see you, boy."

Before Dax could reply, the old man moved to the other end of the counter and started polishing glasses. Everyone knew that Mr. Wallace never gave anyone a drink on the house.

Reid grabbed their drinks and cleared his throat. "You asked me to come and I'm here, so let's talk." He gestured toward an empty table at the back of the room.

"I have to admit I didn't think I was ever going to get you to come down here."

Dax studied the man sitting across from him, so familiar and yet so different.

"The whole way here I asked myself what I was doing."

"I'm glad you kept driving, then," Dax said. "By the way, congratulations on your promotion. One of the youngest assistant district attorneys Chicago's ever had—that's a great accomplishment."

"I guess I should congratulate you on starting up your consulting firm."

"Thought it was time to put down some roots."

"And you chose to do that here."

Dax heard the disbelief in his brother's voice. "I did."

"What am I here for, Dax?" Reid asked, suddenly sounding tired. "What do you want from me?"

Just like with Callie, there was only one way to start, and that was with an apology. "Reid, I owe you an apology. Since I've been back, I've realized how differently Mom treated you. I'm starting to see the memories I had from childhood in a different light. I'm trying to understand what happened."

Reid downed the rest of the contents in his glass. "It doesn't matter. I gave up trying to understand a long time ago."

The look on his brother's face brought back another memory: Reid sitting at the dinner table with his fists clenched in his lap. His mother welcoming Dax home from school with home-baked cookies while sending Reid straight to his room. How many times did she dote on Dax and ignore Reid?

Why didn't their father do anything to stop her?

The memories were like acid in his gut. "Reid, I hate the way Mother treated you, and I'm really mad at Dad for standing by and doing nothing."

"We weren't estranged. Dad came to visit me. Did you know that?"

Dax slowly put his drink down.

Reid's lips curled into a wry smile. "Those law conferences he was always going to? He used those as an excuse to visit me."

"I don't understand."

"Do you want to know why I didn't come to the funeral? He came to see me before he died. I think he knew his time was limited. He came to say goodbye and he told me not to come to the burial. It may have looked like he stood by and did nothing, but I knew he loved me, and I'll never be able to say that about our mother."

Dax tried to process what his brother had just revealed. Dax had never been close to their dad. Sure, they played catch and went fishing, but Dad had kept a wall of detachment between them that he could never climb over. "I wish he would have brought me on one of those trips," Dax said quietly. "I still don't understand why Dad let Mother send you away. I'll always be angry with him for that."

"I'm not. I'm glad. If Mom thought she was punishing me, she was wrong. She saved me."

"How did that save you?"

"If I'd had to stay in that house, I would have run away."

Dax blew out a deep breath. "Reid, I—"

"You're the reason I didn't."

Dax wished he'd known that at the time.

"I don't think you could have done anything," Reid said, as if he could read his mind. "You were just a kid—it wasn't your job."

"I regret everything that happened when we were growing up, everything that I did."

"Is that why I'm here, so you can apologize?" Reid asked.

"That's part of it, yes." Dax picked up a peanut from the pile on the table and threw it back down. "I'm not really sure where to begin. Do you remember Callie Colton?"

"Richard and Minnie Colton's granddaughter? The little girl you used to call names and throw rocks at?"

"Yeah," he said flatly, "that's just one more thing in a long list of regrets." There was no going back, only forward, so he took another swig of his beer and continued. "You left... no, that's wrong, you were sent away after the first summer she came to stay with her grandparents."

"What does that have to do with us?"

"Callie moved here a couple of years ago, after her grandparents died. Mom has been trying to run Callie out of town ever since she came back. Then I came home, and things have escalated."

Reid frowned. "Explain what *things have escalated* means."

"I think Mom is involved in attacks on Callie."

Dax told Reid about the bike, the broken window, and how their mother had been running off contractors, watching his brother's anger grow with each incident. "You're the security expert. What do you need me for?"

"I want to try one more time to talk to her about her attitude and her actions. I don't know, pull her back from the point of no return. I guess I'm hoping if we make a united front, we can get through to her before she gets into real trouble."

Reid drained the rest of his glass. "She's not going to listen to anything I have to say."

"Reid, this is serious. She's going to end up getting arrested—hell, the only reason she hasn't had harassment charges filed against her is because Callie won't do it and Mom's got the sheriff backing her up."

"What set her off?"

"Well…." He crumpled a peanut shell until it became dust. "Callie and I have kind of been seeing each other."

"Kind of?" Reid's eyebrow arched.

When Dax didn't reply, Reid leaned toward the bar.

"I'm going to need more of that bourbon, Mr. Wallace," Reid shouted toward the bar. Mr. Wallace nodded and brought another glass and a bottle over to their table.

"You're right, Mom's behavior is a problem, but I don't think I can do anything to help."

"Maybe, maybe not, but if you could stay around for just a little while, I'd like to have a chance to be a better brother."

"You weren't a bad brother Dax, we're just… different." Reid shrugged. "You were always trying to make Mom happy. You were so eager to do whatever she asked, and I wasn't."

"I didn't want her to yell at me the way she always yelled at you. I thought that if I did everything the way she wanted, I could keep both of us out of trouble. When you were sent away, I was afraid if I didn't agree with everything she said or wanted, she'd send me away too. It doesn't matter what the reasons are. I did a lot of things I'm not proud of. If Uncle Robert hadn't come back and straightened me out, I hate to think about the kind of person I'd be today."

"I haven't seen Uncle Robert in years. I have to give him credit, he reaches out from time to time. I haven't been very good about staying in touch."

"You have your reasons. Maybe you'll share those with me someday."

"Why did you come back?" Reid asked.

"In spite of everything, this is home. I spent enough time traveling around the world to learn that no place is perfect." He hesitated, brow creasing. "What's that saying? Home is where you make it? I want to help Colton. There are good people here."

"And Callie Colton is one of those people?"

"She is."

"How did you get her to forgive you for all of the shit you did?"

"I apologized, over and over again—" Dax hesitated and then put his cards on the table. "—just like I'm going to apologize to you until I prove to you that I want you to be a part of my life." Reid's jaw ticked. "I'd like it if you stayed long enough to meet her," Dax pressed.

His brother sat back, rubbing his hands over his face before letting out a heavy sigh. He glanced toward the bar. "I guess I can stay for a day or two."

"It's pretty sparse at my place, but I know that Uncle Robert would love to have you bunk with him."

"Thanks for the offer, I'll think about it." Reid rubbed his temples. "I suppose Mom will know that I'm here."

"She probably knows already. I don't suppose you want to see her."

"Let's be real here, she doesn't want to see me, and I don't want to see her. I won't see her unless we need to have some kind of intervention."

"I'm hoping it won't come to that."

"So, no, I won't see Mom, but... I would like to go by Dad's gravesite."

Reid's revelations about their father had left Dax feeling like he was standing on shifting sand. Everything he thought was true wasn't the reality. The one truth he could hold on to in that moment was that Reid was here because he'd asked him to come. "I'd like to come with you, if that's okay."

Reid stared down into his empty glass. "I think Dad would like that."

Dax filled both of their glasses and lifted his. "For Dad."

Reid tipped his glass against his and they both downed the contents. Reid chuckled when Dax sputtered and coughed.

"I don't know how you can drink this stuff. The first time I tried it, I couldn't catch my breath for an hour." Dax wheezed.

Reid chuckled. "That's because you weren't drinking the good stuff. This has aged twenty years." He pointed toward the bar. "That man is a master craftsman." He rolled the glass between his palms. "Primus has offered to teach me his recipe."

"Primus? Are you talking about Mr. Wallace?"

"That's his name."

"Well, I'll be damned. I think you might be one of the only people who knows his name." Dax looked from the old man at the bar and back to his brother. If Mr. Wallace could tempt his brother to stay for a day or two, he was all for it. "I didn't realize you were so interested in bourbon."

"It was something Dad and I used to do together. He bought me my first glass of bourbon when I turned twenty-one. We used to go to whiskey bars around Chicago when he would visit."

All this time Dax believed his brother had been denied a relationship with their father, and it turned out Reid had a closer relationship with him than Dax ever did.

"I'm glad you had those times with him."

"And you didn't. I didn't realize…. Here I thought I got to be the only messed-up kid in this scenario. I think that's why I've been avoiding you. I didn't want to hear you talk about how great your life was growing up with Mom and Dad."

"At first, I thought it was. I got tired of being the town bully in high school, but I didn't know how to stop. It was easier to live up to my reputation than try to change it. Thank God Uncle Robert came back." Dax laughed quietly. "He took one look at me and had a dyin' duck fit."

Reid smiled. "I would have liked to have seen that."

"Believe me, I'll never forget it. I've never seen him so mad. He caught me and some of the other boys making plans to try to ambush Callie the next time she rode her bike into town. I'd just gotten a new BB gun and was bragging I could use it to make her pedal faster when Uncle Robert came up behind me and grabbed me by the collar and dragged me back to his cabin. He threatened to horsewhip me until there was nothing but a bloody pulp left, but then he did something that to this day I'm thankful for. He sat me down on the front porch and started talking, and he made me sit there until I began to listen."

Reid shook his head with a sympathetic smile. "I'm glad it was you and not me."

Dax snorted a laugh. "Uncle Robert talked to me for three days straight before I understood the consequences of my actions. Of course Mom pitched a fit, but it was one of the rare times I saw Dad put his foot down. I spent the rest of the summer working on Uncle Robert's farm. The physical work strengthened muscles and the talks strengthened my soul."

Reid looked at him. "Where do we go from here, Dax?"

A small flicker of hope burned in his chest. Reid wasn't shutting him out; they were talking. If he could keep talking the way Uncle Robert had kept talking to him all those years ago, maybe they might have a chance to heal the breach between them.

"I don't know.... You're here, and that means a lot to me. I want you to get to know Callie. I hope the two people I care the most about can be friends."

"I'd like that too."

REID FOLLOWED Dax to the library and just as he hoped, his brother and Callie hit it off.

"You're head over heels for this girl, aren't you?" Reid commented as they made their way over to the Barton Building.

"I am. she makes me want to be a better man—" He stopped and faced Reid. "—and a better brother."

"A partner in life like that is worth… everything."

Reid craned his neck, looking up at the façade. "I always loved this building. There's just something about it." He turned to Dax. "Mother must have pitched a fit."

"There was no way I could have moved back home. It would have been suffocating. Mom put so much pressure on me about being the head of the house after Dad died it was… it was too much. I hated every moment I spent in that house after that. I can come home to Colton, but I can't go back to pretending that house is my home."

Dax led Reid through the main floor of the building and through the partially finished apartments on the second floor before taking him up to the recently finished loft space. His phone buzzed in his pocket while Reid took in the view.

"Hello—"

"Your brother doesn't have the manners to visit his mother. I have to hear he's in town from a friend," she said in a terse voice.

"By friend, I'm assuming you mean Sheriff Crosby."

"It doesn't matter who it is; your brother still hasn't learned how to show the proper respect. What will people say? It's an embarrassment."

Dax moved out of earshot from his brother. "Why do you care? You wouldn't have welcomed him home anyway. Just keep doing what you always do and pretend he doesn't exist."

"Daxton Madden Ellis, how dare you speak to me like that?" his mother hissed. "Your brother has been here for only a few hours and already his bad manners are rubbing off on you."

"When you are ready to show the proper respect and welcome both of your sons into your home the way a mother should, we can talk. Until then, I'm not going to continue this conversation with you."

Reid came over to stand next to him. "Dax, I don't want you to give up—"

Dax held up his hand. "I'm not giving up anything. I'm getting my brother back, and that is more valuable to me. I'd hoped I could have a relationship with both my mother and my brother but if I have to choose, I'm going to choose you. It's hard to accept it but clearly, Mother isn't going to change."

CHAPTER TWENTY-ONE

"I'M GOING on a date with Dax Ellis." No matter how many times she said it out loud, the woman in the mirror didn't look like she believed it.

Callie reached up and fingered the ruffled sleeve of the floral-print blouse she wore. Dax sent her a text that afternoon telling her to dress casual for tonight. She didn't tell Mae about the date, so that meant she was on her own trying to figure out an outfit. She glanced at the pile of clothes on her bed with a wince. Casual wasn't as easy as it sounded. She turned her attention back to the mirror. After an hour of indecision, she ended up in a blouse, jeans, and her favorite cowboy boots, the soft brown leather embroidered with colorful flowers and vines. Mae had been horrified when Callie ordered them from a custom boot maker in Texas, but she loved them and saved them for special occasions, which meant that tonight was the first time she had ever worn them.

She smoothed the hem of her shirt. Should she change back to the pink T-shirt?

The doorbell rang. "I'm going on a date with Dax," she told herself one more time. Large gray eyes filled with a mixture of excitement and just a little bit of trepidation stared back at her.

One look at Dax standing on her doorstep and her brain couldn't come up with a coherent sentence. Clean-shaven and wearing a blue plaid shirt under a dark gray sweater with jeans and work boots, he smiled down at her.

"Evening, Callie."

She smiled back, and the two of them stood there grinning at each other. If she read this scene in a book, she would have given it a one-star review.

"I'll just get my sweater. I wasn't sure what to wear. I hope this is okay for whatever we're doing."

Dax took her hand, tucking it into his arm as he guided her to his truck. "You're perfect," he said as he opened the door for her. She climbed in and he gave her a gentle kiss on the cheek before he closed the door.

He started up the truck, heading away from town with Lucas Monroe playing on the radio.

"I love this song," she said, tapping her fingers on her leg.

"It's one of my favorites too." Dax reached for the dial and turned up the radio.

Through every season.
Down every country road.
You're waiting for me with open arms.
I'll always come back to you.

"His songs always tell a story." She sighed.

"He has a lot of stories to tell."

"You said you served with him, didn't you?"

"I did. I give Lucas a lot of credit for opening my eyes." He frowned slightly. "He taught me you shouldn't make assumptions about people just because of the way they look or the things they say."

Callie thought about her conversation with the reverend back at the cemetery. "People do that to me all the time. They assume things about me because I don't look 'Black enough'"—she used air quotes—"or they expect me to want to go into the music business because my father is a producer."

"That's not you."

He really sees me for who I am, her heart sang. Dax turned off onto a narrow road leading out toward the old Colton Plantation house. She glanced at Dax. He smiled and took her hand. He drove a little bit farther and then he pulled over and turned toward Callie.

"Do you think you can trust me?" he asked.

For the first time, there was no doubt that she did. His eyes crinkled in the corners as he searched hers, and she realized the hands holding hers were trembling. "I trust you," she said in a whisper.

He pulled out a bandanna. "Will you put this on?"

"Isn't this how someone gets murdered in every scary movie, on a country road in the middle of nowhere and the guy blindfolds her?" She laughed.

Suddenly, his warm soft lips pressed against hers in a gentle kiss. "I promise, you can trust me."

A funny, light, floaty feeling came over her as the truck started again. There was something freeing in the trust. They drove for another five minutes and then he must have turned off the road, because the ride became bumpy and she had to grasp for the door handle as she bounced around on her seat. The truck came to a stop, and then there was nothing but silence around her.

"I need you to give me just a few more minutes," Dax said dropping another quick kiss on her lips. Callie listened as he opened the door and got out of the truck. She held her breath, listening, trying to figure out what he was doing.

Her door opened and he guided her out of the truck. He put his arm around her and led her a few steps before he stopped and reached behind her to untie the bandanna. Callie kept her eyes closed, taking in the smell of sweet grass and the crickets chirping. "You can open your eyes now."

They were standing in a field. Dax had mowed a patch of overgrown grass and stretched a large piece of canvas between two cottonwood trees. He'd pulled around and parked the truck so that the bed faced the canvas. Callie turned; the truck bed was filled with blankets, pillows, and a picnic basket. Two lanterns sat on the top of the truck's cab, casting a soft glow.

"We don't have a movie theater so I thought we could make do with this."

"This is incredible, I can't believe you did this for me."

He reached up and cupped her cheek. "I wanted to do something special for you. I thought about taking you for a fancy dinner in Nashville, but"—he swept his arm over the homemade drive-in he'd created—"this just seemed like… us."

Us. "I like the idea of us," she confessed.

"It's all I think about," he said, reaching up to cover her hand with his, nuzzling her palm.

She took a deep breath, inhaling the scent of cut grass that mingled with the sandalwood cologne that he wore. She wound her arms around his neck and pressed her lips to his again. He made a low rough sound deep in his throat, making her toes curl. When they finally broke apart, his eyes were dark with desire and they were both breathing heavily. Kisses from Dax were so much better than any of the fictional kisses she'd ever read. His lips were firm and his hands gentle—she was quickly becoming addicted to them. She grew bolder with every contact, wanting more. She pressed her hands against his chest, reveling in the feel of hard muscle under her palms.

Dax closed his eyes and took a deep, shuddering breath before pulling her hands away. "You are making it very hard for me to be a gentleman." He slipped his hands around her waist and lifted her into the back of the truck. "Ms. Colton." He wagged his finger at her. "I am taking you to dinner and a movie, and at the end of our date I'm going to escort you home and we might sit on your porch for a spell before I kiss you good night. No matter how much you tempt me, I am going to court you like a proper Southern gentleman."

She blinked at him, speechless. It was the most romantic thing a man had ever said to her, and yet if any other man had spoken those words, it wouldn't have been the same. They were special because it was Dax.

He climbed in and pointed toward the pillows. "Get yourself comfortable and I'll get dinner ready."

Callie scrambled toward the back and settled against the pillows and watched while Dax started pulling food and two place settings out of the large basket, then he draped the top with a tablecloth and set the makeshift table.

He turned to her with a sheepish expression and held out a bottle of wine. "I hope I got the right one."

Her eyes grew wide. "Brothers in Arms Syrah. How in the world did you get this?"

"I called the winery, told them I needed a bottle of your favorite wine, and they shipped two bottles overnight."

"I can't believe you did this."

"Is this the one you like?"

"Yes." She brushed her fingers over the label. "It's perfect."

He took the bottle and pulled out two glasses and an opener, holding it out to her. "You're probably better at this than I am, so how about you open it and I'll finish getting dinner ready."

Dax kept sneaking glances while she inserted the opener and pulled the cork. After pouring the deep garnet liquid into the glass, she swirled and sniffed before taking a sip. "The owner of the winery mentioned that you have an excellent palate. She said you would have made a terrific sommelier. I had no idea my girlfriend was so talented." He winked.

Callie paused, the glass at her lips, and then slowly set the glass down, blinking at him. He just called her his girlfriend... and she liked it.

He'd taken the time to find her favorite wine. He was incredibly considerate. He'd spent a lot of time planning this date—it left her feeling open and exposed, but in a different way. A good way. Dax saw her for who she really was, and she liked this feeling too.

"Maybe I shouldn't have said that," Dax said.

She rose up on her knees, moved toward him, and clasped his handsome face in her hands. "I might as well tell you my last secret since you know all my other ones. Do you want to know what my last secret is?" He nodded and she leaned forward until her lips were almost touching his. "I like the idea of being your girlfriend."

His warm gaze met hers, and for a moment the air felt electric. And then he sucked her bottom lip between his teeth before devouring her mouth. By the time they broke apart, the lightning bugs had appeared, dancing around them. "You have to stop distracting me," he growled, "or I'll never get you fed."

She grinned and leaned against the pillows, watching Dax as he went to work piling their plates with cold ham with potatoes and black-eyed pea salad.

Dax told her more about his visit with Reid while they ate.

"Do you think he'll come back soon?" Callie asked.

"I hope so, and if he doesn't, I'll make the time to go to Chicago and see him. I'm not going to waste any more time; we lost too many years already."

"We lost a lot of years too."

"I think in our case we both needed the time."

She wrinkled her nose. "You're right. I don't think we would have had as much in common as we do now."

He brushed a curl from her cheek. "Did you always plan on moving back to Colton?"

"When my dad finally realized I wasn't going to follow him into the music business, he arranged for me to have a job with a publisher in New York. I thought about it for about ten minutes and said no. I've always been a small-town girl at heart. Then Grandma and Grandpa died, and I knew right away I wanted to be here. The old librarian that Grandpa had hired wanted to retire, so it worked out that when I moved here permanently, I could take over."

"The library isn't run by the state?"

"It's a public-private partnership. Grandpa always owned the library, and we have an agreement with the state to use their search engines and things like book transfers."

Dax wouldn't let her help clear the dishes after dinner, so she made herself comfortable and watched the man who with every word and gesture burrowed deeper into her heart. He packed everything back in the hamper and pushed it out of the way before settling next to her.

He held out his arm and patted the space next to him.

She scooted next to him. He reached behind him and pulled out a package of Red Vines and two boxes of Junior Mints and Milk Duds. "I thought we could have dessert while we watch the movie."

"What movie did you pick?" she asked, expecting some kind of action-adventure guy flick.

"*Desk Set.*"

She did a double take. "How did you know it's one of my favorite movies?"

"I did my research."

"Mae," Callie said, with a laugh. Mae was the only person who would know.

"I can't reveal my sources. Besides, my source would knock me into next week if I gave her away."

He gave her one more toe-curling kiss before he tucked her under his arm and with a few clicks of his tablet, the opening credits appeared on the screen. Dax fed her pieces of candy, stealing kisses every now and then while they watched Katharine Hepburn and Spencer Tracy exchange snappy dialogue. When the old-fashioned computer malfunctioned and began to spew punch cards all over the office, Dax doubled over with laughter. Callie enjoyed watching his reactions as much as the movie.

When the final credits rolled, they lay side by side under the stars, talking about the movie, life, and their hopes and dreams for Colton. Conversation with Dax was easy, so much easier than any other man she'd spent time with. He asked questions and made observations that made her aware of just how much he cared about her. Their words became kisses, and this time there was a new level of trust when they made love under the stars. She sighed with contentment wrapped in Dax's arms.

Dax propped himself up on his arm, tracing the worry lines on her forehead. "You're thinking awfully hard. Do you want to share what's going on in there?"

"Not thinking that hard. Just enjoying this moment." She turned her head and looked at him. "Best. Date. Ever."

Dax returned to the field after he dropped Callie off to take down the makeshift screen he'd set up for their date. When he was finished, he sat on the bed of the truck looking up at the stars, replaying his date with Callie. Suddenly an image of his future flashed in his head: sitting with Callie on her front porch, a little girl in her lap looking up at him with big brown eyes that matched his and golden curls just like Callie's.

The wind rustled the leaves in the trees and the air grew heavy with the scent of eucalyptus. He peered into the darkness surrounding his vision. An old woman appeared out of the shadows, her dark brown skin still smooth and her eyes bright despite her age. She grinned at him.

"I'm 104 years old." She lifted her chin. "Colton woman age well," she answered his unasked question. She gazed lovingly at Callie and the little girl in her lap. "There's only so much I can do from this side. When the time comes, you'll have to do the rest."

She faded back into the darkness.

Dax jerked upright. "What do I have to do?" he whispered to the old woman, even though the vision had already disappeared.

DAX HEADED to the bank the next morning, eager to move forward with his contribution toward improving his hometown. An hour later he looked down at the deposit slip in his hand with satisfaction.

"Thanks for all your help, Ash."

"It's my pleasure." Ashton Beaumont glanced around the room to make sure no one was within earshot. "I'm really looking forward to working with you and Callie. There's a lot of good we can do now that we have the Colton Foundation account all set up."

"What would you think about setting up a business association?"

Ashton grinned at him. "That's a great idea."

"There wouldn't be many of us to start with. I was thinking the three of us, Hank, and Tillie."

"I'd be happy to stop by and talk to them tomorrow."

"That'd be great. I'll talk to Callie about it tonight."

Ashton's eyebrows rose. "Tonight?"

"You keep that bit of information to yourself, you hear?"

"Are you kidding me? The last thing I want is to be subjected to the hissy fit my sister's gonna have when she finds out. Your secret is safe with me. But," Ashton's mouth turned down, "you know how this town is. Someone's going to find out and tell your mother. Be careful, Dax. I know she's your mom and has been saying some really terrible things about Callie lately."

Dax sighed. "I know, when the time is right, I'll have to have a hard talk with her."

"Just so you know, half the town has bets going on if that will ever happen."

"Oh yeah, what are the odds?"

"Lately they've been turning in your favor."

"Good to know."

Dax stood up and shook Ashton's hand. He couldn't keep from smiling as he walked out of the bank. He was settling in, finding his place in the community, and he had another date with Callie tonight. The odds were turning in his favor. He planned to have Sunday dinner with his mother to confront her about her behavior and, more importantly, break the news to her that he was dating Callie. She wasn't going to be happy, far from it, but he hoped they could reach some kind of truce in the end.

He walked down the block to his place just as Mae pulled up in front of the building.

"Good timing. I was hoping to catch you," she said.

Dax unlocked the door and stood aside to let her in. "To what do I owe the pleasure of this visit?"

"Well... I thought this was a good idea, but now that I'm here... this is really awkward."

"Am I in trouble?"

"That's the thing I'm trying to help you avoid it."

Dax waited for her to elaborate.

"Spit it out, Mae," he said when she remained silent.

Mae took a deep breath. "Here's the thing, I know you have a date with Callie tonight and I'm sure she has taken care of this, but just in case you wanted to buy... protection, you shouldn't get it at Walker's Pharmacy because everyone in town will know. Trust me, I've learned this lesson the hard way," she said in a rush.

Dax looked at her in stunned silence for a minute before throwing his head back and laughing.

"It's not funny. Callie is my best friend, and I'm just trying to make sure you're being responsible."

Mae's outburst had him laughing so hard his sides hurt. Mae's lips twitched and then she stared, laughing along with him.

"Okay, I'll admit as I said it out loud, I realized how ridiculous I sound. I hope I didn't offend you or anything."

"Not at all, you're looking out for Callie. That's what good friends do for each other."

"Just don't tell her, she'd be mad as hell if she found out."

"Not a word."

Mae looked around the finished main floor. "How are the apartments coming along?"

"Good. Want to take a look? Since you're my first official renter, you get first pick."

Dax led Mae up to the second floor and through the four units. Each space had an open floor plan and the same exposed brick walls that Dax had upstairs in his loft. Mae was thrilled and chose one of the units that overlooked the park. Once they finished, Mae left him to get ready for his date after another promise to never speak of their earlier conversation again.

Dax arrived on Callie's doorstep with a bouquet of yellow flowers in hand.

The door flung open before his knuckles hit the wood. "I saw you coming up the walk."

She smiled and stood back so he could come in. He held out the bouquet and she took it from him, burying her face in the blossoms.

She took a deep breath. "Heavenly, thank you."

"Anything I can do to help?" he asked.

"No, I just have to pull everything out of the oven. Have a seat."

Dax hadn't been in Callie's house since the book club meeting. He was so wound up then he didn't pay much attention to his surroundings. He looked around the tiny bungalow, admiring the mix between old and new.

Callie put the bouquet he brought out and set it on the table and went back to the kitchen, returning with a platter filled with chicken, vegetables, and rice.

"It's nothing fancy," she said as she set the platter on the table.

He caught her wrist and kissed the back of her hand. "It's not the food, it's the company."

"White wine okay with you?"

"You're the expert."

She went back into the kitchen and returned with a bottle of wine. She poured out two glasses, handing him one.

"I've never made dinner for anyone before." She blushed.

He reached across the table and took her hand. "Would it be impolite for me to say I'm glad?"

"No, because I feel the same way."

They grinned at each other for a moment before he let her hand go.

CALLIE HAD butterflies all day getting ready for her date with Dax. Now that he was here sitting at her kitchen table, she wondered why. It felt like the most natural thing in the world to enjoy a quiet dinner with him.

"I stopped by the bank today. The account for the Colton Foundation is set up, and all we have to do now is decide what our next project is going to be."

"I've been thinking about that. It may be a while before we find a doctor who would be willing to move here and run the clinic. What if we provide the funds for the fire department to hire an EMT?"

Dax looked at her thoughtfully. "I like that idea."

"We just have to figure out a way to do it so that the town council can't divert the funds."

"Has that been a problem?"

"I learned quickly not to make any kind of monetary donation when I first started doing this."

Dax frowned. "I hate what my mother is doing to this town."

Now it was her turn to take his hand. "Dax, you can't take on this burden. Grandpa used to say that Colton will only thrive when everyone in the community takes responsibility and pride in the town. A lot of folks are scared of the town council and their influence."

"I just want to make a difference."

"You are and you will, but you have to give it time. Give people a chance to get to know you, and they'll realize that you have good intentions and a good heart."

He rubbed his thumb over her knuckles. "Thank you, Callie."

The room grew warm as he looked into her eyes. They finished their dinner and Dax followed her into the kitchen, carrying the empty platter. "What can I do?"

Callie pointed to a dish towel on the counter. "Do you mind drying while I wash?"

"Nope, not at all."

It didn't take long to get the dishes cleaned up. They stood next to each other hip to hip in her tiny kitchen, their fingers brushing, their touches lingering until they finished and Dax pulled her into his arms and captured her mouth with his.

"I wanted to do that the minute I walked in the door," he said.

"So did I."

He kissed her again, threading his fingers through her hair, pulling her against him. She wound her arms around his neck. He dipped his tongue in her mouth and his tongue danced with hers.

"This is all I've been able to think about since kissing you under the stars last night."

His hands slid down to her hips; she pressed against him and he sucked in his breath.

Callie looked up into his beautiful brown eyes that were filled with desire. He made her feel cherished in a way she'd never felt before.

She let her hands fall to his shoulders and reveled in the feel of his body under her hands. Her mouth found his and she nipped at his bottom lip, eliciting a groan from him.

"Callie, please, I can't let you go." He tore his mouth away from hers, holding her gaze. "Please—"

He didn't get any further as Callie took his hand and led him down the hallway to her bedroom. She reached the bed, turned around, and started unbuttoning his shirt.

"The answer is yes."

When the sun found its way through Callie's bedroom window, they had explored and touched and tasted every inch of each other. She stretched and grinned at the ceiling.

"That may be the prettiest sight I've ever woken up to," Dax said in a low, sexy voice that made her heart flutter.

She reached up with a lazy smile and stroked the stubble covering his jaw. "Good morning," she murmured.

CHAPTER TWENTY-TWO

IT WAS late when Dax pulled up in front of the library. Callie decided it wouldn't be the end of the world if the library opened an hour late so she could spend a little more time in bed with Dax. She cringed when she saw his mother standing on the sidewalk in front of the library. Dax reached over and grasped her hand, giving it a quick squeeze.

"Don't worry," he reassured her, ignoring his own feeling of unease.

Callie jerked forward. "Oh no," she exclaimed jumping out of the truck before it came to a complete stop.

His mother was standing in the doorway. Wait, why was the door open? He parked the truck and rushed in.

Presley stood in front of him, her arms filled with books. She held the stack out to him.

"Oh, good you're here. Take these, will ya? They're old so you can put them over there with the rest in the garbage pile," she said pointing to a jumble of books tossed carelessly in a corner.

"Get out." She rushed over, grabbing the books away from Presley. "GET OUT!" she shouted.

Presley blinked at Callie. "Mrs. Ellis says you're not responsible enough to run the library, so I'm takin' over." She flipped the cotton candy, tangled mess of her hair and smirked. "It's a good thing, too, nothing made sense in here. I'm gonna rearrange everything by color. It's gonna be so pretty."

Dax wrapped his arm around Callie's shoulders. "I know you want to kill her, and I do too, but you know if you make a move, Mother will have Sheriff Crosby here and you in handcuffs before you can finish the job," he murmured into her ear.

He saw his mother come in out of the corner of his eye, but he kept his attention focused on Presley. "I'd like to know how you got in here."

"I let her in," his mother announced.

"How?" Callie asked.

"It's my duty as head of the town council to have access to every building in town."

His mother's gaze flicked to Dax's arm around Callie. She took in a sharp breath but softened her gaze and gave him a placating smile. "Darling, I don't think you understand."

Dax held up his hand. "I understand quite a bit now," he said. "You played the tragic widow after Dad died and everyone took pity on you. And you took advantage of it, ruling over this town as if you were a queen." Dax ignored his mother's outraged gasp and turned his attention back to Callie. "Who owns this building?"

"I do," she said, her eyes never leaving his mother's.

Dax held out his hand palm up. "Give me the keys, Mother."

Dorothy pulled a ring of keys out of her suit pocket. Pressing them to her chest, she shook her head, her mouth pressed in a thin line.

"You are trespassing. Callie has every right to have you both arrested."

"I hope she does," Uncle Robert said from the doorway. He stepped inside with a nod to Dax.

"But Mrs. Ellis said...." Presley pouted.

"Shut up, Presley," Callie and Dax said in unison.

"I want both of you to leave now. I'll have the locks changed on every building on this block, so you might as well throw those out." Callie pointed a shaking finger at the keys in Dorothy's hand.

"Honey, I suggest you call a locksmith other than the one here in town," Uncle Robert said quietly when Dorothy smirked at her.

"That's a good idea. I'm sure we can find someone from Jackson who'd be willing to make the trip," Dax added.

His mother's confident smirk faltered.

"Apparently I won't be doing any more business at the hardware store."

"I doubt many people will once they find out what Billy's been up to," Uncle Robert muttered. "I hope you're happy, Dorothy," he said coming around to face his sister-in-law. "What little business Billy has left will dry up when folks hear that he's been making copies of keys for you."

Dorothy drew herself up, lifting her chin. "I have the right to—"

"Do what, trespass on other people's property?" Callie asked.

Callie stepped out of Dax's arms. He wanted to pull her back and wrap her in a protective embrace, shield her from the animosity radiating from his mother. Callie made it clear more than once that she didn't want anyone to fight her battles for her, so he took his place at her side as she stood in front of Dorothy.

"If either of you set foot on my property again, I will file charges." She looked between Presley and Dorothy. "You have one minute to leave."

"How dare you speak to me like that!" Dorothy poked her finger in Callie's chest, forcing her to step back. "The library wasn't open on time because you were out whoring around with my son. You're a slut, just like your mother!"

In an instant Dax pulled Callie behind him. "Get out NOW!" he shouted.

Uncle Robert stepped up and grabbed the two women by the arm.

"Ouch, you're hurting me," Presley wailed as his uncle pushed them out to the sidewalk, slammed the door, and locked it.

Dax pulled Callie into his arms. He cupped the back of her head as she leaned against him, trembling. "I didn't think they would go this far. We'll get this cleaned up and I'll make sure this never happens again," he said, kissing the top of her head. After a minute she stiffened in his arms and pulled away.

"It's going to take a while to get this mess fixed." Her voice was shaky.

"I'll start making calls to get the locks changed," Uncle Robert said, giving Dax's shoulder a squeeze. He scanned the chaos Presley had created in such a short amount of time and let out a low whistle. "As soon as I can get a locksmith, I'll help you with this."

Dax nodded. The two men exchanged a look. "Take care of her first and we'll clean this up later," Robert said before he slipped outside.

"It's going to be okay. I promise." His stomach churned. His reassurance didn't ring true in his ears, and he could tell by the look on Callie's face that she didn't believe him.

"Dax, I need you to leave. You don't know anything about the library system and I… I just want some time to myself."

"Callie, please, don't turn me away. We're in this together. I don't care about my mother."

"I'm sure you believe that, but she's your mother. My parents aren't perfect, but they're still my parents. You need to go talk to her, Dax."

"I'll go, but I'm going to come back and check on you later, okay?"

Callie gave him a small smile. "Just give me some time to get this cleaned up and then we can talk."

Dax was too angry to talk to his mother. He was the kind of person who wanted to take action instead of talking.

He headed to the barbershop instead of to his house.

"I need your help. My mother and Presley broke into the library this morning."

"What in the hell? What do you mean she broke in?" Nate asked.

The door opened again.

"What the hell is going on?" Jacob asked.

"My mother has keys to every building in town. Callie was late this morning and she used it as an excuse to set Presley loose."

Nate let out a low hiss. Hank's grip on the broom in his hands tightened and his jaw ticked.

"I had no idea. I swear."

"I know that, son," Hank said, his heavy hand falling on Dax's shoulder. "What do you need us to do?"

"Besides give your mother the ass-whoppin' that's long overdue," Nate said under his breath.

"No, that's my job. Uncle Robert is—"

"Right here," he said walking in. "I've got a locksmith coming in from Jackson. He'll be here in a couple of hours."

"I came to let you know, Hank. You'll probably want to have your locks changed too. I'll pay for it since this is my mother's doing."

"I took the liberty of letting the locksmith know that there might be more than just one customer. Tillie has already asked to have him stop by the café. You and I are going to have a talk with Judge Beaumont."

Hank let out a low whistle. "You ain't playin'."

"Nope, not anymore." Robert jerked his head toward Dax. "Come on, let's go."

Nate grabbed Dax by the arm as he walked past. "Don't worry, we can all help. I'll start letting the other folks know."

"Don't have to worry about the bank since they have that fancy alarm system," Hank added.

"We still need to let Ashton know. I wouldn't put anything past my mother at this point," Dax said.

"I think I'll go have a talk with Billy at the hardware store," Jacob said.

"Thanks." Dax grimaced. Colton Hardware was the only place in town where you could get a key made. He had no doubt that Billy was involved in his mother's chaos.

"Not today, Grace," Uncle Robert said to Judge Beaumont's office manager without breaking his stride, heading straight into the judge's chambers. Only the very top of Judge Beaumont's thinning hair could be seen behind the stacks of papers and books on his desk.

The judge looked up, peering over the top of his glasses at them. "By the looks on both your faces, I'm not going to like what you have to tell me, am I?"

Twenty minutes later, the judge took off his glasses and rubbed his eyes. He sat back in his chair with a long sigh. "Does Callie want to press charges?"

"I don't know, but there are others around town who might," Dax said.

"Who are they gonna call to press charges? We both know Jeb isn't good for a damn thing," Uncle Robert said.

"I had my part to play in this mess." The judge pushed a stack of papers to the edge of his desk. "Ever since my Mary passed away, I've buried myself in my work so I could avoid doing the hard job of being a responsible parent and a good member of this community. I dedicated myself to my job instead of my children." He held his hands up. "I'm not making any excuses. I'm going to have to recuse myself from the legal ramifications that come out of this. But I'll help any way that I can."

"I wanted you to know what's coming," Robert said.

"Dax, when the time is right, please apologize to Callie for my daughter's behavior. No," the judge said, shaking his head. "I'll make sure Presley apologizes. It's my responsibility."

"I feel bad for him," Dax said to Uncle Robert as they made their way down the steps of the town hall.

Uncle Robert rested his hands on his hips, looking out over the town square. "It's time to quit talking about regrets and take action."

CHAPTER TWENTY-THREE

THE CHAOS that took Presley just a few minutes to create took Callie the rest of the day to put back together. Dax hovered over her all day until she finally sent him home. She appreciated all the care and concern Dax and the rest of the folks in town had shown. Tillie came by with lunch and a slice of her pecan pie, while Ashton came over from the bank apologizing profusely for his sister and insisting on paying for the locks being changed, not just for the library but for every business in town.

At the end of the day, Callie just needed some time alone, so she told Dax she would see him in the morning. They had a lot to talk about, but it could wait. The situation with his mother was becoming impossible. By the time she came home, the events of the day caught up with her, and she was too tired to bother with making dinner. She'd been sitting at the dining room table with a glass of wine trying to calm her frazzled nerves. The air around her felt heavy. She stood and made her way toward the bedroom, stumbling. She leaned against the wall for support. If she could just lie down for a little bit, she wouldn't be so sleepy. It felt like such a long way to her bed. By the time she made it, she barely had the strength to lie down.

Callie closed her eyes and saw a woman running through the cotton field, her cotton dress billowing out behind her. The gold buttons on the tall man's uniform sparkled in the sunlight as he held his arms out to her. He wrapped his arms around her when she reached him, slipping the scarf from her head, running his hands over her long curls as they tumbled free. She reached up and stroked his beard, her long brown fingers caressing his blond whiskers. The two embraced, and Callie strained to hear their whispered words. The air shimmered around her, heavy with heat and a sickly sweet smell she couldn't identify. The image of the man and woman blurred. Callie struggled to open her eyes, but her whole body resisted.

Suddenly the woman turned and her gaze focused on Callie. The air crackled around them. "Callie, honey, you gotta get out now!"

Someone was banging on the door. Was that part of the dream? A loud bang shattered the scene into a million tiny colored fragments. A voice called in the distance.

"Callie! Callie, you've got to wake up!"

Just as the sound faded away, she felt herself being lifted and carried away. Something was pushing on her chest over and over again. She opened her eyes, and her throat burned as she tried to scream and get away from the shadowy figure that hovered over her.

"Callie, Callie, I'm not trying to hurt you." Dax helped her sit up and pulled her into his lap as she struggled against him. He wrapped one arm around her, while he frantically typed into his phone with the other hand. "Shh, it's going to be okay, but you've got to let me help you get to the hospital."

"There's a gas leak." Dax's voice sounded muffled and distant.

Callie tried to speak, but her words came out slurred and disjointed. She was being lifted again, floating in Dax's arms, and then everything faded into blackness.

THERE WAS a beeping sound, slow and steady, and then it became faster. She tried to move and realized someone was holding her hand. She frowned. Her eyelids felt so heavy. It took all her strength to pry them open.

"She's waking up, get the nurse." Callie turned toward the voice, squinting to find Dax.

"What—?" she croaked, her voice muffled from the oxygen mask covering her nose and mouth.

The doctor came in, pulling the stethoscope from around his neck. "Mr. Ellis, why don't you give me a minute to look at my patient."

Callie tried to move the mask, but the doctor pushed her hand away and adjusted the mask back in place. "We need you to keep this on for a little while longer, okay?" he said, patting her on the shoulder.

Callie looked over at Dax and his uncle hovering in the doorway with Jacob. Dax kept his eyes on her with a grim expression while the doctor checked her vital signs before Robert put a reassuring hand on his shoulder and ushered him into the hall.

"Miss Colton, I'm Dr. Anderson. Do you remember what happened?" the doctor asked as he checked her pulse.

Callie shook her head.

The doctor's lips pressed into a thin line as he listened to her heart for a moment before he continued. "There was a gas leak in your house. You are very lucky your friend got you out in time. I'm going to keep you here for another day just as a precaution. You might feel a bit disoriented, but that will pass."

She wrinkled her forehead, trying to focus. The doctor finished his examination and Dax came back in, pulling up a chair at Callie's side, taking her hand back in his. Robert and Jacob joined him a minute later.

"Good to see you awake," Robert said in a gruff voice as he leaned over, placing a gentle kiss on her cheek.

Callie frowned. She tried to talk, but her throat was raw and the oxygen mask made it difficult.

"Shh, don't say anything," Dax said, kissing her hand clasped in his. "We can talk in the morning."

The door burst open and Mae rushed in, pushing Dax out of her way. She threw her arms around Callie. "Oh my God, Callie, are you okay?"

Callie tried to smile behind the mask. She reached up and gave her a weak pat on the back.

"The doctor just came in. She's going to be okay," Dax reassured Mae.

"Mom and Dad are on their way." Mae turned to Dax. "You can go now." She dismissed him.

Dax growled, tightening his grip on her. "I'm not going anywhere."

Callie looked between her best friend and Dax. They stared at each other, locked in a battle of wills. Robert cleared his throat. "Son, you could use a rest. Why don't you let Mae take a turn?"

Dax opened his mouth to protest. Callie gave his hand a reassuring squeeze. He leaned over and kissed her forehead, letting his lips linger for a moment. He hovered over her. "I won't be gone long."

Callie nodded. He tried to take his hand from hers, but she couldn't bring herself to let go. The heart monitor reflected her distress, the beeping increasing again.

Mae sighed. "Okay, you win, Dax." She got up from her perch on the bed. "I'll come back in the morning."

Once Robert ushered Jacob and Mae out of the room, Dax climbed into the bed and pulled Callie into his arms, kissing the top of her head.

He stroked her arm. "Try to sleep, sweetheart. I'll be here when you wake up, I promise."

Feeling safe in his embrace, Callie drifted off.

She was alone when she woke up again. The nurse came in and removed the oxygen mask, exchanging it for a smaller tube fitted into her nose. Once she helped Callie use the bathroom and got her settled again, Mae came in, wrapping her arms around Callie.

"I can't imagine what life would be like without you. I was so scared when Dax called." She broke down crying. "Do you remember anything about what happened?"

"I came home and had a glass of wine. And then I got so sleepy." She shuddered. "Mae, I was dreaming. It was so crazy. There was a man and a woman in a field of cotton. The connection between them made the air shimmer. And then... the woman turned to me and told me I had to get out. I tried to move, but everything felt so heavy. I heard—" she scrunched her forehead, trying to remember "—hammering, I think, and then I fell asleep."

A single drop lost its grip on Mae's lashes and slid down her cheek. "Oh, honey, the hammering was Dax banging on your door. He smelled the gas and when you didn't answer, he broke it down to get you."

Callie frowned. "I don't remember; everything is still kind of hazy."

Fragments of memory flashed through her mind of the events, faster and faster.

Dax found her crying softly in Mae's arms.

Mae let go and Dax took her place. Callie buried her face in his shoulder. "I was going to talk to you in the morning. You were trying to help me, and I fought you. Oh, Dax, I can't believe I did that."

"It's okay." Dax stroked her hair. "I'm not going to let you go ever again, whatever happens.... No matter what my mother does, we're going to stand together."

Callie sniffed and nodded, slipping her hand into his, weaving their fingers together. "You're right."

The doctor came in. Looking at their clasped hands, he cleared his throat. "I'm going to assume you don't mind my discussing your case with your... friend here?"

"I'm her boyfriend, and I'm not going anywhere," Dax said.

The doctor nodded. "Miss Colton, your oxygen levels look good as well as your vitals. I'm willing to release you if you will promise to take it easy for a few days once you get home."

"She will," Dax said, giving her a stern look.

The doctor reviewed her care instructions, advising Dax on any warning signs to look for that would mean she needed to come back to the hospital. Once the release papers were signed, he bundled her into his truck, and they headed back to Colton. Dax passed her house, instead heading straight into town and pulling up in front of his building. "Dax, what are we doing here?"

He leaned against the steering wheel and looked at her with his mouth turned down. "Callie, Nate thinks someone may have tampered with the gas line at your house. Until we know it's safe, you're going to stay here with me."

"I don't believe it. The notes and the other stuff are one thing, but this is… crazy."

Dax put his arm around her. "We're in this together."

She nodded and blew out a shaky breath. "Okay."

Callie was surprised at how much work Dax had done when she entered the loft. A large rug anchored the center of the room, and a long leather sofa and two chairs upholstered in a gray fabric on either side of a large wood coffee table created a seating area. There was a desk in the same midcentury modern style against the wall of windows overlooking the town square. Callie noticed the binoculars and looked at Dax with a raised eyebrow.

"Just making sure my girlfriend is safe," he said with determination.

He took her hand and led her through the doorway to the large master suite. A massive king-size bed sat against an exposed brick wall. Dax continued the midcentury decor in the bedroom with two low nightstands and a dresser that matched the clean lines of the bed frame. The bed was covered in a soft gray blanket and matching pillows. He pointed to a bag on the bench at the foot of the bed. "Mae packed some things for you."

"That was nice of her."

"How about a nice hot shower or bath?"

"I would like that, thank you."

A large soaking tub and massive walk-in shower took up one whole wall. Callie wandered over to the tub and ran her hand along the edge. "This is huge. Two people could fit in here," she said.

"When you're feeling better, we can give it a try, but for now it's all yours."

"I think just a hot shower for now."

"I'll just be outside. Call if you need me."

The water felt like heaven. Callie lathered her hair, washing away the antiseptic smell from the hospital, replacing it with the sandalwood scent of Dax's shampoo. She stayed under the spray, letting the warm water relax her muscles. When her fingers began to prune, she reluctantly turned off the water and wrapped herself in the soft fluffy towel Dax had left for her, along with her toiletry bag.

She sighed with relief when she opened the bag, glad to find her comb and hair oil. It would have been a hair disaster otherwise. Callie rubbed the oil into her hair and combed through the tangles. She dug out her toothbrush and toothpaste and brushed her teeth. Feeling more like herself, she came out of the bathroom to an empty bedroom. She'd just finished putting on her pajamas when Dax appeared with a tray.

"I thought you might be hungry," he said. "I've got soup and a sandwich." Dax motioned for Callie to climb into bed and carefully placed the tray on her lap. She managed a few spoonfuls of soup and a couple of bites from the ham sandwich Dax had made before her eyelids began to droop. She barely noticed when Dax took the tray. She felt the mattress dip and Dax tucked her into his side.

"What made you come last night?" she asked in a sleepy voice.

Dax's arm went around her. "You wouldn't believe me if I told you."

"Tell me anyway."

"I heard a voice, a woman's voice, and she told me I had to go to you. I didn't even think about it. I just got in my truck and started driving."

Callie couldn't quite believe it. When she wasn't so tired, she'd tell him about her vision.

"I don't want to be the reason you don't have a relationship with your mother," she murmured, half asleep.

"You, Reid, hell everyone in this town is more important to me than being in my mother's good graces. Time has passed her by, and she didn't keep up. She wants to live in a world that doesn't exist anymore. I can't help holding on to some small hope that she'll change her ways. That's what's in my heart, but in my head, I know that's not going to happen.

Callie nodded. She understood what it was like to hold out hope that your mother or father could be a better person, the loving parent they were supposed to be. They would be better parents, she thought as she drifted off to sleep.

Muffled voices brought her out of a deep sleep. It took her a moment to recognize where she was. She jumped up only to realize that her legs were still a bit wobbly. She followed the sound of voices to the kitchen and found Dax, Robert, Jacob, and Mae leaning around the large island, deep in conversation. Dax looked up with a smile that didn't quite reach his eyes and reached out for her. Callie put her hand in his and he pulled her to his side.

"Good morning," he murmured, nuzzling her neck for a moment before giving her a quick kiss that made her whole body tingle.

"More like good afternoon," Mae said.

"Oh." Callie tried to get up. "I have to get to the library. It's been closed for too long as it is."

"Don't worry, the Jewels are helping out. You should have seen Opal doing story time for the kids, making up funny character voices. You should consider hiring her," Mae said.

"I'll just go over and check in," she said, trying to get up again.

"No, Callie, the doctor said you still need to rest." Dax shook his head.

Jacob leaned forward. "It would be better for you to stay here for a few days."

Callie took in the serious expressions of everyone around her. "What's going on?"

"You don't remember what I told you last night, do you?" Dax asked.

Callie bit her lip and shook her head. "I guess my mind is still a bit fuzzy," she confessed.

Uncle Robert moved to her side and wrapped his arm around her shoulders. "We just want to make sure you're safe." His mouth turned down. "The gas leak was no accident."

Everyone at the table shared his grim expression. She should be worried or afraid, but she wasn't. "I'm not going to hide," she said, with quiet determination. She looked at Dax. "We aren't going to let fear take over our lives. I'll stay here for now, and I'll rest for another day or two, but I'm going back to my library. I love you all, but you can't stop what you're doing with your own lives to watch me."

"That's easier said than done," Mae said.

Callie stood up. "I'll be careful," she reassured the worried faces around her, "but I'm done living in the shadows and trying not to make waves." She brushed away the wrinkles on Dax's forehead. "We're going to be okay."

CHAPTER TWENTY-FOUR

IT WAS the next morning, and Callie was spending her first day back at the library. Dax had just sat down at his desk when the doors of the Barton Building slammed open with so much force the glass windows on the main floor rattled.

"How could you!" The crack of her hand against his cheek echoed.

In all the years his mother had berated, judged, and chastised him, she never laid a hand on him. Dax never thought there was a line he could cross that would escalate her judgment to physical punishment; now he knew otherwise. He looked down at his mother. The lines around her lips were etched in deep trenches. Her love for him had twisted into something ugly over the years, and he envied his brother's exile for the first time.

"Mother," he said between clenched teeth, "I'm going to assume this is about Callie." He stepped back as she stood in front of him with her fists clenched. "She's okay, by the way, thank you for asking."

"You brought that whore into your home!" she spat out.

He willed himself to speak calmly. "You've lost the right to pass judgment. I would only give that right to someone I respect."

Her cheeks tinged pink, clashing with the artificial bloom of youth she had applied that morning. She moved toward him, her whole body shaking. The heart of the little boy who worshipped his mother raced; the grown man held himself still and didn't look away from her furious gaze. "I won't lose you to a n—"

"Don't you dare say it."

"She's not worthy of you."

"Why, Mother? Is it because she's half Black? Does it really matter that much to you? There was a part of me that always accepted you were a racist. That was when I was young and didn't know the hate you were teaching me was wrong. And that's the thing—" he slowly shook his head "—you're wrong if you think that you are better than anyone else around here."

Her voice took on a pacifying tone that made his gut clench. "Dax, my precious boy, I'm your mother. I want the best for you."

She moved to put her hand on his cheek. Dax jerked away. In spite of her placating words, the cold calculating glint never left her eyes.

"What about Reid? Do you want the best for him?" He moved out of his mother's reach again. "Is that why you sent him away?" He looked into her icy glare. "Was giving all of your love to me and not him best for either of us?"

His mother's placating smile slipped, and her mouth twisted into a scowl. "Your brother has always been difficult. It was better for everyone for him to go to boarding school."

"You didn't even let him come home for the summer—only Thanksgiving and Christmas, and even then, you only allowed him to stay for a day or two. I was the one who was bad. I bullied this whole town. Why didn't you send me away?"

Dorothy started to reach out to him again, but she hesitated and let her arm fall back to her side. "You've never been bad; you treated people the way they deserved to be treated. Reid wouldn't listen to me; you were always so obedient."

"Seriously! What is wrong with you?" He saw his mother flinch, but he didn't care. "Can you hear yourself? I'll never forgive myself for how I treated...." He couldn't bring himself to say her name in front of his mother. "And the worst part is... the worst part is that you encouraged me." He turned away, unable to look at the woman who raised him. "You need to leave," he said.

"I am your mother. I will always know what is best for you and I will not allow you to betray me with that whore."

He turned his back to her. The cold, hard edge in her voice sent a chill through him. He waited, staring at the tiny fissures and cracks in the brick walls until he heard the click of the door closing. There was something deeper going on, and he didn't understand it. Her insistence on his loyalty made his skin crawl.

The door opened again. A tall man with a shaved head and rich dark skin walked in. "What in the holy hell is going on around here that you need me to come all the way down from civilization to this godforsaken place?" he demanded in a deep voice.

"If you want to call Detroit civilization, then we need to talk about your standards," he teased before grabbing his friend into an embrace and slapping his back. "It's good to see you, Isiah."

"It's good to see you too, man."

Jacob came in and clapped his hand on Isiah's shoulder. "You're a sight for sore eyes. Welcome to Colton."

Isiah Owens had served with Dax and Jacob and retired along with them, choosing to move to Detroit and use his degree in engineering to take a position with the fire department as a fire marshal.

"I appreciate you making it down here on such short notice," Dax said. He called Isiah as soon as Nate told him he suspected the gas leak wasn't an accident.

Isiah shrugged. "I haven't taken any vacation in a long time, and to be honest I needed a break from investigating burned-out abandoned buildings. The city's trying to make a comeback, but it has a long way to go."

"Small-town or big-city renewal isn't easy." Dax nodded with understanding.

Isiah crossed his arms and looked from Jacob to Dax. "Do you want to tell me about this incident that happened with the gas leak?" he asked, cutting to the point.

"Let me take you upstairs. I'll make us some coffee and we can talk."

Isiah nodded and followed them upstairs, admiring Jacob's handiwork along the way. He blew a long whistle when they walked into his loft on the top floor.

"This is impressive. You made yourself a nice setup here."

"I have to admit I was skeptical when I first saw this place, but it came out better than I expected," Jacob agreed.

Dax set up the coffee maker while Jacob and Isiah sat on the new metal stools that lined one side of the large island.

They made small talk while the coffee brewed. After they caught up for a while, Isiah set his cup down and raised his eyebrow. "So, do you want to tell me what's going on?"

"The short story is that there was a gas leak at my girlfriend's house. Our local fire-EMT, Nate Colton, suspects that the leak was created intentionally, but he's not sure."

"You need me to take a look," Isiah stated, nodding with understanding. "What does the police report say?"

Jacob snorted. "This is a small town. There's a sheriff and that's it and he's not good for shit." He slapped Isiah on the back. "Welcome to small-town politics."

"It's complicated. There's some other things I need to tell you, and you might not like me very much when I'm through." Dax took a deep breath and plunged in, telling Isiah about his history with Callie. It wasn't easy, especially when he saw the fury that ghosted over Isiah's expression. When he finished, he waited for Isiah's censure.

His friend sat for a long time with his jaw clenched. When he spoke, his voice was gruff. "I'm not sure what to say here. As a Black man, the idea of you tormenting a little brown girl makes me sick to my stomach. I need you to know that. As your friend, I know you're not that boy. You've been a loyal friend, a brother-in-arms, and someone I respect." Isiah looked at him. "You've earned forgiveness from the one person that matters; you don't need mine."

"I'd like it just the same."

Isiah nodded. "Like I said, you don't need my forgiveness. It won't give you absolution. I will say this: you treat my mother and sister like queens, you always call my father sir and respect his opinion and ask him for guidance. I can't ask for a better person to have as a friend."

"I know it's hard to imagine, but there's going to come a day when the only person you need to ask for forgiveness is yourself," Jacob added.

Isiah stood up. "When can I take a look at your girlfriend's place?"

"I can take you over there now," Jacob offered, "and you can bunk with me while you're here. Callie is staying with Dax for now. I'm sure he would tell you he doesn't mind, but I think he would rather have his privacy."

"I feel you," Isiah said.

It felt good to have the guys with him again. He missed this easy banter between friends. Once Jacob and Isiah headed over to Callie's house, Dax went over to the window to look out over the park again. There was nothing out of place, but he couldn't get rid of the uneasy feeling that churned in his gut. His phone buzzed. Dax smiled when he looked down at the caller ID.

"Hey, Reid, thanks for returning my call."

"How's Callie?" Reid asked, sounding anxious.

"She's fine, Reid." Dax frowned. "Where are you? You sound like you're in a wind tunnel."

His brother laughed. "I'm driving with the top down."

"It must be a nice day in Chicago?"

There was a pause. "I'm not in Chicago."

"Oh?"

"I'm just outside of Memphis. I should be there in less than two hours unless I get pulled over."

"You're on your way here?"

"My little brother's girlfriend was almost killed." He cleared his throat. "I want to be there for you."

Dax swiped at the wetness on his cheeks. "Thank you."

"Hang in there. You can fill me in on whatever's going on when I get there." There was another pause. "You tried to warn me, and I didn't listen. I don't know what I can do, but I'll help you with Mom."

Reid arrived just as Jacob and Isiah returned from Callie's house. Jacob greeted Reid. The two met briefly on his last visit and fell into an easy camaraderie. Dax introduced Reid to Isiah, and it turned out that although they'd never met in person, Isiah had consulted on a case Reid prosecuted. They chatted for a few minutes about the case before Isiah turned to Dax.

"Your fireman's suspicions are valid; the gas leak wasn't an accident," he said with a curt nod.

"The line behind the stove was loosened so that gas was coming directly into the house," Jacob added.

"She's lucky the house didn't explode," Isiah said.

Dax shuddered. Reid put a steadying hand on his shoulder.

"Jacob and I are going to Jackson. I'll pick up a kit and dust for fingerprints."

"Thanks, I appreciate you being here, Isiah."

"It's how we do. You know that."

His chest tightened. Whatever happened next, he trusted these men with his life and, more importantly, Callie's.

"Talk to me. I can see the wheels turning in your head," Reid said when they were alone again.

"I don't know. I have a lot of suspicions, but no real evidence yet."

"Since you haven't said it, I'll ask: do you think Mom has something to do with this?"

"I don't want to."

"But a part of you believes she is," Reid said quietly.

Dax nodded. His instincts were rarely wrong, and it hurt to acknowledge that his mother could be so cruel.

"Listen, Mom and I don't have a good relationship. We don't have any relationship, but I don't want to think she's capable of doing any real harm any more than you do. I know I just met her, but I like Callie and I like the two of you together. I don't know if the reason is about race, class, or whatever, but Mom's behavior toward her is way out of line."

"I'm really glad you're here." Dax noticed the dark circles under his brother's eyes. "What time were you up this morning?"

Reid gave him a sheepish grin. "I couldn't sleep after you sent me the text about Callie. I made up my mind around three in the morning that I wanted to be here, and I was on the road by four thirty."

Dax looked at his brother with surprise. "What about work?"

His brother avoided his gaze. Wandering over to the windows overlooking the park, he pressed his hand against the glass, craning his neck to look around the town square before he turned back to Dax.

"The thing is, I've been thinking about coming back ever since my last visit. I know it doesn't make any sense. I swore I would never set foot in this town again but..." He shrugged. "...here I am. I have two weeks of vacation and I want to spend it here." He held his hands up. "Don't think it's all about you. Mr. Wallace, Primus, offered to teach me about making bourbon. It's something I've been interested in for a while now." He sighed. "I need something more in my life than work."

"I don't care what the reasons are, I'm just glad you came home. Will you have dinner with Callie and me tonight?"

"That would be great."

"You're welcome to stay here with us, if you'd like."

"I think I'd better bunk with Uncle Robert. I have a feeling three's a crowd."

"Thanks, Reid. Dealing with Mom isn't going to be easy, and I'm really thankful that you're here."

"We're brothers, where else would I be?"

CHAPTER TWENTY-FIVE

CALLIE GLANCED up from her desk and Reid's gaze met hers. "You don't have to babysit me, you know."

Reid turned the page on the book he obviously wasn't reading. "I honestly don't mind." He looked around the room. "I like it here."

It wouldn't be right to say things had returned to normal after the gas leak at her house. She and Dax fought about her going back home, so she compromised and agreed to stay with him for a few days until Isiah had done a thorough inspection of the house. She smiled softly—not that she minded waking up with Dax every morning.

Callie was surprised that Reid decided to visit, but also happy for Dax. They had dinner together the night before and she loved watching the two brothers reconnecting and forming new bonds. Reid had been at the library all morning. She knew Dax had asked him to check in on her while she was working, but all the attention was starting to wear on her nerves. Still, Callie understood people meant well, and she was touched by the love and concern everyone showed her.

Callie got up from her desk and pulled another book from the shelf. "Have you read this one?" she asked, handing Reid a copy of *Whisky Women*.

Reid took the volume from her hand. "No, I haven't."

"It's about Elizabeth Bessie Williamson, considered the greatest female distiller, and other women like her who were pioneers in the industry." Callie smiled. "I noticed you're reading a lot about distilleries, and Dax mentioned you've been spending a lot of time with Mr. Wallace. Are you interested in making your own?"

"There's an urban distillery in Chicago that had a class. I don't really have time with my caseload, but if I had the time, I'd like to give it a try someday."

Callie pulled out a chair and sat down. "I know how busy you are, and I really appreciate that you took the time to come down here. It means a lot to Dax."

Jacob poked his head through the door that connected the library to the bookstore. "Hey, Callie, I've got a question for you. Can you come here for just a minute?"

"Sure." She turned to Reid and said, "Do you mind?"

"Go." Reid waved his hand toward the bookstore. "I'll give a holler if anyone comes in."

Dax walked into the library to find his brother standing in front of a small, framed picture on the wall. "Where's Callie?"

"She went next door to talk to Jacob. Have you seen this?" Reid asked, pointing at the picture.

Dax moved to stand next to him. It wasn't a piece of artwork, it was a piece of history. Callie had a copy of her grandfather's NAACP card framed so that both the front and the back of the card were visible. The front of the card read.

Richard Colton

P.O. Box 85

Colton, Mississippi, 39192

1954

Member: $2.00

"We've come so far and yet we have so far to go," Dax said reading the six points listed as reasons to join the organization.

1. To educate America to accord full rights and opportunities to Negros.

2. To fight injustice in Courts when based on Race prejudice.

3. To pass protective legislation in State and Nation to defeat discriminatory bills.

4. To secure the Vote for Negros and teach its proper use.

5. To stimulate the cultural life of Negros.

6. To stop lynching.

"I can't imagine what he must have seen in his lifetime," Reid said.

"Callie told me her grandfather worked alongside Medgar Evers."

"That's amazing."

"I'm so grateful she gave me a second chance. I'm so thankful for the history she's shared with me."

"It's been nice getting to know her. I like the two of you together. You belong together."

"I love her," Dax said.

"Over my dead body."

They both turned to see their mother standing in the doorway, her face twisted into a mask of rage. "Why are you still here?" she said, staring at Reid.

"Reid has every right to be here, Mother."

She closed the door and walked toward them, fingering the pearls at her neck.

Reid squared his shoulders. "I haven't come by the house, Mother—"

"Don't call me that," she spat at Reid, interrupting him. "I was never your mother."

"I know I've never been the son you wanted me to be—"

Dorothy's laugh sent a shiver down Dax's spine.

"That's just it," she continued, "you aren't my son—"

"Mother," Dax cut her short. "Don't be cruel."

"I'm being honest. Reid isn't my son." Dorothy's gaze was riveted on Reid. "Your father never stopped loving her, your bitch of a mother or her kind. That's why you were his favorite. All those secret visits—your father and son weekends—did you think I didn't know?"

Reid's jaw hardened. "Dad loved you."

Dorothy shook her head. "No. We were already engaged when I caught the two of them together. He swore it was over. We had to go through with the wedding—what would people think?" She smiled, wistfully. "It was a beautiful wedding, everybody said so, and for a few months I believed he could learn to love me, but he couldn't stay away from her." She twisted her lips and focused on Dax. "She lured him, the same way that whore has tricked you into carrying on with her. Why can't they settle for their own kind?"

"I don't care," Dax said. "Reid is my brother."

"Half-brother," she corrected. "And now I'm going to take care of this." She reached into her purse and pulled out a gun. "I'd hoped to get rid of her, but I'll start with this mongrel and then take care of the other one later."

The door opened and the sheriff walked in. "Dorothy," he said. "I've been looking for you."

She flashed him a distracted smile. "Oh, Jeb, thank goodness you're here."

"Dorothy, my love, put the gun away."

"No."

"You don't want to do this," the sheriff said, moving carefully toward her until he was close enough to rest his hand on her shoulder.

She briefly nuzzled his hand before adjusting her grip on the gun. Her eyes flickered toward Dax for a second before glaring at Reid again. "Jeb was the only one who understood what it was like for me. When your father forced me to raise this mongrel child. The shame of it was so terrible. I'd heard whispers, but I never imagined someone like your father would sink so low." She smirked. "I guess that's why they call it jungle fever, except in your father's case it was incurable. He was always hanging out, picking up the wrong kind of girls at that juke joint."

She waved the gun at Reid. "We were only married for a month when he told me he got some whore pregnant. She was going to get rid of it, but he begged her to keep it. He didn't know I was already pregnant." A tear rolled down her cheek. "We weren't living here. I moved to Memphis to be with your father while he finished law school. She gave birth right after I miscarried. She didn't want you either. You were light enough your father brought you home and begged me to pass you off as mine." She sniffed and her face twisted into a mask of hate. "As if you could ever replace a child of my own."

She glanced at Dax. "Thank goodness I had you."

Dax flinched. "He was just a baby—it wasn't his fault."

Dorothy sneered at Reid. "When someone told me that they saw you kissing a boy, I wasn't surprised. I never wanted you, and I wasn't going to have a deviant living under my roof. It gave me the perfect excuse to send you away. Dax," she swung her attention back his way, "sweetheart, can't you see now how much I sacrificed for you? I saved you from this filthy boy."

Dax pressed his lips together and shook his head.

Jeb began to reach slowly for the gun. "Yes, my love they're ungrateful children. They don't deserve to have a wonderful woman like you for a mother," he said in a placating tone while he wrapped his hand over hers. "We'll figure out another way, but you can't do this. I can't see my love go to jail."

Dorothy's eyes grew wide. "They won't send me to jail. I'm a pillar of the community." She looked at Jeb with confidence. "You're the sheriff. You won't let them."

"Darling, look around, there are witnesses."

"Dax won't say anything. Deep down he knows I'm doing what's best. He'll thank me later."

Dax took advantage of the brief moment of distraction and knocked the gun out of her hands.

"No," Dorothy howled.

Dax tackled Jeb before he could reach for his gun, pinning him to the floor.

"Don't touch me," Dorothy screamed as Reid held her.

Jacob rushed in and pulled the handcuffs off the sheriff's belt. "I've got this," he said cuffing his hands together. Dorothy wrestled out of Reid's arms and ran over to the sheriff. She reached up and cupped his cheek. "My darling Jeb, why didn't you kill her when you had the chance?

"You fucking bitch, this is your fault," she spit at Callie as she came in behind Jacob and rushed into Dax's arms.

"Shut up," Dax growled.

"I'm the law here—you can't do nothin' to me," Jeb sneered.

Nate came in and grabbed Dorothy just as she let go of Jeb and lunged at Callie.

"Take your hands off me." She spat on Nate's face while he wrapped her hands in soft restraints.

Nate wiped the spit from his cheek. "I'll be happy to add assault and any other charges that are made against you. Not that adding assault to your attempted murder charge will make much of a difference."

Jacob yanked the sheriff to his feet.

"You'll pay for this," the sheriff said.

"Come on." Nate jerked his head toward the door. "Let's get them over to the jail."

THE REST of the afternoon passed in a blur for Callie. It was horrible having to relive watching Dorothy point a gun at Reid. When she first heard Dorothy's voice, she started to go back toward the library, but Jacob held her back, put his fingers to his lips, and shook his head. When they saw the gun, Jacob pulled her aside and crouched by the door, waiting. Everything played out in slow motion—watching Dax disarm his mother and then attack the sheriff before he could reach for his gun.

She shuddered thinking of what could have happened if Dax hadn't been successful.

"Are you okay, ma'am?" the officer taking her statement asked.

"Yes, it's just... I still can't believe it."

The officer nodded and looked over his notes again. Callie glanced toward the street lined with patrol cars from the next town over. She was allowed back into the library, which was now a crime scene, just long enough to retrieve the threatening notes she'd received. The officer put them in a manila envelope. "That should be all for now. We'll let you know if we need anything else."

"Thank you."

Dax and Reid had finished up their interviews as well, and they all stood in front of the library watching Dorothy and the sheriff as they were led outside in handcuffs.

Dorothy had pleaded for Dax to help her, her tone swinging wildly between cajoling and threatening. By the time she was taken to the patrol car she was belligerent, her head held high. "Don't you know who I am?" she declared. "This town will not survive without me."

By now word had spread, and most of the town was crowded along the sidewalk across the street from town hall.

"Oh honey, bless your heart. You ain't that special," Tillie said loud enough for everyone to hear.

Dorothy glared at her through the patrol car window, her face contorted into a mask of rage as the car passed by. The sheriff had his chin to his chest as he was led down the stairs and pushed into a separate car.

"Goodbye and good riddance," Nate muttered under his breath.

CHAPTER TWENTY-SIX

THE DAY that followed the arrest of Dorothy Ellis and the sheriff was chaotic, filled with interviews with the state police and county prosecutor's office. Callie couldn't help but worry that Dorothy and the sheriff would use their influence to get off the hook, but Dorothy's confession opened an investigation that was already revealing more crimes. It turned out Dorothy had been using the town funds to pay for her criminal activities that included paying two of the sheriff's nephews to write the threatening notes and throw the brick through the library window.

Isiah and Jacob were talking at one end of the porch while Reid and Uncle Robert were sitting together at the other end when Callie and Dax arrived the next morning.

"Y'all need coffee?" Uncle Robert asked.

"I'd love a cup," Callie said.

Uncle Robert gave her a pat on his way inside. Callie leaned against Dax. She felt the need to reach out for him often to reassure herself that they had all made it through Dorothy's attempted attack safely.

Isiah and Jacob approached.

"I was able to talk to the prosecutor." Isiah's expression was grim. "I hate to tell you this, Dax, but your mother is likely to go to jail for some time."

Dax nodded. "I can't say I'm surprised."

Uncle Robert came out and handed Callie a cup of coffee. "I failed you, honey."

"What do you mean?" Callie asked.

"I should have paid closer attention to what was going on."

"Uncle Robert, this isn't your fault. In a way we all let Colton down. Maybe it was from fear, or tradition, but no one wanted to go against Dorothy and the sheriff."

"Callie's right," Dax said, "you don't have anything to apologize for. I'm the one who should have confronted my mother long before I even moved here."

"No," Reid stood up and faced his brother, "you're not taking this burden on yourself. This isn't your fault, Dax. The seeds of this were sown long before we were born." He looked around at everyone assembled on the porch with a somber expression. "Before any of us were born. You could argue the seeds were planted by the first person enslaved on the Colton Plantation."

There was a moment of silence while each of them felt the weight of Reid's words.

Callie set down her cup and gave Reid a hug.

"Mae's parents came by this morning," he said when she let go.

"Why?"

Reid glanced at his brother.

"No more secrets, whatever it is," Dax said.

"Joseph thinks he might know who my mother is," Reid said. "He had a cousin, Rosie, and Joseph told me he saw her with Dad a few times."

"Did Joseph tell you what happened to her?" Dax asked.

Reid shook his head. "No, but he offered to help find out what he can."

"I wish I could stay and help, but I've got to get back," Isiah said.

"I don't know how to thank you," Dax said, shaking his hand.

"I know you'd do the same for me."

"You say the word and I'm there."

After Isiah said his goodbyes, they stayed on the porch talking about what would happen next. The town had some major hurdles to overcome. Dorothy and the sheriff weren't the only ones in trouble. Emma's father, the third member of the town council, would also be under investigation for any part he may have played in the misuse of the town funds.

"I'd like to slap the three of them into Sunday," Uncle Robert grumbled.

"Nothing will happen for a while, and the town will probably be put into receivership until a new town council can be appointed," Reid said.

Callie sighed. "What a mess."

Dax put his arm around her. "Maybe that's what needed to happen. Everything had to be torn apart so we can build it back again."

She nodded slowly, thinking he was right. She wasn't worried, though. Together with Dax and the rest of the people who loved Colton, they would recover from the damage the town council had done, and Colton would be a better place than it was before.

Uncle Robert excused himself, leaving the three of them on the porch.

"What else can I get you?" She rested her head on Dax's shoulder.

He drew her even closer and kissed her temple. "Just be here."

"I'm not going anywhere," she answered before glancing at Reid. His eyes were bloodshot. He looked exhausted. "What about you, Reid, are you okay?"

His broad shoulders shifted. "When I looked in the mirror this morning, I didn't know who I was looking at."

"I'm still looking at my brother," Dax said.

Callie studied the differences between the two men. Dax was slightly taller than his older brother and Reid's hair had more curl. They didn't need physical similarities to connect them, not when they were bound by love.

Reid's arms crossed over his chest. "I keep replaying what Mom... Dorothy said."

Callie shuddered. "I'll never get that scene out of my head."

"I don't even know who she is anymore," Dax said grimly.

Reid was still troubled. "She's going to go to jail. It's unavoidable; she's confessed to multiple crimes."

"I know. And on one hand, I feel bad for her, but she needs to be punished for what she's done."

"She...." Callie shook her head. "What a terrible thing, to carry this secret around until it broke her. She wasn't allowed to grieve for the baby she lost."

"I'm so angry with Dad right now. For what he did to Dorothy, for what he did to my mother, to me." Reid's voice had a slight tremor. "I thought we had this special bond, and the whole time he was lying to me."

"He lied to both of us."

"I can't believe I'm half Black," Reid said looking down at his hands, outstretched before him.

"Does it bother you?" Callie asked, looking at him with concern.

"No, but everything I thought I knew has changed, and it's going to take some time to… I don't know," he exhaled, "get to know myself again."

"I can teach you the secret handshake when you're ready."

Reid gave her a half smile.

"Everyone's experience is different, but I'm here whenever you want to talk," Callie offered.

"I'd like that."

Callie looked at Dax. "What happens now?"

"We start over." He looked over at his brother. "Together as a family."

"I know it's not true, but I feel kind of orphaned."

"I'm going to say this as many times as you need to hear it. We're brothers, half Black, half White, gay, you're my brother." Dax sighed and shook his head. "I'm not Dorothy. My love for you is unconditional."

"I love you too."

"Then that's all that needs to be said until you want to say more."

Despite his brother's offer to stay with them at Callie's house, Reid decided to stay with Uncle Robert.

Dax hugged his brother. "Just promise me you won't stay away for too long."

"We lost too much time. I won't let that happen again."

Reid walked them to their truck and gave Callie a hug, whispering in her ear, "Take good care of him."

They drove back to Callie's house and instead of going inside, Dax sat down on the porch swing and pulled her into his lap.

"How are you, really?" she asked.

He took a deep breath. "I know this is going to sound strange, but I'm thankful. You're safe now and I have my brother back in my life."

"What do you need, Dax, what can I do to help you here?" She put her hand over his heart.

"Can we go for a walk?"

"Where do you want to go?" she asked.

Dax reached for her hand. "It doesn't matter, as long as we're walking in the same direction together."

They walked toward town. The air was still warm, but the heat of the day was gone. The lampposts surrounding the park flickered on just as they made their way into the town.

They walked along two blocks that made up half of the town square and then started down the next block. When they reached the library, Dax stopped and took both of Callie's hands in his. His eyes locked with hers for a moment before he dropped to one knee.

"I know how much you love this place, and I want to replace the memory of what happened here with something good."

Callie squeezed his hands, holding back tears, not from sadness but of pure joy.

"Callie, you are the love of my life. I will only be half the man I can be without you, because you're the other half of me. Will you marry me?"

Callie couldn't hold back her smile. "You are the only man I will ever love. I can't imagine my life without you in it. Yes, I'll marry you."

Dax stood and drew her into his arms, sealing their promise with a kiss before reaching into his pocket and pulling out a ring and sliding it on her finger. Callie looked down at the simple round diamond surrounded by smaller yellow ones.

"I hope it's okay."

"It's perfect." She glanced toward the park. "It reminds me of the gazebo surrounded by yellow roses."

"That's exactly what I had in mind when I had it made." He reached up and caressed her cheek. "I'm hoping you'll want to get married under the gazebo and continue the tradition."

"There's no other place I'd want to take my vows with you. But the tradition isn't why we're going to have a long and happy life together. We found a way to move forward from the past, with love and forgiveness. I'm glad you came home, Dax. When I came to Colton, I had a vision for bringing the town back to life and... I thought I could do it all myself." Her eyes shone with happiness. "Now I can't imagine this journey without you by my side." She looked around the park. "This is a good place, not perfect, but no city or town is. But you know what? Perfect doesn't give us a chance to grow."

Dax kissed her forehead. "I'm looking forward to every day I get to grow with you."

CHAPTER TWENTY-SEVEN

IT WAS that magical time of day when the day ended and the birds in the trees began to welcome twilight with a song. Dax looked around the park with pride. The whole town had come together to make their day special. This day showed the promise of what Colton could be. More than a town, a community. The air shimmered and shifted, the scent of eucalyptus washed over him. He looked around and saw her. The same old woman he'd seen before, smiling and nodding at him.

Uncle Robert straightened his tie. "If you don't breathe, you're going to pass out before your bride gets here."

He wasn't nervous, far from it. He glanced over to where he saw the old woman, but she was gone. A rightness settled into his bones. Dax took a deep breath and gazed at their friends and family seated around the gazebo. It was the end of summer, and the light filtering through the trees bathed them all in a warm glow. The columns and railing around the gazebo were covered in garlands of yellow roses, freesia, and peonies. Their heady scent filled the air. Lights had been strung across the park and a stage and dance floor had been set up on one side. Dax kept the band he'd hired a closely guarded secret. He couldn't wait to see the look on his bride's face when Lucas Monroe serenaded them for their first dance.

Speaking of his bride, he looked toward the library for the hundredth time, anxious for Callie to come out escorted by Mae's father. Her parents' absence was the only disappointment on their day.

"Don't worry," Reid said, slapping him on the back, "you'll get to see her soon enough."

Jacob and Isiah joined them. Dax looked over his groomsmen in their gray suits with yellow ties and grinned. "You two clean up well. Thanks for standing up with me today." He held out his hand to Isiah. "I appreciate you coming back down for the wedding."

"Oh, he's not just here for the wedding." Jacob grinned, rubbing his hands together.

"Oh?" Dax looked at his friend.

"I'd like to introduce y'all to Colton's new sheriff," Jacob announced.

"I just signed the paperwork this morning."

"That's great. Are you sure you're ready to give up life in the city?"

"It's going to be an adjustment, but I need more than a career. I want to be a part of a community where my neighbors are my friends. I like what I've seen here, the way you all support and care for each other. Hopefully your kids can grow up with mine someday."

"And I'm looking forward to being here and spoiling my nieces and nephews," Reid quietly added.

Dax looked at his brother with wide eyes. Just when he thought he couldn't be any happier, the day got better.

Reid shrugged. "You and Callie are my family. We missed out on too many years together. I don't want to miss any more."

"You just gave Callie and me the best wedding present we could ever ask for."

"Gentlemen, it's time," Judge Beaumont announced, peering at them over the rim of his glasses.

There had almost been an all-out war between the ministers of the two Baptist churches vying to marry them, each hoping their service would be rewarded with a large donation to their congregations. When the judge called and offered his services as a conciliatory gesture for Presley's involvement in Dorothy's schemes, they were happy to accept. The judge's offer may have been another part of Presley's punishment as well. Dax glanced to the lone figure standing under a tree at the corner of the park dressed in black, her face hidden by a hat with... wait, was that a... veil? He rolled his eyes. Other than wreaking havoc in the library and believing his mother's lies, Presley hadn't done anything illegal. She had been spoiled and coddled by his mother. Without her influence, Dax hoped that she would learn the same lesson he had. That kindness was a gift and forgiveness had to be earned, second chances didn't happen every day, and if you were lucky enough to get one, you had to treasure and nurture it until it bloomed and grew.

His groomsmen lined up with Reid at his side. Patting the pocket with Callie's ring, he gave Dax a quick thumbs-up.

The library door opened, and he caught his first glimpse of his bride. Ruby began singing Etta James's "At Last" in a strong, clear voice that carried across the park. Emma came out first followed by Mae, wearing matching pale-yellow dresses with gray sashes that coordinated with the groomsmen's suits. Callie came out on her uncle's arm. Her curls were pulled into a low bun with a cluster of roses tucked behind her ear. She wore a strapless chiffon dress with a yellow sash, carrying a bouquet of yellow roses. His breath caught. When she reached the steps of the gazebo, Joseph placed Callie's hand in his. "Love each other long and love each other well," he said. He placed a kiss on Callie's cheek before joining his wife in the front row.

Dax thought he would burst with love and pride. Callie beamed at him. Her eyes sparkled. She mouthed *I love you.*

Dax turned to his bride. "I love you so much," he said.

The judge cleared his throat. "We haven't started yet," he admonished them, to a chorus of laughter.

Judge Beaumont looked out at the guests. "Ladies and gentlemen, the bride and groom have asked me to welcome you all here today to witness their vows. Callie and Dax have chosen to write their own vows and will recite them now."

Callie handed her bouquet to Mae and placed both her hands in his. Her hands trembled, but her gaze was steady and focused solely on him. Dax took a deep breath and began. "Callie Ann Fischer Colton, I was half a man until you made me whole and my life complete. I will love and honor you every day." He reached up and caught a tear before it could fall. He cupped her cheek and pressed his forehead to hers. "I will always cherish the gift of your trust and forgiveness," he whispered, brushing his lips against hers before standing back again.

The judge cleared his throat and glared at Dax over the rim of his glasses. "We haven't gotten to that part yet."

Dax tried to look properly mollified, but he couldn't hide the smile that tugged at his lips.

Callie squeezed his hands. "Daxton Madden Ellis, love doesn't always follow an easy path. Ours took many twists and turns before we could stand here now. When I couldn't see the end of the road, you held my hand and walked beside me. I will love and honor you every day. I look forward to the years ahead building a life with you. I will always cherish the gift of finding our way to each other again."

Neither one of them paid any attention to what the judge said next. The world faded away and it was just the two of them. He looked into her gray eyes that he'd started out tormenting and ended up dreaming about every night. He marveled at the beauty and love standing before him. He would spend the rest of his life trying to be worthy of the gift of Callie's love.

The judge cleared his throat again. "You may salute your bride."

Callie lifted her face to his, radiant with love and trust. She reached up and wrapped her arms around his neck. "My husband," she whispered.

"My wife," he answered.

Their kiss was celebrated with cheers and applause from their guests. When they finally broke apart, Callie's cheeks were flushed and her eyes were bright. The stars were just beginning to shine as Dax took his wife's hand. Mae came forward and laid a broom tied with a yellow ribbon at their feet. They jumped and Dax led his bride down the gazebo steps into the loving embrace of their friends and family. Callie was right: love didn't always follow an easy path, but through forgiveness and hope, they found their way forward.

Keep Reading for an excerpt from
The Way Home
Mockingbird Bridge Book Two
by Eliana West

THE
WAY
Home

MOCKINGBIRD BRIDGE

BOOK TWO

ELIANA WEST

Mockingbird Bridge Book Two

A letter from the past will transform their future…

Taylor Colton always loved the crumbling plantation house passed down through his family for generations. Now he's bringing his popular renovation reality show to the small town of Colton, Mississippi, so he can bring the plantation house known as Halcyon back to life for the cameras.

After an ugly breakup, Josephine Martin needs a new start to heal her broken heart in peace. A hidden letter reveals a family secret that leads her to Colton to protect her family's history and honor a promise made before the Civil War… and to a house she didn't know was hers.

Suddenly, Josephine must decide if she's ready for the challenge of restoring a run-down mansion and its history, and Taylor's facing a challenge he can't charm away. Together, they must untangle a tragic history, a rocky relationship, and risk everything they love. Can they overcome the past to find their way home?

Scan the QR code below to order

CHAPTER ONE

JOSEPHINE RILEY swatted at the dust bunnies drifting through the air in the attic of her parents' house. The floorboards creaked under her father's feet as he moved another box from the pile in the corner.

"Are you sure it's up here?" she asked, anxiously peering over his shoulder.

"Here, take this," he grunted, handing her a box, "It should be, we haven't gotten rid of anything up here since we bought this house." He stopped and stretched his back. "We need to have a garage sale," he announced, looking around the room.

Jo tried to keep the impatience out of her voice. "Let's find the trunk first."

"I don't mind helping you look, sweetheart, but all this work because of a dream?" He looked down at her with concern, "The last few months have been stressful. Maybe you should see a doctor."

"I did, and I have a clean bill of health, Dad."

The same dark brown eyes she'd inherited studied her for a moment before he gave a brief nod. "Okay."

Jo didn't keep secrets from her dad; in many ways he was her best friend. But how could she tell him about the voice she'd started hearing a few weeks ago, the one that told her about the letter she was looking for now? So she lied and told her parents she'd had a reoccurring dream that there was a letter hidden in a trunk that passed down through her family for generations. The part about the doctor was true; when she started hearing the voice she went in for a full physical, but there wasn't a medical excuse she could use to explain the voice that came to her one day telling her to "get me my house."

Together Jo and her father shifted the boxes out of the corner until a large trunk appeared. They pushed the piece into the middle of the room under the dim light of the bare bulb in the ceiling. She swiped away the dust on top and the wood glowed a warm golden brown. The dips and groves were the markings of work that was done by hand without the benefit of and precision of modern tools. The wood was arranged a chevron pattern on the top. and it was clear the person who made it put a great deal of care into it.

"*My husband Amos made it for me,*" the voice in her head whispered.

"Are you sure about this?" her father asked.

Jo took a deep breath and nodded as she pressed the latch and opened the lid of the trunk. The hinges creaked, releasing a faint musky smell and revealing an old yoyo quilt. It looked so fragile she expected it to fall apart when she picked it up, but the stitches held firm. Underneath the quilt there were pictures, cards, and letters scattered among other small items. She would have to go back through and organize all of this later; right now she needed to focus on finding the letter—one letter in particular. *Are you sure it's here?* She asked the voice in her head.

"*It's here,*" the voice said.

Her father peered over her shoulder as she ran her hands over the faded floral paper that lined the lid. She found the edge and carefully peeled back the paper, revealing a small panel of wood. She pressed against it, and it popped into her hand. Her breath caught when she saw the envelope behind it.

"Well, I'll be damned," her father gasped as Jo pulled it from its hiding place.

Her hands shook as she read the writing on the front. In bold handwriting, it was addressed to an Ada Mae Colton with A. M. Colton listed for the return addressee.

Her father knelt down next to her, peering over her shoulder as she pulled the piece of parchment out.

September 7th, 1860

Ada Mae,

I will refrain from calling you my dearest. I know how those endearments upset you.

Halcyon is no longer a home now that you are gone. I can't bear to be in the house with Julia,. I have sent her to the house in Jackson and do not plan on ever letting her set foot in Halcyon again. Now I wander this house alone, and thoughts of you and our son haunt my dreams at night. It is the sharpest knife wound to my heart to hear that you have married, but I know it is for the best. I know he is a good man, you would not settle for anything less, and that assures me he will be a good father to our son.

War is coming, and I will have to fight. You should be safe where you are. I do not believe Illinois will join the Confederacy, but guard your freedom papers closely. Enclosed are enough funds for you and your family to flee north as far as Canada if need be. I have made arrangements with my solicitor that when the time comes for me to depart this earth, Halcyon will pass to you and our son.

You will forever be in my heart,

Absolem

"I heard stories, but I didn't believe them." Her father's deep voice shook with emotion.

She looked at her dad in surprise. "What stories?"

"My great-granddaddy used to tell me how we were descended from a freed slave, free before the Civil War. He said his great grandfather was a man named Stephen, and we had mixed blood because Stephen was the son of the man who owned his mama, a confederate general." He shook his head. "I didn't believe him, who would want to believe that, it would mean…." His jaw ticked.

Jo wrapped her arm around her father, leaning against him, "It's okay, Dad."

He gently took the letter from her. Holding the delicate parchment in his large hands up to the light, he studied the document.

"Dad," Jo spoke softly, "I want to go and see Halcyon."

Her father pressed his lips together. "It's probably long gone."

"It's still there, I looked it up."

"Why do you want to do this, what are you hoping to find?"

"Honestly, I'm not sure, but I know I need to see it with my own eyes."

"Do you want me to go with you?"

She stood on tiptoe and placed a kiss on her father's cheek. "Thanks, Dad, but I'll be okay."

He tucked the letter back in the envelope. "We better go tell your mother about this. Your brother and sister will be here soon. We'll talk about it over family dinner."

Jo suppressed a groan. Sunday dinners at her parents' house were an exercise in patience for her. Her older brother Marlon and younger sister Brooke shared a close sibling bond that she was left out of. She was a textbook middle child and she hated it. Ambitious and outgoing, her siblings only cared about being seen at the right parties and events in

Chicago's thriving social scene. They looked down on Jo as the awkward sister and were constantly reminding her what a disappointment she was.

Dinner was the disaster she knew it would be. Her siblings thought the idea of Jo going to see an old house in the Mississippi Delta was crazy. As bad as it was, that night wasn't much different from every other Sunday dinner. Her siblings teased and made pointed comments about her ex-boyfriend while her mother tried to play peacemaker, still clinging to a vision of family harmony that just didn't exist.

When her sister made an exceptionally cruel remark about the end of her last relationship, she'd had enough. Jo jumped up from the table, taking her plate into the sanctuary of the kitchen.

"You know your mama hates to see good food go to waste," her father said, walking in as she scraped the contents of her dinner into the garbage.

"Sorry, Dad," she muttered.

He leaned against the counter, folding his arms. "Your brother and sister—"

"Please, Dad, you need to stop making excuses for Marlon and Brooke." She leaned against the counter, mirroring her father's pose. "I've never really fit in with this family. Sometimes I wonder if we even share the same DNA."

Her father winced and put a comforting arm around her. "I hate that you feel that way."

"Just because we're family doesn't mean we have to get along or even be friends."

"I'm worried about you. I know it's been hard to get over what happened with Oliver and Courtney."

"How can I get over it when I'm constantly being reminded of what happened?"

"I could kill him for hurting you the way he did."

"It doesn't matter. He and Courtney are engaged, and Oliver got his wish and gets to pretend he's a big tech tycoon."

"With your technology," her father growled.

When she met Oliver Cox at a tech conference two years ago, he swept her off her feet with his dazzling smile and compliments. It wasn't easy to be a woman in her field, let alone a Black woman, and a lot of men were dismissive of her capabilities, but Oliver was different. He constantly complimented her on her programming skills, and she reveled in dating someone who shared her love for writing code and developing new programs. Her friends all thought he was amazing, especially her best friend Courtney. All of the signs were there and yet she missed them, so she was completely blindsided when Oliver took one of her ideas for a new systems integration program and used it to sell it and himself to one of the top tech firms in Silicon Valley. When she accused him of stealing, he fought back with falsified documents to make it look like she was the one trying to steal his code. He told his story to anyone who would listen, and within weeks her career and reputation were destroyed. If that weren't bad enough it turned out that he'd been cheating on her with her friend Courtney for the last six months of their relationship. Her small group of friends became nonexistent when she found out that they all knew about Oliver and Courtney and kept it from her. Over the last few weeks, she wavered between being embarrassed at being so naive and humiliated that her friends had all been laughing at her behind her back.

Jo blew out a shaky breath. It had been two months, and the sting of betrayal was still sharp.

"We could still sue," her father said with hope in his eyes.

"No, you know how difficult cases like that are to prove. And you know what," she smirked, "he's going to have a hard time developing any other programs. The emperor has no clothes."

Her dad snorted a laugh, shaking his head.

Jo sobered. "I won't lie, it still hurts." She sighed. "A weekend in Mississippi will do me good. I want to see the place that should have been our home."

Her father rested his hands on her shoulders. "Our family left Mississippi before the Civil War. We went from being slaves to becoming doctors, lawyers, and," he gave her an affectionate smile, chucking her under the chin. "systems architects. Our home is here."

Later that night, Jo stood at her dining room table with a glass of wine, looking over the various papers, letters, postcards, and photographs there were in the trunk. Her father's family history was laid out before her. She sorted everything into piles by date. There were WWII letters home from her third great-grandfather, along with a small journal filled with notes from Army nurses' training from his sister. A registration card for the Pullman Porters union from Ada Mae's son Stephen, along with other mementos that spanned over a hundred and fifty years of history, but nothing more from Ada Mae.

She'd introduced herself to Jo shortly after she started speaking to her. *"I'm Ada Mae Riley and I'm one hundred and four years old. A promise was made and you're the one who's going to make sure it's kept."*

"Why me?" she asked. "There are generations here that could have done what you want."

"But you is the one I want," The voice softened her tone. *"You remind me so much of him, so impatient with the world and yet so weary to really live in it. There's nothing more for you here, but there's a home waiting for you at Halcyon."*

"Explain it to me again," she muttered.

"You're gonna get me my house."

A few days later, Jo looked out the window at the unfamiliar landscape of low flat buildings surrounded by land with only a few small patches of water instead of the vast freshwater ocean of Lake Michigan as the plane descended into Jackson. By the time she made the hour drive from Jackson to Colton, she had convinced herself this was the worst idea she'd ever had. The green fields gave way to a small cluster of low buildings next to railroad tracks. She drove past an old train depot following the GPS directions to a large brick building with Town Hall etched into the gray stone above the door.

She found her way to a room marked Office just inside the main entrance. An older woman, her hair cut into a severe bob, sat typing away at an ancient computer. She peered at Josephine over the tops of her bright red reading glasses that matched the red lipstick that only emphasized the wrinkles on her pale skin. "Can I help you?" she asked in a tone that suggested she wasn't going to be much help at all.

Before Jo could answer, a woman who looked to be about the same age as her and sharing the same dark brown skin, with close-cropped hair that emphasized eyes so dark they were almost black, came through another doorway marked Mayor. "Grace, have you seen the printout for..... Oh, hello," she said with a friendly smile.

"Hi, I'm Josephine Riley. I'm here looking for... well, I'm not exactly sure," she said with a nervous laugh.

She came forward with her hand outstretched. "I'm Mae Colton. It's nice to meet you. Why don't you come on back to my office and we'll see if we can figure out what you need."

The older woman, Grace, cleared her throat. "Mayor Colton, I'm sure you have better things to do than help this person. I'm sure I can take care of whatever she needs."

"Grace, why don't you see if you can find the files I asked you for two days ago while I speak with Miss Riley," Mae answered with a raised eyebrow.

Grace pursed her lips and glared at them as Mae led her past the front desk and into her office. Jo looked around and wondered if she had just wandered onto the set of *Mad Men*. Mae sat behind a huge oak desk that dwarfed her petite frame. There were two chairs covered in dark burgundy vinyl to one side and a smaller version in front of the desk. "Take a seat," she said, gesturing to it.

Jo sat down and pulled the envelope from her bag. "I'm here about Halcyon."

Mae wrinkled her nose. "The plantation house? What about it?"

"I'd like to see it, and I'm interested in—" She cleared her throat. "—I'd like to buy it."

She would explain to her parents later that she'd never intended to come to Colton for just a weekend. She was ready for a fresh start and planned on making her move permanent.

"Well," Mae sat back with her eyes wide, "this is interesting. Can I ask why?"

Jo handed Mae the envelope. "I recently came across some documents that show our family has a connection to the house."

Mae looked down at the handwriting on the front and drew in a breath. When she pulled out the sheaf of paper and started reading, she gasped, looking from the letter to Jo and back again. "Holy shit," she whispered. "Grace," she yelled, still looking down at the letter.

Grace popped her head in the door.

"I need all of the files you have on Halcyon, tax records, and who the current title holder is. If you don't have them here, call over to the county office and have everything they've got sent here."

Grace frowned/ "What in the world do you need information on Halcyon for?"

"Damn it, Grace," Mae snapped, "just do what I ask for once! Sorry," she grumbled when Grace left. "I was just appointed the interim mayor after... well, there was an incident a couple of months ago and the town was put into receivership. I was asked to serve as interim mayor and," she held her arms out, "here I am. It's been a bit of an adjustment for some people." She tilted her head toward the doorway.

Jo gave her a sympathetic smile. She couldn't begin to imagine the challenges of running a small town.

Mae carefully folded the letter and put it back into the envelope, handing it back to Jo. Her face suddenly lit up. "You realize what this means, don't you?"

Jo shook her head.

"We're probably cousins." She grinned. "The roots of the Colton family tree run deep and are so damn tangled it's hard to figure them out, but if you're Black and you descended from one of the enslaved people who worked on the Colton Plantation, odds are we're related.

"Of course y'all are related. I was one of eight, and the only one who got to leave. She don't even know she was named after me," Ada Mae said with a wistful sigh.

Jo held up the letter pointing to Ada Mae's name in the corner. "This could be your namesake."

Mae tapped her lips. "You know, I was always told Mae was a family name, but I never knew who is was for." She sat up straighter and grabbed her phone, holding up a finger. "Hi Mom, I'm bringing company for dinner tonight. No," she shook her head, "not him, it's a surprise." She hung up the phone and rubbed her hands together. "Now that that's taken care of, let's take a drive over to Halcyon." She dropped her voice to a whisper. "She works slower than molasses," she said, jerking her thumb toward the front desk.

Mae explained that the park across the street was named after Colonel Absolem Madden Colton, and Jo shuddered. It was one thing to read about history online, but to see it in person brought the reality of what she was about to see crashing down on her. She twisted her hands in her lap as Mae's Jeep zipped down the road. Mae explained that Halcyon was only ten minutes outside of town across Mockingbird Bridge. The way Mae was driving, it was quicker than that. She turned down the long driveway, and Jo got her first glimpse of Halcyon. Her whole body shook as they pulled around a large oak tree that stood at the center of a circular driveway at the front of the house.

"Are you okay?" Mae asked.

Jo gave her a shaky smile. "I'm okay."

"I'm sorry we can't go inside, but we can walk around the outside."

ELIANA WEST, the recipient of the 2022 Nancy Pearl Award for genre fiction, is committed to embracing diversity in her writing. That means she doesn't limit herself to a single genre. Instead, Eliana welcomes every story that comes her way with open arms. She aims to create characters that reflect the diversity of her community, with a range of social backgrounds, ethnicities, genders, and sexual orientations. Eliana loves to weave in historical elements whenever she can. She believes everyone deserves a happy ending.

From small towns to close-knit communities, Eliana West loves stories that bring people from different backgrounds together through the common language of unconditional love and acceptance. Eliana is a passionate advocate for diversity within the writing community. She is the founder of Writers for Diversity and teaches classes and workshops, encouraging writers to create diverse characters and worlds with an empathetic approach.

When Eliana isn't plotting her characters' happy endings, she can be found embarking on adventures with her husband, traversing winding country roads in their beloved vintage Volkswagen Westfalia, affectionately named Bianca. Whether it's traveling abroad or exploring locally, Eliana and her husband are always willing to get lost and see where the adventure takes them.

Eliana loves connecting with readers through her website: www.elianawest.com.

Follow me on BookBub

THE
WAY
Beyond

MOCKINGBIRD BRIDGE

BOOK THREE

ELIANA WEST

Mockingbird Bridge Book Three

When she finds out his secret, will he lose her for good?

Jacob Winters has a secret: he's come to Colton undercover as an FBI handler. He didn't plan to stay, but the small town has charmed him with a sense of community that he hasn't felt in a long time. And his attraction to the beautiful Mae Colton complicates things even more. Jacob doesn't do relationships—he won't risk making memories he might regret.

Mae Colton loves her little town of Colton, Mississippi, and doesn't want to leave. In fact, instead of moving on to bigger things—namely a political career in D.C.-like she'd planned, she wants to run for a second term as mayor of Colton. But not everyone in town supports this choice, including the commitment-phobic Jacob Winters.

Mae is ready to make their secret relationship official and go public, but that would break Jacob's one rule. When a threat against Mae's life forces him to admit the truth of his feelings, he has to race to save the woman he loves before it's too late.

Scan the QR code below to order

A
HIDDEN
Heart

MOCKINGBIRD BRIDGE

BOOK FOUR

ELIANA WEST

Mockingbird Bridge Book Four

Rhett Colton has spent the last two years working deep undercover for the FBI. He's forsaken his friends and family to keep his community safe, but now that his mission is over, he's haunted by what he's done and is having a hard time returning to his previous life. Only two things are keeping him from becoming totally lost—his dog, Rebel, and the beautiful new town veterinarian.

Jasmine Owens is ready to start over in the charming town of Colton, Mississippi, by opening her own veterinary practice. Jasmine knows what it's like to constantly have her abilities questioned, but she's strong enough to persevere. When she agrees to board Rhett's dog while he's away in D.C., they begin talking every night over the phone and she realizes Rhett isn't the man she thought he was. He's so much more and sparks quickly fly on both ends.

But when new threats surface, Jasmine and everyone in Colton's safety are threatened. Rhett will need to make a decision. He's always sacrificed everything for his job, but is he willing to risk their relationship too?

Scan the QR code below to order

Four Holly Dates

ELIANA WEST

An Emerald Hearts Novel

Four dates
A chance to reconnect
A different way to embrace the magic of the holiday season

Soccer star Nick Anderson is new to Seattle. He's thrilled to see the shy girl he remembered from high school when he visits the local Children's Hospital. Unfortunately, his excitement is one sided. With the help of her friends, he's got four chances to show Holly another way to celebrate the holiday season.

Holly Williams had worked hard to become a pediatric nurse at Seattle Children's Hospital. The only problem is she hasn't taken the time to enjoy it. Now the popular guy she secretly crushed on in high school is asking her out not just for one date but for four.

As Holly and Nick get to know each other again, they each learn what the holidays are really all about.

Scan the QR code below to order

Summer
of Noelle

ELIANA WEST

An Emerald Hearts Novel

Star midfielder for the Seattle Emeralds, Hugh Donavan looks forward to his visits to Children's Hospital and spending time with the young patients. What he looks forward to the most is seeing one nurse who's captured his attention.

Noelle Williams is ready to open her heart again, but she isn't interested in dating a professional athlete after a disastrous marriage to one, no matter how kind and charming Hugh is.

With encouragement from friends and one special little patient to live her life to the fullest, Noelle agrees to one date with Hugh.

Will the magic of summer in Seattle lead to love?

Scan the QR code below to order

AN EMERALD HEARTS NOVEL

BE THE
Match

ELIANA WEST

An Emerald Hearts Novel

A senseless accident leaves Ryan Blackstone a single father. His son, Leo, survives, only for the hospital to discover he has leukemia. Ryan's only hope to save him is a bone marrow donor.

A donor registry reveals a perfect match for Leo but unearths an unsettling family secret: Ryan's wife's brother isn't dead. Then they meet, and Ryan realizes Dylan could save him as well.

Dylan McKenzie stopped thinking about his family's betrayal when they kicked him out twelve years ago. They would rather say he is dead than gay. So the news of his sister's death comes as a shock. Dylan is afraid being pulled back into the family will hurt him again, but meeting Ryan and Leo upends his plan to keep his heart closed.

Ryan almost lost everything. Now he must decide if he can gamble losing his family to have everything he's ever wanted. Together, he and Dylan could be the perfect match.

Scan the QR code below to order